RUMORS IN EDEN FALLS

A SWEET BEST FRIENDS TO LOVE ROMANCE

TINA NEWCOMB

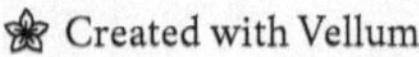 Created with Vellum

To that best friend we all have -

the one who cheers us up after the storm.

CHAPTER 1

"We've been dating for five weeks and I've never met your parents."

Leo Sawyer watched Gayle pull a string of gum out of her mouth, then twirl her finger around, collecting the line before sucking it off with a "pop" of her lips, like she was eight instead of twenty-eight.

Just one of her many habits she thought adorable and he found irritating.

"I've told you about my parents. They're usually so stoned they wouldn't remember meeting you, much less remember your name."

"Has Phoebe met them?"

They'd already discussed this on more than one occasion. "Yes, because I've known Phoebe forever."

"Do they remember her name?"

"Yes." *On a good day.*

She stretched out another strand of gum.

"Can you not do that in a restaurant?"

"This is a café." She glanced around. "Besides, no one cares."

I do.

"If I made you choose between Phoebe and me, who would it be?"

Easy choice. "There's nothing—"

"Going on between Phoebe and me," Gayle finished for him, trying to mimic his voice. She leaned forward, resting her arms on the table, her brown hair falling like a dark curtain on both sides of her face. "Except you're always together. If you're not, you're on the phone or texting each other. Almost every one of your sentences mentions her."

"You're the one who's bringing her up tonight."

When he first met Gayle, he'd been attracted to her energy and youthful nature. Now—not so much.

Gayle chewed with her mouth open, her gum snapping loudly. "She spends the night at your house."

Yep, Gayle hadn't been happy when she unexpectedly showed up at his house last Saturday morning, and Phoebe answered the door in a pair of his sweatpants and an old San Francisco T-shirt. "She stays in the guest room."

"Right. Like I believe that."

Everyone in Eden Falls believed he and Phoebe Adams were more than just friends, so why not Gayle? He didn't bother to argue since he couldn't force her to believe him.

"I'm normally not the jealous type, but I'm jealous of her. She's pretty."

"You're pretty."

Gayle scoffed. "You're supposed to say I'm a step higher."

"A step higher?"

"Yeah, like, *she's pretty, but you're beautiful,*" she said, again, attempting to sound like him.

He smiled. "Okay. You're beautiful." Which she was, in her free-spirit, carefree way.

"It's not the same if I have to tell you what to say."

He searched for a graceful exit to their conversation. Him canceling their Wednesday night date might be the cause of Gayle's grumpy mood, but he'd already committed to help Phoebe's sister, Izzy, move some furniture when a problem with the rental truck forced her to change the date at the last minute.

The waitress stopped next to their table and picked up his empty plate. Gayle had barely touched her dinner, but pushed her plate toward the edge of the table, signaling she was finished. "Can I get you anything else?"

"Just the check." Leo pulled his wallet out of his pocket.

"Excuse me. I'd like a piece of apple pie," Gayle said. "With ice cream."

Their waitress glanced at him with lifted brow.

"Just one, thank you."

"You could have asked me," Gayle said after the waitress turned away.

"You're right, but since you didn't eat dinner, I assumed you wouldn't want dessert."

"Would you have asked Phoebe?"

He wouldn't have to ask. "Phoebe never turns down dessert."

"How does she stay so skinny?"

High metabolism. "She's a cop. She works out a lot."

His phone vibrated, but he didn't pull it out of his pocket. Gayle was already antsy enough about his relationship with his best friend. If it was Phoebe, he'd call her back after dinner.

"I hear your phone, Leo. Aren't you going to answer?"

"Whoever it is can leave a message."

Gayle stretched her long legs out, plopping her heels on the seat next to his. *Not in a restaurant* ran through his mind. Again.

"You already know who it is. You might as well answer."

The waitress delivered the pie, and Gayle pulled the wad of gum out of her mouth and stuck it on her knife.

Why save it? She carried multiple packs in her purse.

"You never answered my question. If you had to choose between Phoebe and me—"

"I shouldn't have to choose. Why are you making this an issue?"

"I don't like to share." She nibbled at a bite of pie.

Gayle was about to draw a line in the sand and wouldn't be happy when he stepped over. In a way, Phoebe saved him. For that reason, he would always choose her. Life took them in different directions after high school, but he found his way back. Phoebe was his anchor in any storm.

He didn't like talking about his childhood, but he decided to share a minimum to get his point across. "My parents disappeared a lot when I was a kid. They'd go for groceries and stay gone for days. Phoebe was always there for me. I'm close to her entire family."

"No one had a great childhood."

Phoebe and her sisters did. "I'm simply saying, if forced to choose, I'd pick the Adams family over everyone else."

Gayle took another tiny bite of pie. "Have you ever kissed her?"

A sweet memory—one he'd never forget—floated through his mind. "Once. When we were nine."

His cell chimed with a text.

Gayle rested an elbow on the table, head in hand. "Did you tell Phoebe we were on a date tonight?"

He and Phoebe talked several times today, so, "Yes."

"And she still interrupts."

"If it *is* her, she wouldn't call or text if she didn't have a good reason." Leo shifted on the bench, feeling a little antsy himself.

"Then you better read the text. Maybe it's an emergency."

He tugged his phone free.

Call me when you're alone.

K, he texted back, then pocketed his phone.

"Phoebe?"

"Yes."

"Important?"

Must be or she wouldn't have texted. "She didn't say."

Gayle pushed the bowl of dessert away, the equivalent of one normal bite gone. "Call her. I have to go home anyway." She stood, wound a winter scarf around her neck, and pulled on a knit hat.

He started to get up, but she put a hand on his shoulder to hold him in place. "It's been real, Leo, but I don't see this working for me. You should be honest with yourself and admit you're in love with your *best friend*," she said using air quotes around the last two words.

"I'm not. At least not in the way you're implying."

"Right. You keep telling yourself that." She grabbed her coat and left Noelle's Café.

From his seat at the window, he waited until Gayle crossed the street and climbed into her car before he reached over with a napkin and pried her gum off her knife so the waitress wouldn't have to. After Gayle drove past, he called Phoebe.

"Where are you?"

He could tell something was wrong by her tone of voice. "Noelle's. Where are you?"

"Henry's."

"What are you doing in Harrisville?" he asked.

"Long story. Can you come?"

"I'll be there in fifteen," he said, grabbing his coat at the same time. He dropped a few bills next to the register and waved to the waitress. "Thanks. Keep the change."

The drive from Eden Falls to Harrisville was a straight

shot once he turned onto the highway, and the roads were clear despite the falling snow. Fifteen minutes later, he exited, taking a bridge over the river, then turned right at a rundown strip mall. Henry's, a twenty-four-hour diner that excelled in greasy food, sat at the far end. Ever since high school, he and Phoebe met at Henry's after a breakup—whether for celebration or commiseration. It was their place.

When he pulled in, he spotted Phoebe through one of the plate glass windows. Beautiful, wicked-smart, funny, quick-witted, snarky—all words to describe his best friend. Vulnerable—not so much, yet, that's how she looked tonight sitting at their usual booth.

The first time he met her, some older kids were teasing him about his hippie parents and geeky, outdated clothes. She'd shoved through the gathering crowd with fists raised.

So, it wasn't surprising that she became a cop, defender of the weak—protecting those who needed someone in their corner. Phoebe was that person.

Once inside, he slipped onto the opposite bench of the booth. "Hey, gorgeous. Did you and Brad have a disagreement?"

Phoebe pushed her blonde hair over a shoulder, revealing red eyes. He could count on one hand the times he's seen Phoebe cry.

Leaning forward, elbows on the table, he reached for her hands. "Phoebs, what's wrong?"

"Brad broke up with me."

He could count on one finger—now two—the number of times a guy broke up with her instead of the other way around. "Did he say why?"

"He doesn't believe you and I are only friends. He said I depend on your opinion too much."

Leo chuckled. "Did you tell him you never listen to me?"

She smiled, but it didn't quite reach her pretty brown

eyes, which cracked his heart. He hated to see Phoebe hurting.

"Were you serious about the guy, Phoebs?"

"We've been dating for three months."

"That's not what I asked. Do you love Brad?"

"No," she said, a look of guilt sliding across her face.

What's this about? Phoebe had only been heartbroken over a guy once. She usually dated for two or three months, then broke things off when the guy started getting serious. She and Leo shared the same attitude about marriage and children. Neither wanted to travel down that road.

Strangers would likely think they were witnessing a romantic moment if they saw him holding her hands. Slipping into a romantic relationship with Phoebe would be like wrapping himself in a warm blanket on a cold night because he already loved her more than anyone else in the world. But then he'd lose his best friend, and that would be like losing a limb.

He worried that one day a man would come along and sweep Phoebe off her feet, and he'd have to back away so she wouldn't be forced to choose—because she might not choose him. Every once in a while, that thought caused him a sleepless night.

"Look at it this way. You don't have to be embarrassed by his annoying habit of picking his teeth in public anymore."

"True."

"And no more stinky feet."

She wrinkled her nose like a bunny, a habit carried over from childhood. "I shouldn't have told you that." Her eyes misted over.

"What's with the tears?" He moved to the other side of the booth and wrapped his arm around her shoulders. "This isn't like you."

She swiped a napkin under both eyes. "I don't know what's wrong with me tonight."

"Is work going okay?"

"Yes. It's not work. I'm…"

"Flabbergasted because you're the one who usually does the breaking up?"

Phoebe snorted—a habit that seemed to run rampant among the five Adams' sisters. "No. Well, yes, but that's not it."

The tired waitress shuffled to their table. "You two want the usual?"

"Yes, please," Phoebe said.

"Add onion rings to my order, Esther," Leo added.

"You want blueberry pancakes with onion rings and a chocolate shake," Esther said rather than asked.

Phoebe held up two fingers. "Make that two orders of onion rings, and can I have some peanut butter on the side?"

"You two are weird," Esther muttered, then shuffled off to the kitchen.

Leo leaned forward so he could look into Phoebe's eyes. "What? You're going to order your own onion rings rather than eat all of mine?"

"Shut up and tell me about your date with Gayle."

He lifted a shoulder. "We broke up too. Gayle also doesn't believe you and I are just friends."

"Maybe we should line her and Brad up."

"Maybe." *His stinky feet and her disgusting gum habits might be the perfect match.* He tucked Phoebe's hair behind her ear so he could see her face.

She looked at him, her brown eyes intense. "Want me to talk to her? I can try to convince her you're not my type."

There was another problem with Gayle. Leo's one-eyed dog creeped her out. He might be able to overlook her gum-smacking, bubble-popping habit, but her not liking his dog was a deal-breaker. "It probably wouldn't have worked out in the end anyway."

"Because of Willy?"

"How can you not love a sweet dog with only one eye? Shouldn't that endear him to her even more?"

Phoebe picked up a packet of sugar. "I like Willy. Though, to be honest, it did take a little time to warm up to him. Not because of the one-eye thing. More the shedding all over my clothes thing."

Leo leaned back on the bench seat. "I'm done with women for a while."

Phoebe scoffed. "That will require a cell with bars."

"I see you haven't lost your sense of humor."

Esther delivered their chocolate shakes and Phoebe's side of peanut butter. "Pancakes and onion rings will be up in a minute."

"Thanks, Esther," Leo said.

Phoebe dipped her spoon in the peanut butter, then scooped up a bit of chocolate shake. "Sorry about Gayle. Despite her gum habit, I kinda liked her."

"Yeah, well, you might change your mind when I tell you she said I needed to choose."

"Wouldn't be the first time a girlfriend told you to do that. Remember Rachel?"

"How could I forget?" Rachel was his only serious girlfriend in high school. And to say she hated Phoebe would be an understatement.

"Sorry about that one, too. I know you liked Rachel."

"Not after she insisted I choose between you and her. It didn't help that I called her 'Phoebe' more than once."

She cuffed him on the chest, the exact reaction he'd expected. "Dork."

"At least I didn't do it during a make-out session like you did with Billy what's-his-face."

"Yeah, that was pretty bad," she said with a laugh.

"Bad?" Leo nudged her. "I got a black eye from your little mistake."

"You need to let that incident go, Leo. We were freshmen."

Esther delivered their pancakes, and Leo moved to the other side of the booth. "Billy wasn't. He was a junior and on the wrestling team."

"Sorry you got a black eye." She picked up her fork. "Hey, didn't you just eat dinner at Noelle's?"

"That was just an appetizer," he said, taking a huge bite. Nothing like pancakes to soothe the ache of a breakup. Only when he was halfway through his stack did he realize Phoebe wasn't stealing bites off his plate. Instead, she was staring at something over his shoulder. He glanced behind him to see what caught her attention.

An agitated man in his early twenties sat kitty-corner from them. His knee bounced nervously as he picked at a plate of fries and eyed everyone in the diner—a total of seven people including the cook and Esther.

When Esther went to the register with someone's check, the guy jumped up and pulled a gun.

"Give me the cash, lady," he hollered, his hoarse voice echoing around the small space.

Phoebe bolted out of her seat in an instant. When Leo started to get up, she put a hand on his shoulder. "Stay there."

She approached the man and he pivoted, pointing the gun at her chest. "Don't move!"

Leo's heart dropped to his stomach. Easing his phone from the table to the bench, he punched in 911, then silenced the volume so the guy with the gun wouldn't overhear the dispatcher.

Phoebe raised her hands in surrender. "Hey, I'm all for

robbing the rich. I just need to use the restroom. It's on the other side of you." She took a step forward.

"I said don't move." His shaking hand terrified Leo. The gun might go off accidentally.

His first instinct was to dive at Phoebe and knock her to the floor, but would the guy get a shot off before he could cover her?

"Mister, look, I really need to use the restroom. My onion rings are about to make a reappearance. If I can just slide past you so everyone here doesn't have to watch me puke, that would be great." She looked at Esther. "Tell Frank he should check the ingredients before adding rat poison to the batter."

As soon as the man's attention turned to Esther, Phoebe closed the distance in a flash. Sweeping out a hand and the opposite foot, she knocked both the gun and the guy to the floor. Then she pounced, agile as a cat, kicking the gun out of reach before flipping the guy facedown and pinning him to the floor.

Before Leo could react, Esther's eyes fluttered, and she dropped to the floor in a heap.

"Check Esther," Phoebe said.

To Leo's relief, a lone siren wailing in the distance grew louder, setting him in motion. He ran around the counter.

The guy struggled, but Phoebe held him tight. "Is she okay?"

"I think so. She's breathing." Leo patted Esther's soft, wrinkled cheek. "Wake up, Esther. It's over."

Leo didn't blame the older woman. His stomach was spinning at a sickening speed, and sweat beaded along his hairline. Sure, he'd seen Phoebe in action many times over the years. She could take down a guy twice her size in a heartbeat, but he'd never seen anyone point a gun at her heart.

"You okay?" she asked.

Anger bubbled up from a place he rarely visited. "No, I'm not okay. You could have been killed. What you did was reckless and irresponsible, and just like that stupid movie we watched last weekend. What were you thinking? He pointed a gun at your chest, Phoebs!" He swallowed when his voice cracked.

She had the audacity to grin.

The next thirty minutes were a blur of activity while two of Harrisville's finest rushed in, revived Ester, and hauled the would-be thief away. While Phoebe answered questions, Leo sat at their booth, rattling like a dried-up leaf skittering down a sidewalk.

Phoebe set a cup of coffee in front of him and sat down, leaning her head on his shoulder. "I was doing my job, Leo."

He wrapped his hands around the warmth of the cup, trying to soak it into his shaking body. "Your job is in Eden Falls, not Harrisville."

"My job is anywhere I am. I took an oath to serve and protect, and I did what any police officer would have done. Besides, I was afraid he'd hurt Esther if I didn't act."

He turned to look at her. "What about you? You're not invincible, Phoebe. You think you are, but you're not."

She smirked. "I was tonight."

"No, you were lucky tonight."

Minutes later, Leo got in his truck and followed Phoebe back to Eden Falls. When she turned off for Town Square and her apartment, he tapped his horn in farewell and headed up the mountain toward home.

Willy met him at the door with his usual happy greeting. Leo needed his dog's unconditional love and friendship more than ever tonight. He sat on the kitchen floor and let Willy pretend he wasn't a sixty-pound dog and too big to climb into Leo's lap.

When he'd found Willy wandering around on his parents' farm, the mangy animal looked like he could use a good meal and a friend. The dog shadowed Leo at a safe distance while he did a few odd jobs around the place to help his dad out. Once he finished for the day, Leo opened his truck door to leave and spotted Willy sitting near the front bumper, shaking like a leaf. Although Leo had never thought of having a pet, all it took was a quick gesture from him, and the dog jumped into the cab. That's how he became a pet owner.

Phoebe and her sister Stella named him after the pirate, One-eyed Willy, from the movie *Goonies*.

Leo finally disengaged, poured dry food into Willy's bowl, and left the dog wolfing down his dinner while he went to stand in front of the wall of windows that overlooked the small town of Eden Falls, Washington. The lights were blurred by the falling snow, but it looked picturesque in the distance.

Soon Willy came to stand beside him, his tail wagging so hard it slapped against Leo's leg. He patted his dog's head. "Hey, boy. Phoebs and I—and I use the word 'I' lightly—saw a little action tonight. She jumped in, and I froze."

He couldn't imagine what life would be like without Phoebe. She was his lifeline, his sunshine on a cloudy day, his salvation from parents who were so doped up most of the time they couldn't pronounce his name, let alone remember they had a son.

All his childhood memories involved Phoebe and her family. Her four sisters considered him a surrogate brother, and he loved filling that role. Her dad, Neil, called him "son" as often as "Leo." And Phoebe's mom, Beverly, had made a place for him in their home. He wouldn't have survived without the Adams family. He would have grown up in foster care, probably in another town, without Phoebe and her parents.

How would Sunday family dinners feel without Phoebe at the table? Would they continue the tradition? The thought made him sick to his stomach.

He flipped on the gas fireplace and sat on one of two butter-soft leather sofas. Willy jumped up and rested his head on Leo's thigh.

Gayle's *Have you ever kissed her* question stirred a memory from childhood.

It had been a sunny spring day, with birds singing and a breeze ruffling through the leaves. He and Phoebe were sitting side by side in one of his favorite hideout spots next to the river when he told her his plans to kiss a girl for the first time.

"Who?"

A golden-haired angel and the most popular girl in the fifth grade. "April."

Phoebe wrinkled her nose bunny-style. "She thinks she's so hot."

"'Cuz she is."

Phoebe flipped her long, blonde braid over her shoulder. "Well, I'm meeting Scott behind the school after my soccer game tomorrow."

Leo gritted his teeth in annoyance. Phoebe was always competing with him. Trying to be the first at everything. "Are you going to kiss him?"

"I'm thinking about it," she said, her tone as defiant as a nine-year-old could manage.

"You're only saying that because I'm going to kiss April."

"Am not."

"Are too."

"Well, so what? You're not the only person who can kiss."

He turned to her and crisscrossed his legs. "Do you even

know how? I mean, besides kissing your grandma or something like that."

"I know how as good as you do, Leo Sawyer."

A sudden thought interrupted his mad. "Do you think we should practice first? Like on each other? Then we'll know what we're doing with April and Scott."

Phoebe raised her eyebrows, and her cheeks turned pink. "You mean…kiss?"

"Well, yeah. I can tell you if you're doing it wrong before Scott does."

"And I can tell you before April laughs her head off."

"Hey!"

Phoebe glanced around, but they'd picked this spot because no one ever came down this way. They'd been fishing and sharing secrets here since they were little. She turned to him and crisscrossed her legs, so close their knees touched. "How do we start?"

"I guess we just touch our lips together."

Leaning forward, she gave him a quick peck but jerked back when their noses bumped.

"Ouch," he said, his eyes watering. "Turn your head."

She giggled and rubbed her nose. "Are you going to tell April to turn her head?"

"If we bump noses, I am. And you're supposed to close your eyes," he ground out. Leo hated that he didn't know what he was doing. By the fourth grade, a guy should know certain things, and this was probably one of them. His parents never told him anything. He always ended up learning on his own or asking Phoebe, but there were certain things a guy couldn't ask a girl.

"You're not supposed to say things like that either. In the movies, the man and lady just move their heads around. And you only know my eyes were open because yours were."

"I don't watch kissing movies. Let's just try again."

"Wait." She tugged lip balm out of her pocket and applied a generous amount. "Your lips are dry."

"Are they supposed to be greased up?"

"Makes sense. If you're moving your lips around and twisting your heads, they'll slide easier," Phoebe said, holding out the lip balm.

Leo greased up and handed the tube back. "Hey, it tastes like oranges," he said, licking his lips. He liked oranges.

"Don't lick it all off," she ground out. "I don't have that much left."

"I just tasted it. Geez, I'll buy you another one." With what, he didn't know. Most of the time Phoebe's mom or dad gave him money for school lunch because his parents forgot. He couldn't count on his parents to buy groceries so he could make a sandwich.

She blew out a breath. "Should we count to three?"

"Do they count to three in kissing movies?"

A frown creased Phoebe's brow again. "No, they just look into each other's eyes, then they kiss."

Leo leaned forward, elbows on knees, and Phoebe did the same. He stared into her brown eyes. He'd always thought her eyes were pretty, like a gorilla he saw at the zoo on a field trip in the third grade. "Is this long enough?"

"I guess. You have dirt on your nose."

He smirked. "Good thing you're not kissing my nose."

"Well, don't rub it on me."

Enough with the talking. Leo leaned forward and pressed his lips to hers. She smelled like oranges. The lip balm made his lips tingle.

She snickered. "How long do we stay like this?"

Leo pulled back and shrugged. "Jake said you're supposed to touch tongues."

"Gross! How does he know?"

"He said he kissed Natalie last week, and they touched tongues."

"Well, I'm not touching tongues with Scott. That's too gross. And my dad would get mad if he found out."

"Will he get mad if he finds out that we're kissing?" He really liked Phoebe's dad and didn't want to make Neil mad.

Phoebe lifted a shoulder.

"Let's just try it. I don't want to mess up when I kiss April."

Phoebe wrinkled her nose again. "Okay, but don't tell anyone, or I'll punch you."

"Like I want to tell anyone I kissed my best friend. You're like a guy."

"Hey, I can say the same thing about you being a girl!"

"Just hold still." He wrapped his hands around her upper arms and touched his lips to hers. "Open your lips, Phoebs," he mumbled against her mouth. When she did, he slipped his tongue between her teeth. His heartbeat kicked so hard he immediately leaned back and stared at her. Was he having a heart attack? That's how his grandma died.

"What are you looking at?" Phoebe asked.

"You're doing it wrong," he blurted, the only thing he could think to say.

"How do you know?"

"Your tongue isn't supposed to be all stiff."

"Yeah, well, you're supposed to brush your teeth. Go practice with somebody else." She jumped to her feet and stomped away.

After that day, they went their separate ways to master the more refined art of kissing.

CHAPTER 2

*P*hoebe let herself into her apartment, and the deafening silence pressed in on her the second she closed the door. Snow and the cold weather didn't help her mood, either. Life had a way of kicking you when you were down and then dancing on the remains. Instead of just dancing, she had a whole team of cloggers pulverizing what was left.

She dropped into a chair, toed off her boots, and planted her heels on the coffee table. She rarely spent time feeling sorry for herself, but her world seemed to have tipped on its axis, and all the connecting parts were spinning out of control. Running amok. Like a roomful of her sister's second graders in the middle of a sugar high.

Thinking of Stella's second graders turned her thoughts to her sisters. Three of the four were either married or engaged, each moving forward, while she was mired in quicksand with no visible handholds to pull herself out.

And she blamed this massive upheaval of her orderly life on a crazy psychic who went by the name of Madam Venus, Goddess of Love.

Last year, as they passed each other on the sidewalk, the kook reached out and touched Phoebe's abdomen. "You're going to have twins."

Phoebe had grabbed the woman's arm and got up close and personal. "You touch me ever again and I'll arrest you."

The corners of the woman's eyes crinkled, and her mouth curled up like the Cheshire Cat.

Minutes later Phoebe snorted and scoffed about the whole incident. She'd never been the motherly type, never thought about having kids. Kudos to her sister for spending five days a week in a room with twenty-five seven-year-olds.

Except now, months after the clash, she had marriage and babies on her mind day and night. She found herself watching families with a yearning she didn't fully understand. But she knew she wanted what they had. She wanted a husband and a home with twins running down the hall, their little feet scampering through the kitchen while she cooked dinner. The thought of freshly washed hair as she tucked them into bed with a story or two brought the sting of tears to her eyes.

One big problem—after tonight, there wouldn't be a man in her life. She knew Brad wasn't "the one," but for some reason, when he said things weren't working for him, she suddenly wanted to hog-tie him and drag him to the courthouse to get married.

Could she imagine a life with Brad?

No. His habit of picking his teeth in public really did turn her off. *But* she could imagine herself with twins—not that she believed Madam Venus. All that woman did was open Phoebe's eyes to possibilities she hadn't considered.

"Except I can't do it alone," she said to the empty apartment, dropping her head to the back of the chair.

Turning her head, she scowled at the Christmas decorations still littering the room four weeks into January.

Normally a little OCD when it came to untidiness, she lacked the energy to box up the ornaments and take down the artificial tree. Somehow, the festive trimmings made her apartment seem a little less lonely.

After messy sister Stella married Rowdy Garrett and moved out, Phoebe enjoyed having a clutter-free apartment for a couple of weeks. No more finding Stella by following the trail of clothes, shoes, and wet towels.

Tidy sister Izzy moved in while she started renovations on the Victorian house she bought. As soon as the attic apartment was finished, Izzy moved out, leaving Phoebe alone again. Only this time, instead of feeling happy to have her apartment to herself, a hollow loneliness filled her and the space.

She found herself leaving dirty dishes in the sink, clean laundry in the basket, and even a wet towel on the bathroom floor—anything to give her a feeling of someone else living with her.

Yep. Every bit of this baby-hungry mess was that lunatic psychic's fault.

As much as Phoebe hated to admit it, that day changed everything for her. Life didn't seem as rich or robust as it had before. And as hard as she tried to ignore what Madam Venus said, her outlook about getting married and having children had changed.

She dug her buzzing phone out of her coat pocket and glanced at the message from Leo. **You awake?**

When Izzy went to talk to Madam Venus about buying her Victorian house, the psychic told her Leo would be the father of Phoebe's twins. She and Leo shared a great laugh over the visionary's prediction when Izzy told them at lunch that day, but over time Phoebe stopped laughing.

Yep.

Just wanted to say sorry.

For?

Henry's. I know you were only doing your job, but seeing a gun pointed at your chest scared me.

And that was her problem. She and Leo had been best friends forever. They'd shared everything from losing baby teeth to time in detention, breakups to makeups. He knew more about her than her sisters, so it wasn't fair to him that she suddenly struggled with sentiments she never had before constantly bombarding her.

She'd tried to shake it off, tell herself it was a bunch of psychological mumbo-jumbo. The power of suggestion had wormed its way into her brain and replaced reasonable thought.

Phoebs? You still there?

I'm here. You're forgiven. Go to sleep.

Breakfast at Noelle's?

I can't. I have an early morning meeting at the station.

Movie at my place tomorrow night since both of us are single again?

Their movie nights were getting harder and harder to endure, but she couldn't just disappear from Leo's life. So, she'd put on a happy face and pretend like her feelings hadn't changed. **Sure. See you tomorrow.**

~

In the conference room the next morning, Phoebe pulled out a chair next to Mac Johnson and reached for a cinnamon roll. Patsy's Pastries always supplied Eden Falls police force's monthly mandatory meeting with a box of fresh pastries.

"How's the new baby?" Phoebe asked Mac. His wife had delivered a son a few days before Christmas.

"Five weeks old today and adorable. I can't believe how

fast he's growing. The fact that Noelle and I made him amazes me."

Phoebe swallowed around the sudden tightness in her throat.

Mac's shoulders raised and lowered with a deep in and out breath. "I missed the first six months of Beck's life, so I'm enjoying every minute."

"I don't blame you. How is Beck adapting to a little brother?"

"Great. Better than I imagined. It was just the two of us for eight years, so I worried about him getting used to having a woman in the house, but he took to Noelle immediately. Then we surprised him with a baby pretty soon afterward, but he's been really helpful. He loves holding Lucas and has even changed a few diapers. Sometimes I think Beck likes the two of them better than me."

A little over a year ago, Beck's biological mom—a woman who had dropped a six-month-old Beck on an unsuspecting dad's doorstep—decided to sue Mac for custody. Noelle swooped in to help by offering a marriage of convenience, and somewhere along the way, Mac and Noelle fell in love. After some convincing from Noelle, Beck's mom dropped the suit and instead visited him in Eden Falls several times a year.

"You'll always be Beck's hero."

Police chief JT Garrett entered the room with his assistant, Helen, who handed out assessment reports, helped herself to a blueberry pastry, and left.

Layne Yancy and Eli Atkins walked in and took seats, followed by Drew Zahn, and their small police force was complete. After pastries were passed and coffee cups filled, JT called the meeting to order. They discussed agency operations, clearance rates—which were high—and arrest rates—which were low for their small town. Their response time continued to be on target, and they only received one citizen complaint from Rita Reynolds last month, a record for them. They usually averaged five from the squawking, birdlike lady.

"Though Rita grumbles about everything from her parking tickets to the color of the sky, we still need to take every complaint seriously and work toward improvement," JT said. He glanced at the newest member of Eden Falls Police Force. "The complaint is aimed at you this month, Eli."

"Maybe you could grow some facial hair to cover that boyish chin of yours," Phoebe suggested. Eli looked younger than his years and was too cute for words. She'd wondered more than once if he and her younger sister Adelaide might hit it off.

Eli shook his head. "People always take me for younger than I am."

"Which won't be a bad thing when you're older," Mac said.

"We all know Rita isn't happy unless she's complaining about something or someone." Layne reached for a second pastry. "She's really reaching with this one."

"I've assured her that Eli is old enough to be on the force, and that, yes, she still has to pay the speeding ticket he gave her." JT stood and moved around the table. "Before we adjourn, I want to make you all aware of the hero in our midst. Even though she was unarmed, Phoebe took down a revolver-wielding man in Harrisville last night."

Phoebe stood and curtsied to the hoots and hollers of congratulations.

"Want to tell us what happened?" JT asked.

"It's not a big deal," she said, taking her seat. "The guy was on something, and when he pulled the gun, I just acted on instinct. I didn't want him to hurt Esther."

"He pulled a gun on Esther?" Layne exclaimed.

Drew looked around the table. "Who's Esther?"

"Esther has worked at Henry's Diner since Mac, JT, Phoebe, and I were kids," Layne explained. "Henry's was our late-night hangout when we didn't want the prying eyes of Eden Falls—namely Rita—reporting back to our parents." Layne glanced back at Phoebe. "Is she okay?"

"She fainted and hit her head on the floor," Phoebe said. "An ambulance took her to the hospital, but when I called this morning, a nurse told me she'd been treated and released."

"Phoebe gets our officer of the month award." JT set a huge, frosted, trophy-shaped cookie in front of her.

Phoebe knew JT's wife—an amazing chef—created the cookie, as well as most of the fast-disappearing pastries. "Aww, this is the perfect award. Tell Carolyn thank you."

"I will." JT looked at each one of them. "I want to thank all of you. You make *my* job much easier because of the great job you do. Layne and Phoebe, have a good day. The rest of you, enjoy your Saturday off."

Phoebe started her shift by walking around Town Square while Layne followed up on a call that had come in during their meeting.

The morning was sunny but bitter cold, not unusual for the first of February. She poked her head into a few of the shops, waved to Dahlia Dallas, who was unlocking the door of her salon. Another block down she helped Maude clear an icy spot on the sidewalk in front of Pages Bookstore.

Life in a small town was all about helping each other. Most residents had lived in Eden Falls their entire lives, with a few transplants thrown in here and there. Maude was a native, but Dahlia had come from somewhere else. They all worked together to make their quaint town a pleasant place to live and a memorable place to visit.

When she neared Noelle's Café, she noticed Rita

Reynolds' car sitting in a no-parking zone. At the risk of being the recipient of next month's citizen's complaint, she went inside and found Rita sitting at the counter working on a breakfast big enough to feed three men.

Phoebe stopped next to her. "Morning, Rita."

The tiny woman swiveled on her stool and looked up, her thick-lensed glasses making her eyes look double their size.

"Sorry to interrupt, but you're in a no-parking zone. *Again.*"

Squawk! Rita flapped her arms like she might take flight. "I only ran in to grab a coffee."

"Yet here you are, sitting at the counter, eating a full-on breakfast."

Several people in the café laughed. Yes, with Rita's loud squawking, they'd attracted an audience.

"Why are you harassing me? Women are supposed to stick together."

"You've been told, more than once, that you aren't allowed to park in the no-parking zone. Move your car. Now."

The woman frowned. "You're just as mean as Mac Johnson. He's the biggest bully on the force."

"Mac is a big teddy bear, and everyone in here knows it."

Rita leaned close and sniffed loudly enough for the crowd to hear. "Is that alcohol I smell on your breath?"

"Nope, you smell one of Patsy's cinnamon rolls, but nice try. I heard you used the same trick on Mac last year. You went too far when you told his mom he'd been drinking on the job."

More laughter echoed around the café.

"I'm going to tell your mom about your harassing nature," Rita said, shaking a bony finger under Phoebe's nose.

"You do that *after* you move your car."

Rita took her sweet time bundling up against the cold and

storming out. Phoebe trailed behind to make sure Rita actually moved her car.

After the Bird Lady fiasco, Phoebe walked back to the station and climbed behind the wheel of a patrol car, but didn't drive far. A block off the square she pulled onto the long driveway leading to the gorgeous Victorian her sister was renovating. One side of the first story would be turned into a tea and sandwich shop as soon as the kitchen renovations were completed, the other side housed Making Memories, Izzy's event planning business. She'd turned the second story into offices for their dad's real estate company. And Izzy lived in the apartment on the third floor.

Phoebe stomped the slush off her boots before entering the grand foyer. The tea shop would serve simple breakfast and lunch items. Phoebe scoffed when Izzy mentioned opening the shop to cater to a need in the surrounding area. She didn't think there would be a clientele, but she was wrong. Izzy got calls every day asking about the opening date. Once they finished renovations on the screened-in porch and warmer weather hit, Izzy could add even more seating. By simply moving the tables and chairs, she could use the area for small events like retirement parties and birthday celebrations.

The door to Izzy's office stood ajar, so Phoebe pushed inside—and stopped mid-stride. Izzy and her fiancée were half-lying on a sofa making out like teenagers. She cleared her throat, then laughed when Izzy toppled onto the floor before Gunner could catch her.

"A little early morning nooky before work?"

"How about learning to knock, Phoebs?" Gunner grumbled as he helped Izzy up.

"The door was open." Phoebe held up her coffee mug. "So, I thought I'd say hi on my way to the kitchen for a refill. Don't let me interrupt."

"You already did." Gunner flashed Phoebe a scowl. "Can't you get coffee at the station?"

Izzy straightened her sweater and waved Phoebe toward the kitchen. "Gunner just made a fresh pot. Come on back."

"When's Gunner going to get to this part of the renovation?" Phoebe asked, squinting when they entered the kitchen with its flamingo-colored cupboards and lime green walls. She'd often wondered what possessed Madam Venus to paint the kitchen such horrendous colors, but the answer became pretty clear after Phoebe's encounter with her.

"He starts next week," Izzy said.

Gunner opened a cupboard and took down a huge travel mug.

"'Bout time." She quickly grabbed the coffee pot and filled her mug before he could empty it into his own.

He scowled.

Izzy patted his chest before disappearing into the walk-in pantry. She came out carrying a bag of coffee beans.

"How're the wedding plans coming along?" Phoebe asked before taking a sip of the hot goodness.

"We're keeping things small the way Stella did. Just family and close friends for the wedding at the church, and the reception will be at The Dew Drop Inn since we won't be finished with the screened-in porch in time."

"You can change the wedding date, push it back a couple of months."

"No, we can't," Gunner growled, sounding more grizzly than man. "We're getting married next month."

Phoebe laughed. She liked that he, one of the good guys, was so anxious to marry her sister.

He and Izzy were transforming the Victorian from a run-down mess to a showpiece. Phoebe's archenemy—Madam Venus—had bought the house several years ago, painted every room garish colors, and let weeds overtake the once-lush yard until she moved to a location closer to Harrisville when she couldn't conjure enough business in Eden Falls. Now she and Izzy were great friends.

Phoebe stayed away whenever she saw Madam Venus's 1970s Suburban in Izzy's driveway.

"Have you decided what you're going to do in here?" Phoebe asked, waving a hand toward the gaudy paint job.

"Oh, I haven't told you. Gunner found the perfect cupboards at a salvage yard in Spokane. The owner said he'd make a trade for these."

Gunner wrapped his arms around Izzy from behind, and she looked up at him with big doe eyes. A wave of jealousy washed through Phoebe. The feeling only lasted a moment, then ebbed like a tide receding over white sand. Thanks to that ridiculous psychic, Phoebe now wanted exactly what her sister was planning—a traditional wedding with flowers and vows and a pretty cake.

"Why would someone want these cupboards? They're horrible." The paint was flaking in places and gloppy in others.

Izzy rested her arms over Gunner's. "The man said he can sell them."

Phoebe selected an apple from the bowl on the kitchen table and took a bite. "I came to tell you Tim's trial is next week in Harrisville. He's been charged with residential burglary, which means he unlawfully entered your house with intent to commit a crime against you or your property."

"I don't believe Tim meant me any harm."

"Izzy, if he didn't intend any harm, why would he have disconnected the gas line behind the stove?" Gunner asked.

"He told his attorney he didn't disconnect anything. According to Tim—" Phoebe pointed at Gunner's chest "—you're the one who didn't hook the stove up right."

"Except Gunner hadn't started working on the kitchen yet," Izzy said.

"Why residential burglary rather than breaking and entering?" Gunner asked.

"A technicality. He didn't actually break in since he used the bomb shelter tunnel from the garage to the basement to get inside. The prosecutor has to prove two points. One, that Tim entered the house, which we have proof of the night we caught him on camera. Two, that he entered with specific intent to commit a crime against you or your property, which we don't have."

"He walks?" Gunner asked, his voice sharp with anger.

"If the prosecutor can't prove that Tim entered with intent, the burglary charge may be dropped or dismissed. Tim is saying he came here to protect Izzy from you."

Her sister and Gunner shared a look so intense, so intimately sweet, that Phoebe could undress and neither one would notice. She took a bite of the crisp apple, breaking the silence, and swiped a knuckle under her lower lip to catch a drop of juice.

"What are we supposed to do now?" Gunner asked.

"You're supposed to do what Madam Venus said. Keep my sister safe."

"I bolted a door over the opening in the basement, so he won't be coming in that way again. Once spring hits I'll do something about the tunnel opening in the garage." Gunner poured the freshly brewed coffee into his travel mug and pulled Izzy close. "I have to go. I'll see you for dinner."

"I can't wait."

"Me either." He gave her a lingering kiss. "Love you."

"I love you, too," Izzy said, sounding a little breathless.

Phoebe was happy to see her sister in love and even happier that she'd fallen in love with someone local. She had no idea Izzy had feelings for Gunner or vice versa and was a little surprised by the way their relationship played out, but they balanced each other so effortlessly.

She held up a hand. "Bye, Gun."

"See ya, Phoebs. Oh, and spend some time learning how to knock."

Phoebe snorted in reply.

Izzy watched her fiancé walk to his truck from the kitchen window, dreamy expression in place. Phoebe couldn't remember ever feeling the urge to stand at the window and watch a man leave. She'd dated so many guys, she lost track in her early twenties. Not one made her consider marriage, or left her longing for more.

Her thoughts turned to Brad while she tried to identify the emotions behind her melancholy and decided she must be disappointed because she didn't have any enduring feelings for the man. So why did the sense of loss linger?

"What's wrong?"

Phoebe glanced at her sister, whose eyebrows were puckered over her nose. "I don't know. Just feeling out of sorts for some reason."

Izzy went to a cupboard and pulled down a box of tea. She made her selection and grabbed a mug from another cupboard, all the while grinning like she just grabbed the last candy bar off a grocery store shelf.

"I guess you believe that medium's prediction that you'd fall in love in this house?" Phoebe said.

Izzy poured hot water over the tea bag, then set the kettle on the stove. "Even though I didn't believe her at the time, I have to admit she was right."

"Simple coincidence."

Izzy raised her eyebrows while she dunked the tea bag. "Madam Venus would call you an unbeliever."

"She'd be right." Phoebe took a sip of her now-lukewarm

coffee and grimaced. "I need a new mug. This one doesn't keep my coffee warm more than ten minutes."

Izzy laughed and reached for the coffee pot. "Here's some fresh."

Phoebe dumped her coffee in the sink and held the mug out for a refill.

"How's Brad?"

He broke up with me. "We're not seeing each other anymore."

"Big surprise. How long did this one last? One month? Two?"

Phoebe lifted a shoulder in a what-does-it-matter shrug. Her family members were used to her buzzing through men, and they took it in stride when she didn't invite the same guy to a family dinner more than two or three times before she moved on.

"Soon there won't be any men left to date, and you'll have to marry Leo and have the twins Madam Venus predicted for you."

Screwing the lid on her mug, Phoebe headed for the door. "I gotta go. Thanks for the coffee."

Phoebe walked through what used to be the billiards room, which now served as Izzy's office space, with her sister following. The original gunmetal-colored walls were now a soft gray, and flames danced in the ornate fireplace, radiating heat against the cold day. Izzy also arranged a seating area near the window on the side that would over-look a garden in warm months.

She'd sectioned off an area in the front of the room for her assistant. The sofa Phoebe caught Gunner and Izzy on this morning sat under the front window with a gorgeous view of the mountains, which were wearing their winter finery.

Phoebe stopped a moment to look around. "I really like what you've done with this room."

"Thanks. I like how comfortable it feels. I hope my clients agree."

"They will. It's a calming room for frenzied brides."

Izzy planned and executed gala events at an art gallery for several years before moving back to Eden Falls. Her past experience, plus a cheerful personality and an eye for detail, would bring in clients, and happy clients would spread the word. Izzy would soon have more business than she could handle.

Izzy touched Phoebe's arm. "I shouldn't have said that about you and Leo. I'm sorry. And I'm sorry about Brad."

Phoebe waved her apology away. "You know me. I'll have another date by this weekend."

"So true. I always envied you being able to move on so easily. Have you ever been in love?"

Phoebe forced a laugh. "Why, when being single is so much fun?"

Izzy studied her for long enough that Phoebe felt the sting of tears, so she turned away and headed to the foyer. "Is Dad in his office yet?"

"I'm not sure."

Phoebe took the stairs two at a time to the second floor. Her dad's long-time receptionist's desk sat empty and, from where she stood, Phoebe could see her dad's office door was closed, so he was either with a real estate client or not in his office yet. Saturdays were big open house days.

Izzy was waiting near the front door when Phoebe went back down the stairs.

"Find your smile, Phoebs."

"I'll work on that." *Along with my knocking skills.*

CHAPTER 3

*L*eo couldn't believe the rotting-from-the-ground-up fence at the entrance to Sawyers Organic Farm could bear the weight of the snow. His parents' property, including the house and all the outbuildings, either needed major repairs or should be razed. Years of neglect left sheds falling in on themselves, the barn was missing half a roof, and the porch steps were tilting dangerously. What used to be a working farm wasn't working anymore.

His truck's wheel jerked in his hands as he maneuvered over the deep ruts and quagmire of frozen mud. Dear old dad refused to let Leo bring in a grader to smooth the driveway. He wouldn't accept any of the financial help Leo offered, insisting Leo's money came from selling out to the *establishment*. Permanently mired in his hippie beliefs, Rock Sawyer wouldn't budge on that subject.

Born in a Northern California commune, where his parents practiced free love and experimented with any drugs they could get their hands on, Leo arrived five weeks early. Against Rock's wishes, someone called an ambulance, and Leo was transported to a hospital for care. Which turned out to be helpful, since he needed to be weaned from his mom's Oxycodone addiction.

He didn't learn any of this from his parents but from others living in the commune who were free with not only love but information—even with a kid who didn't understand what the word Oxy meant.

Parking next to an SUV he didn't recognize, Leo climbed out of his truck and studied the ramshackle house with the missing bricks and a roof that should have been re-shingled years ago. His parents had relocated from California to Washington state when his mom inherited the farm from her mother—a move that probably saved Leo's life.

His childhood wasn't easy. He never knew when his parents would disappear for a week—or two—to follow the Grateful Dead from one concert to another. He'd lived in terror that they might never come back, and suffered the crushing guilt that sometimes he wished they wouldn't.

Their 1960s psychedelic van, parked around back, reminded him of The Mystery Machine from the Scooby-Doo cartoons he used to watch after school with Phoebe. Except his parents' van was rusted through in a few spots, sported more dents than not, and had been missing a back fender since Leo was a kid.

Grabbing the five grocery bags off the passenger seat, Leo trudged through the weeds and snow until he reached a path to the back door. His knock went unanswered, so he let himself into the aged farmhouse kitchen. Toeing out of his boots, he left them on a braided rug his mom made years ago. "Summer Breeze" by Seals and Crofts floated in from somewhere down the hall, and the easily identifiable scent of marijuana hung as dense as early morning mists.

"Sage?" he called, setting the bags on the table. He looked out of the window over the sink and spotted his dad near the barn with another man.

A moment later his mom swirled into the kitchen, a joint between index finger and thumb, wearing a colorful skirt that dusted the floor with an oversized sweater probably snagged from Rock's side of the closet.

"Hi, honey."

He bent to kiss her cheek. Though his mom was still beautiful at seventy, living a wild, drug-crazed life had taken its toll. She held out the joint.

"Mom…"

"I know, I know, Mr. Strait-laced, *I-don't-do-drugs*," she said, before bending over in a coughing fit.

He grabbed a glass from the cupboard and filled it with water.

She took a sip and then another. "One hit isn't going to hurt you. In fact, it might help relax some of your uptightness," she said, her voice rough, even when she could talk again.

"I'm not uptight." *Except when I'm here.*

His mom shrugged. "It's legal now, so you can stop worrying about me breaking any laws."

They'd had this conversation more times than he could count, starting about the time he turned eight. At twelve, he'd shouted, "It will hurt me if I turn out like you!" then regretted his harsh words when he saw his mother's crestfallen expression.

He unloaded the grocery bags and put away cheese, eggs, and milk while his mom watched with glassy eyes. "Who's outside with Rock?"

"An appraiser."

Leo straightened and slowly turned toward his mom, his brain trying to catch up with what Sage just revealed so nonchalantly. "You're selling your mom's farm?"

She walked over to the window and took another hit, holding the smoke in her lungs for about three seconds before blowing it toward the ceiling. "Your dad will be seventy-three this summer. We can't keep up with the planting and maintenance anymore."

He couldn't count the times his dad refused his help or his offer to hire help. "I thought you loved this place."

Lifting a shoulder, which he would have missed if he wasn't facing her, she took a long drag. "Times change."

"Where will you go?" He hated the desperation he heard in his voice. Pent-up childhood memories rushed back with a force that left him dizzy. He might be a grown man, but a part of him still worried that his parents would abandon him and disappear forever.

His desperation turned to anger. More at himself than with his parents. He always came last with them. First came drugs, music, commune friends, optional clothing, and the farm. Then, if they had time—or remembered—Leo.

"We haven't really decided. Somewhere warm. Rock hates the cold."

Leo nodded. Somewhere warm would be far away.

They'd moved to Eden Falls when he was five. The first things Rock complained about were the cold and snow.

Leo went back to the table and finished putting away the groceries.

"Your dad also hates it when you bring food."

"I know."

"He says it's your way of lording your money over us."

They'd also rehashed this argument more times than he could count. His parents had a little fruit and vegetable stand out by the road and sold some of their produce to local restaurants in summer and fall months. Other than that, they didn't have any other *legal* income.

Leo turned to her. "Do you believe that, Sage?"

"Sometimes I think you forget where you came from."

How could I ever forget?

He started kindergarten in the middle of the year and was immediately drawn to a little, brown-eyed blonde who shoved through a group of his tormenters, fists raised.

She befriended him despite his ill-fitting garage sale clothes and hair almost as long as hers. When she discovered he was pitifully behind others in his grade, Phoebe taught him the alphabet. In return, he taught her the words to every Beatles song and showed her how to roll a joint with the paper from a stick of gum and some dried grass found behind the school.

Phoebe Adams and her family rescued him from a lonely life.

They welcomed him into their home, where he experienced what the words "parent" and "family" meant. Until then he had no idea families sat at tables and ate their meals together. Or that fathers laughed and played games with their kids, and mothers made sure you took a shower and used shampoo and soap and toothpaste. How many times had he climbed out of the shower at Phoebe's, only to have Beverly tell him to climb back in and wash *everything*?

Neil and Beverly Adams never hesitated when he showed up at dinnertime or lunchtime, or even for breakfast some weekends. They always had plenty of food and were happy to share. Beverly bought him several changes of clothes, pants that fit, shirts and socks without holes, and shoes that didn't hurt his feet because half the sole was missing.

About the time he turned eight, Neil built a bedroom in the basement for the nights when Leo's parents didn't come home. Beverly added a bed and dresser and a nightlight that he used, but only after he was sure the Adams girls were tucked into their own beds.

Being alone on a dark farm outside of town had been pretty scary when he was a kid. He would call the Adams house, and Neil would arrive ten minutes later with an invitation for ice cream and a bed with real sheets, a soft pillow, and a warm blanket.

He felt safe when he stayed with them. They provided stability and consistency. And love.

The Adams home became his safe haven with people who cared about him, surrogate parents who checked his homework, gave him a curfew, and expected him to do his part. They even added him to their family chore chart, and he needed to complete those chores just as their five daughters did if he wanted an allowance.

Suddenly he had money to buy school lunch or bread and peanut butter when there were no groceries at the farm.

Neil and Beverly taught him how to work and get along with others. He didn't have to hoard food under his bed or hide an extra dinner roll in the pocket of his jacket.

Most importantly, they taught him that their love was unconditional and always available.

So no, Sage, I'll never forget where I came from.

"I bring food because I love you and Dad, and I know you don't have much income right now. I would even fix up this farm and hire employees to do the work for you if you'd let me."

He held up a hand when she opened her mouth to argue because she always did. Same with his dad. "I know you don't want my money, but I made it honestly by selling a company I built with my own two hands. If that's selling out to the establishment, so be it. I'm not ashamed of my hard work. I'm simply trying to help my parents because I can."

He'd offered the same kinds of things to Phoebe's parents —their dream house wherever they wanted to build, new cars—multiple times, but they also declined.

Sage's eyelids drooped as they talked while she nodded in time to the Rolling Stones "Satisfaction," zoned out to everything around her, including him.

Rock would probably dump the milk out and the cheese would rot in the fridge just to show him they didn't need his help. Leo didn't understand why he kept trying.

Because they're my parents, and I wouldn't be here without them.

~

*A*fter work, Phoebe walked into Dahlia's salon to meet sister number four for their every-eight-week hair trim. Stella, already sitting in a chair at Misty's station, waved.

"I'll be right with you, Phoebe," Dahlia said.

Phoebe turned to the waiting area and dropped into a chair.

"Squawk! I heard you were some kind of hero yesterday."

She glanced over at Rita, who was peering at her in the mirror from Dahlia's chair. Her eyes didn't look so huge without her thick-lensed glasses.

Phoebe picked up a magazine, glad Rita wasn't holding a grudge after she cut the woman's breakfast short this morning. "Not a hero. Just doing my job."

"Delores at the Harrisville post office told me a man pointed a gun at you."

"What?" Stella screeched.

"Squawk!"

Thanks, Rita. "It was nothing," Phoebe said to her sister. "The guy tried—"

"Phoebe! Mom would have a heart attack if she heard."

"So don't tell her." Phoebe thumbed through the first few pages of the magazine, then backtracked when an article titled, "The Pitfalls of Falling in Love with Your Best Friend" caught her eye.

"Delores said Phoebe took him down with a karate chop."

Phoebe shook her head at the woman who, just this morning, accused her of having alcohol on her breath. "There was no karate chopping."

Dahlia glanced over her shoulder. "You should teach a self-defense class at Get Fit."

"Urp!" Misty covered her mouth and sprinted for the bathroom.

"What's wrong with that girl?" Rita demanded. "If she's sick, she shouldn't be in here spreading her germs around. Stella, you go home and take a shower immediately after Misty's done."

Stella caught Phoebe's eye in the mirror and mouthed, "Misty's pregnant."

A shiver raised the hairs on Phoebe's arms. Back in October, Madam Venus congratulated Misty's husband, Beam, on the conception of a new baby. Their daughter just turned two and Misty swore she'd never get pregnant again.

Phoebe looked back at the magazine article while trying to convince herself that Madam Venus and her predictions were nothing more than coincidences. Phoebe had years to fall in love with Leo, with hundreds of people suggesting they already were in love, but they'd never been more than friends.

Madam Venus was crazy.

Yet so many of her predictions were coming true.

No! She wouldn't let herself get pulled into the psychic's farce.

Dahlia whipped the cape off Rita's shoulders with a flourish. "There you go."

Rita leaned forward and studied her reflection in the mirror. "It doesn't look any different."

"You wanted a trim, and that's what I gave you. The evidence is on the floor," Dahlia said, grabbing a broom.

Rita frowned as she settled her glasses on her nose and

bent to look at the hair Dahlia swept toward a vacuum in the corner. "That's not worth paying for. You barely cut anything off."

Dahlia turned toward Rita. "It's still going to cost you thirty-five dollars."

"Thirty-five dollars! That's highway robbery." She glanced at Phoebe. "You need to do something about this."

Phoebe closed the magazine and stood, slipping off her uniform coat. "How long have you been coming to Dahlia for a haircut, Rita?"

Tiny Rita climbed down from the chair and grabbed her coat, stabbing her arms in the sleeves. "Since she opened."

"Eight years…right, Dahlia?"

Dahlia nodded, heading for the register.

"Eight years with inflation," Phoebe said to Dahlia. "I'm surprised you aren't charging fifty bucks by now."

"Thirty-five it is," Rita said, setting some bills on the counter and hurrying out of the shop.

"No tip, again. Thanks, Rita," Dahlia muttered after the door closed.

Misty came out of the bathroom looking a little green. "I'm going to sue Madam Venus."

Stella laughed. "For what? She predicted another baby. You and Beam proved her right."

"She caused this!" Misty jabbed a finger at her stomach. "Sophia is still in diapers!"

"I'm pretty sure a night with your husband caused that," Stella said, adding her signature eye roll.

"Ready?" Dahlia asked Phoebe. "Just a trim?"

Phoebe sat in the chair and Dahlia swiveled her toward the mirror.

"What would you recommend?" Phoebe asked. "If you could do whatever you wanted?"

Dahlia lifted her brows with a smile. "How about a shoulder-length cut? A little longer than Stella's."

The thought of Dahlia cutting off her hair was scary and exhilarating at the same time. She'd worn her hair long and straight—which she usually braided or put up in a bun—her whole life. Maybe it was time for a change.

She glanced at Stella, who went extreme a few months earlier, telling Dahlia to chop off her hair, and she looked adorable. But Phoebe wasn't adorable like her sister. School-teacher Stella had a fun, bubbly personality, while Phoebe, a police officer, tended to be more serious, even when off duty.

"Stella's hair has some natural curl to it. Mine is stick straight. Will it take much maintenance?" Right now, she was a wash and go girl, unless she took the time to add some curl.

Dahlia lifted her heavy hair. "I'll bet your hair has as much curl as Stella's, but it's weighed down by the length." She held a loose ponytail shoulder height. "This is the length I have in mind."

"Let's see," Stella said.

Dahlia swiveled Phoebe's chair to face Stella.

"I think you should do it. Try something new." Stella shrugged. "It'll grow back if you don't like it."

"Keep it long. Men love—Urp." Misty covered her mouth and ran for the bathroom again.

Something new might take her mind off husbands and babies and Madam Venus. And Leo. Something new might be just what she needed to help climb out of her funk.

Phoebe took a deep breath. "Let's do it."

~

*L*eo pulled an iron skillet of nachos out of the oven and set it on a trivet on the coffee table. He pointed at his dog's nose. "Those aren't for you."

Willy's tail moved back and forth while he lifted his nose,

sniffing the air and pretending not to notice the nachos.

Back in the kitchen, Leo adjusted the oven temperature, slipped the spinach artichoke zucchini bites in, set the timer for fifteen minutes, then checked his watch. Phoebe should be here by now. He grabbed napkins and two glasses of water and set everything on the coffee table before he picked up his cell phone and quickly texted Where are you?

At the door.

Willy barked, his tail wagging, right before Phoebe walked into the kitchen and slipped out of her coat.

"Hey." Leo did a double-take. "You cut your hair."

She turned in a circle. "Do you like it?"

He swallowed. Phoebe had always been beautiful, but now…he had no words.

The smile dropped from her face. "You don't like it."

"No. I mean yes. I like it a lot. You look…" *Gorgeous.* "It looks amazing."

"Then why did you hesitate?" she asked, toeing off her boots. She disappeared into the laundry room for the slippers she kept here for movie nights.

Grateful when the timer went off, he turned back to the oven. He didn't like the funny feeling scrambling through his chest like a lizard searching for a place to hide. "You just caught me by surprise. I've never seen you with short hair."

She shrugged. "Neither have I."

"What made you decide?" Keeping his back to her, he pulled out the artichoke bites and set the baking sheet on the stove.

"I just felt like a change. Those smell delicious." She circled the island and stopped near his side.

"Yeah, I saw the recipe on the internet today and thought I'd give them a try." He grabbed a spatula.

"What movie are we watching?"

"Go pick something. I'll be there as soon as I get these on

a plate." Because he needed a long minute and a deep breath while he cursed Madam Venus for putting the idea of him and Phoebe together in his head.

We're just friends. Something he needed to remember. He couldn't risk losing his best friend and the only *real* family he'd ever known.

He carried the plate into the living room and set it on the coffee table, where Phoebe was helping herself to some nachos. "Thanks. These are as good as always. You should be a chef."

His becoming a chef was something he and Phoebe had talked about since they were kids. Because he needed to fend for himself, he learned to cook. He loved coming up with unique recipes and trying the results on Phoebe, who was a great cook herself.

Phoebe leaned forward and plucked two artichoke bites off the plate. She popped one in her mouth and closed her eyes. "Mmm, this is delicious, Leo."

He chanced a look at her lips. She wore a soft pink lipstick, which she rarely did. Why tonight? *We're just friends.*

He looked away and loaded his plate with nachos. "Thanks. Did you pick a movie?" he asked as he settled back into the sofa cushions.

"Yep. It's already in the Blu-ray."

"What did you pick?"

"Action adventure," she said with a mischievous grin.

"Perfect." As soon as he hit play, he groaned. "Not *The African Queen* again, Phoebs."

"You said I could pick." She tucked her feet under a throw.

"I meant pick something we both like."

"You can pick the next movie."

He knew Phoebe. He'd be watching the second movie alone because she'd be fast asleep before this one ended.

Willy settled near his knee, and he reached down and

rubbed the dog's soft ears. "You want a treat, boy?"

"I'll get him something," Phoebe said, hopping off the sofa. "I'm going to get a soft drink. Do you want anything?"

"No. I'll stick with water."

She pointed at his nose. "No changing the channel."

He smirked but didn't reach for the remote the way he normally would, because that would end in a wrestling match, which wouldn't be smart, considering his muddled feelings.

"Are you sure you don't want anything?" she called from the kitchen.

He heard her pop the top of a soda can and the rattle of ice falling into a glass. "Nope. I'm good."

Willy trotted into the room carrying a carrot. The silly dog loved his vegetables.

Phoebe followed, setting her glass on a coaster, and plopping down on the sofa. "Are you okay? You seem a little off."

"My parents are selling the farm."

"What?" She reached for the remote and paused the movie. "Where are they going?"

It felt good to tell someone, to unload just one of the many burdens his parents dropped on his shoulders. "Sage said somewhere warm."

Phoebe moved closer and wrapped her arms around his neck. "Leo, I'm so sorry."

His throat closed at her touch, her closeness, and he silently cursed Madam Venus again. He would not ruin his friendship with Phoebe by acting on his feelings. If those feelings didn't pan out for both of them, another important element of his life would vanish.

"Rock was outside with an appraiser this morning when I stopped by." He leaned away from her soft, spicy smell until she unwound her arms and sat back a bit.

"Maybe it won't happen. You know Sage and Rock. They

aren't the most reliable."

Like he could forget. He felt like he'd lived his whole life in fear of what his parents would do next. A small part of his brain tried to reason that once Rock and Sage moved away he'd finally be free of the worry he'd dragged around since childhood. He wouldn't have to make his weekly trips to make sure they had food. He wouldn't be waiting for the next phone call from JT Garrett saying they'd been picked up for transporting illegal substances.

Except now, he'd have to worry about them in a distant state, farther away, harder to get to if they were in trouble or needed him. He scoffed silently. They would never call him if they needed help. Whenever they were arrested or detained, JT was always the one who called him. Never them.

"I'm sorry, Leo. What can I do?" Phoebe asked.

There was nothing anyone could do. He'd deal with the situation the way he always did. Meanwhile, anger rioted just under the surface, making his skin feel too tight and his head hurt.

"I'll go back on Monday and try to talk to Rock. I'm sure he won't listen, but I have to try."

He also wanted to check on how much they owed in taxes. More than likely there was a lien on the property. If his parents were determined to leave, he couldn't stop them, but he could help by paying off the taxes so they could leave with enough money to buy another place.

He'd also visit Eden Falls' only attorney and see if he could get some answers. Phoebe's dad, a real estate agent, might have some answers, too. He'd see Neil tomorrow for Sunday dinner, but this wasn't something he wanted to discuss in front of the Adams family.

Leo hit the play button on the remote. "Let's start *The African Queen* so you can fall asleep and I can watch something else."

CHAPTER 4

*P*hoebe's cell rang early Monday morning, and the screen lit with Leo's handsome face. She let the call go to voicemail. Since it was her morning off, she'd set a goal for herself and didn't want to risk being distracted.

At church yesterday, Preacher Brenner talked about cleaning out the attics of the congregation's lives to make room for growth. She decided to take it literally. Well, not too literally since she didn't have an attic, but she did have a living room full of Christmas decorations that should have been put away a month ago, and a brain that seemed to be running on fumes.

She also decided to take a step back from Leo so she could sort out what was going on inside her heart, head, and ovaries. She didn't want him—or anyone else—to suspect her feelings for him were expanding into something more than friendship. Especially if it turned out she was just experiencing a biological productivity midlife crisis.

Saturday night was hard until she fell asleep on his comfy sofa. She woke early Sunday in the same spot, but with a down comforter tucked around her.

Rather than stay for breakfast, which she usually did, she snuck out, head down, like she was doing the walk of shame.

Later, when she saw Leo at church, of course, he asked why she left, and she stumbled through the lame excuse that she woke up with a stiff neck and decided to go home for a hot shower. He'd studied her for a long moment, probably thinking, *I have hot water at my house.*

During Sunday dinner at her parents' house, she kept her distance. Life without Leo was unimaginable, so she couldn't take the chance of running him off because she wanted to change the rules. And he needed her to be there for him if his parents really did leave.

After a fitful night, grogginess fogged her brain. Hoping the exertion of packing boxes would get her adrenaline flowing, she went into the kitchen for coffee only to realize she ran out and forgot to stop at the store.

A silver ornament slipped through her fingers when her phone rang a second time. She performed a juggling act but lost in the end, and the ornament shattered on the hardwood floor.

Great.

She reached for one of the larger pieces, then jerked back when the shard sliced her thumb.

Fantastic.

Her cell rang a third time, and she thought about shoving it in the freezer on her way to the bathroom. She held her right hand under the running water and, with her left, searched the medicine cabinet for a box of bandages. Opening the box with her teeth, she peered inside. Empty.

Yep, this day is getting better by the minute.

She washed the cut, trudged back to the kitchen, and folded a paper towel into a strip. Pulling out her junk drawer, she shoved items around looking for a tape dispenser, and then remembered she used the last of the tape to wrap Christmas presents.

Dropping into a chair, she peeled the paper towel away. The cut didn't look deep enough for stitches. She applied pressure and watched blood seep through the paper towel.

All I wanted to do was clean my attic.

Someone knocked on her door. The image of Madam Venus in all her gypsy glory popped into Phoebe's head. *If it's her, she's getting a punch in the nose.*

When she yanked the door open, Izzy took a step back. "Whoa, are you okay? I got worried when you didn't answer your phone."

"I'm fine," she said, opening the door wider. "I didn't answer because I've been trying to clean my attic."

"You don't have an attic."

"Metaphorically."

"Oh," Izzy said, a puzzled look on her face. She pulled a strand of Phoebe's hair. "I know I told you yesterday at church, but I love your hair. The style is so cute on you."

Leo didn't say much about her hair Saturday night or Sunday. *Doesn't matter. You didn't cut it for him.* "Thanks."

Izzy touched the knot of hair on top of her head. "I wish I could wear mine shorter."

"You should try. If you don't like the shorter cut, you can always grow your hair out again," she said, echoing Stella's comment.

"Maybe after the wedding." Izzy turned toward the living room. "Okay. Now I get the metaphorical attic. I've never seen your place so messy."

"I'm trying to get my Christmas stuff put away." Feeling close to tears, she turned away. She could probably count on one hand the number of times she'd cried since she gradu-ated from college, and no way would she add to the count today. In that sense, she took after her mom. Her dad was the tenderhearted softy of their family.

Izzy shed her coat. "Want help?"

No, she wanted her sister to leave. "I don't work until tonight, so I have all day. I can get it done," she said, glancing down at her hand.

Izzy frowned. "You're bleeding."

She lifted the bloody paper towel off her finger. "I dropped an ornament."

"Let me put a bandage on it." Izzy took her hand and leaned close.

"I don't have any bandages or tape or coffee—" her voice cracked. *Oh, no.* She was going to do the unthinkable and burst into tears.

Her sister's frown grew. "Phoebe, what's wrong?"

"Nothing." She cleared her throat.

"Something." Izzy caught her arm and tugged her over to the sofa. "Tell me what's wrong."

Phoebe fell back into the cushions and covered her face with both hands. "I don't know."

Rummaging through her purse, Izzy produced a bandage. She hopped up, disappearing down the hall, then reappeared with a tube of antibiotic ointment. "Did you wash your hand?"

"Yes." Phoebe swiped at a stupid tear that escaped despite her rapid blinking.

Izzy squeezed some antibiotic on the bandage and wrapped it around Phoebe's thumb. Then she put her head on Phoebe's shoulder. "Talk to me, Phoebs. What's going on? Is it Vera's prediction?"

"Yes."

"And Leo?"

"I don't... Maybe." Phoebe pushed up from the sofa and

paced around the Christmas bins and back. "If I ever see that goddess of love again, I'm going to arrest her."

Izzy smirked. "What'll you charge her with?"

"Disturbing *my* peace."

"What's going on with Leo?"

Nothing. And everything. Her heart fought against her decision to distance herself from him. What would he say—or, more importantly, do—if she told him she didn't want to be *just friends* anymore? Would it be so awful to see where a relationship might go? Even if a relationship didn't work out, they'd always remain friends.

She'd keep telling herself that until she believed it.

"I don't even like kids," she said, hoping Izzy wouldn't notice she'd changed the subject.

Izzy snorted. "Yes, you do."

"Okay, but I don't like babies."

"Phoebs, you like babies," Izzy said, sounding exactly like their mother when she reprimanded one of her daughters.

Phoebe held her arms wide. "How would I know? I've never been around any. The only babysitting I did as a kid was watching four sisters."

"You mothered both Stella and Adelaide when they were babies."

"I didn't really have a choice when Mom and Dad went out."

"Yes, you did. There's taking care of children and *taking care* of children."

Possibly true. Phoebe made it sound like taking care of her younger sisters was a drudgery, when really she hadn't minded at all. "You're a dork."

Izzy smiled. "Get dressed. I don't have a client until eleven, so I'm taking you to Noelle's for breakfast."

She stopped at the front window and stared out into the cold. "I don't feel like going out."

"Phoebe," Izzy said, sounding like their mom again.

Phoebe had to turn and look. *Nope, still Izzy.*

"Get dressed and brush your teeth. You'll feel better."

She could tell by Izzy's determined expression that she wouldn't let up, so Phoebe slogged down the hall. Despite what she said about not wanting to go out, she didn't want to be alone either. As soon as Izzy mentioned breakfast, Phoebe realized she was starving. She pulled on warm leggings and a long sweater, brushed her teeth, and slipped on snow boots. Her hair had survived a night of restlessness, so she simply spritzed on a product Dahlia had sold her, flipped her hair over her head twice, and fluffed it with her fingers. *Good enough.*

By the time she walked into the living room, ever-efficient Izzy had cleaned the artificial tree of ornaments and packed them away.

"Thanks, Number Three."

"You're welcome."

While Izzy drove into town—only a couple of blocks from Phoebe's apartment—they chatted about the latest wedding Izzy was planning. Seemed the bride and groom were pretty laid-back, but both mothers were making life miserable for everyone. "The bride's mother insists on sage and silver. The groom's mom wants navy and silver. The bride and groom don't care. One mom wants a sit-down dinner, the other wants buffet style. Everything is a fight. The two dads came to one meeting as mediators, but they ended up being no help, so they walked to Rowdy's Bar and Grill for sandwiches and a drink—I imagine they were pretty stiff ones."

Phoebe snorted out a laugh and it felt good. "Sounds like loads of fun."

Though frigid, the day was beautiful, and she appreciated Izzy's insistence on going out.

"I'm afraid the bride and groom will get fed up with the whole thing and elope."

"Can't say I'd blame them."

Izzy rounded Eden Falls town square and pulled into a parking space in front of Pages Bookstore. "Me either, but then I'll lose the wedding."

"Yeah, sorry if that happens."

They entered Noelle's Café to a warm blast of heat.

"We don't have any vacant tables," a waitress said.

Phoebe looked around the café and spotted Mac and JT in a booth big enough for four. She was too hungry to wait, so she hauled her sister along and stopped next to JT's elbow. "You guys have room for two more?"

JT did the same double-take Leo had. "I didn't recognize you, Phoebs." He scooted toward the window. "Sure, we have room."

She pointed at the empty spot "There you go, Iz."

"Wow, I didn't recognize you either." Mac also moved over, making room for her. "I like the new cut."

"Thanks." She and Leo both went through school with JT and Mac. She'd been like one of the guys, following along with whatever trouble they got into.

"Why the change?" JT asked.

"Just needed something different." Her hair would definitely take some getting used to, both the length and the look. When she passed the bathroom mirror yesterday morning, the shorter cut stopped her in her tracks.

She glanced around. "Why's the café so busy this morning?"

Mac shrugged.

"Your wife owns this place and you don't know?"

"My wife is still on maternity leave, but she'll be thrilled when I tell her the place was packed."

"Noelle offers comfort food, which draws people in, especially on cold mornings," JT said. "The café is always crowded when it's cold."

"I want my bed when it's cold," Phoebe said.

Mac chuckled. "Then why are you here?"

Phoebe pointed across the table at her sister. Thank heavens her sister managed to get her out of the house and into the sunshine. She could always finish cleaning up Christmas later this afternoon.

~

*L*eo climbed out of his truck and walked to the kitchen door of his parents' house. Through the window, he could see his dad sitting at the kitchen table. He knocked and waited for Rock to glance toward the window. When he didn't, Leo let himself in. No need to kick off his boots. The floor was just as filthy as it was on his last visit. The bottoms of his socks were so black after that visit, he threw them into the trash when he got home.

"Hey, Dad."

Rock, eating the Cheerios and milk dropped off, nodded. "I see you brought more groceries. You can take them home with you."

Leo didn't feel like getting into a back-and-forth with Rock this morning. "Mom said you're selling the farm."

"Yep."

"What did the appraiser have to say?"

"He thinks we can sell the place in no time."

I doubt that. Leo sat across from his dad. "That's good news for you and Mom. Where will you go?"

"We're headed to Green Valley, near LA."

"Another commune?"

Rock looked up for the first time. "They're called intentional communities nowadays. Your mom likes this one because of their greenhouses."

"Would you let me grade the driveway and fix the porch? The house would sell—"

"Nope. Don't need your help."

Leo looked at the stained kitchen cupboards, the peeling wallpaper, and the same linoleum floor that had been there when they moved in almost thirty years earlier. His parents hadn't updated a single thing in the house or on the property in all those years.

The set of Rock's jaw told Leo that his dad would move whether the farm sold or not. Any potential buyer would likely be facing a lien on the property for back taxes—money his dad could never come up with. "Okay, how about I *lend* you the money to move? You can pay me back as soon as the farm sells."

"That's a good idea, Rock," Sage said from the kitchen doorway. Leo hadn't heard her come down the hall. Rock used to say she could be stealthy as a cat. Seemed it was still true.

"We could leave sooner, and be in sunny LA while it's still cold and snowy in Washington," she added.

Leo saw the hope in her eyes and could almost hear the wheels turning in Rock's mind, his reluctance to accept his son's help weighed against warmth and sunshine. Normally his dad would have said no immediately. That Rock was taking time to think through the offer amazed Leo.

Sage moved behind Rock, resting her hands on his shoulders. He settled back in his chair, staring somewhere beyond Leo's left shoulder.

"What do you think, Rock?" his mom asked.

"I'd want a contract," his dad said, keeping his gaze on anything but Leo.

"I can have Owen Danielson draw one up," Leo said in a rush, afraid his dad would change his mind. "How much do you think you'll need to move and get settled?"

"A couple hundred bucks."

They'd need more than two hundred dollars, but they could come up with a figure later.

His mom's shoulders relaxed and she smiled at Leo.

Since his dad agreed, Leo decided to venture a step or two farther. "Do you owe back taxes? That could be a huge deterrent for a potential buyer. I can pay the taxes off—a loan," he quickly added when Rock opened his mouth, probably to argue. "After the farm sells, you can pay that back too. I'll tell Owen to include it in the contract. We can even work out a payment schedule if you need."

Leo didn't need a contract, but he'd have one drawn up if it eased his dad's mind. He'd be happier if his parents would just accept the money as a gift.

Rock looked down, slowly circling the interior of the bowl with his spoon. "I want the contract to say you won't use any money to fix up the farm before it sells. No grading, no repair work. Nothing."

Leo nodded. He'd won a major battle by getting his dad to accept help moving to California. As much as he didn't want them to go, Leo knew he couldn't keep them here. "Are you listing the house with Phoebe's dad?"

His mom patted Rock's shoulders. "Yes. He came out this morning before you got here."

Leo wondered why Neil hadn't called to give him a heads-up about his parents move.

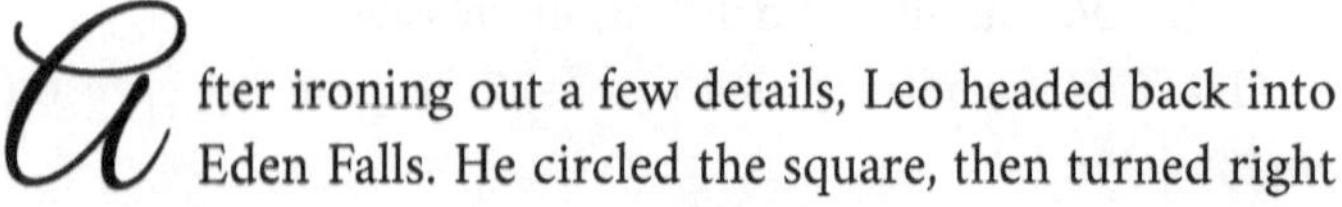

*a*fter ironing out a few details, Leo headed back into Eden Falls. He circled the square, then turned right and parked at the curb of Izzy's beautiful Victorian home. Izzy and Gunner were breathing new life into the historic place after Madam Venus left it a wreck.

He entered the grand foyer and took the stairs to the second floor two at a time. "Hi, Elise. You look beautiful today."

"Oh, phooey," the woman sitting behind the reception desk waved a hand at the same time a girlish blush touched her cheeks.

"Is Neil with a client?"

"No. He just got in." She picked up the receiver and pushed a button on her phone. "Neil, Leo's here to see you. Okay." She hung up. "You can go in."

He winked at the sweet lady who'd worked for Neil Adams since Leo was a kid. "Thank you, Elise."

Izzy had turned the five spacious bedrooms on this floor into offices for her dad and his agents. When Leo walked in, Neil was leaning back in his chair, one foot propped on an open desk drawer, leafing through a pile of papers.

"Hey, Neil."

"Hey, son. How are you this morning?"

"Okay, I guess." Leo dropped into a chair in front of Neil's desk.

Neil unhooked his heel and leaned forward. "I guess you've talked to your parents."

Leo nodded. Neil was always more of a dad to him than Rock. Leo wasn't sure why his biological parents leaving Washington hit him so hard. By today's standards, he would have been removed from his neglectful parents' home and placed into foster care. Instead, he'd been lucky enough to be embraced by Beverly, Neil, and Phoebe, along with four other surrogate sisters.

"I stopped by the farm this morning, hoping they'd let me

grade the driveway and fix the porch. The place is deplorable. Who's going to buy it in that condition?"

"Whoever does will most likely buy it for the property and raze the house and all the outbuildings."

Leo didn't want that to happen. "I talked Rock into letting me help them with moving expenses."

"That's a big step for your dad," Neil said with raised brows.

"But only if I have a contract drawn up."

Neil leaned back with a nod. "That sounds like Rock."

"What's the appraised value?"

"Just shy of eight hundred thousand."

"Do you think it will be on the market for long?"

"I think a developer will snap it up in a heartbeat and subdivide it."

Another thing Leo didn't want to see happen. His dad constantly accused him of selling out to the "establishment" but wasn't selling to a developer the same thing? "Did Rock put in any stipulations about me?"

"No. Why?" Neil studied him a moment and then smiled. "Are you thinking of buying the property?"

"It crossed my mind. But I'm afraid if Rock finds out he won't sell to me."

"Why would he care who buys the farm?"

Leo scoffed. "We're talking about my dad, Neil. He makes no sense three-fourths of the time. Especially if it involves money or help or me."

"What would you do with the property?"

Leo had considered that question all weekend. "Continue what my grandma started. Make it a working farm. Build a farm-to-table restaurant—*the restaurant Phoebe and I talked about.* Set aside a specific area to grow vegetables for the food banks and the homeless shelters in the area. Block off an area for a community garden. The land is only a few minutes from town, so people could plant and grow their own vegetables. Create jobs. Fix the bar or build a new one so Izzy will have a place to hold events besides The Dew Drop."

There was so much good he could do with the property that size. Clear the hill in the back for sledding in the winter. And open the pond for kids to fish in summer. Hold fun events that would bring in tourists, which would help local businesses.

"I've always been impressed with your creative approach to helping others, Leo. Maybe you should suggest all this to your dad and skip the middleman," Neil said, pointing a thumb at his own chest.

"I don't want to take the chance of him adding a clause to the contract that will prevent me from buying."

Leo stood and walked to the window. When Izzy first bought this house, the front yard was a jungle. She'd already cleared a lot of the debris, but she had a long way to go yet.

"I've wanted to clean up that place for years," Leo said. "I offered to clear more land and hire employees, but Rock refused any help from me."

"He and Sage have property and federal liens on the farm."

"I figured as much. I told Rock I'd pay all that off with the promise he'd pay me back when the farm sold. Do you have the total? Rock wants it added to the contract."

"Of course." Neil rubbed his hand along his jaw. "What if your dad finds out it's you buying the property?"

"How? Once he and Sage leave, they won't ever come back." Dang, his throat tightened until he felt like he might choke to death. "If I have to, I'll have someone else buy the property then—"

"Quitclaim it over to you," Neil finished. He stood and moved to Leo's side. "I'm sorry, son."

That was the second time Neil called him "son" in ten

minutes. Rock hadn't called him "son" in thirty-four years. He swallowed around the lump and lifted a shoulder. "It is what it is. My parents won't change, and I need to stop hoping that they might."

Leo watched Izzy turn into the driveway and pull around the house. "Look what Iz did for this place. I can do the same with the farm."

"I have no doubt," Neil said, patting Leo's shoulder. "Personally, I think your idea for the property is great, and I'll help you any way I can."

After Neil gathered the totals of the liens, Leo walked to Eden Falls' only attorney, Owen Danielson, whose office was in the Victorian right next door to Izzy's. He stepped inside the reception area and smiled at the brunette behind the desk. He'd heard Owen hired an out-of-towner.

"Hi. I'm Leo Sawyer."

She stood and shook his extended hand. "Hi, Leo. I've heard your name mentioned around town. It's nice to have a face to go with it. I'm Ronnie Coleman."

"I've heard your name mentioned too. How do you like Eden Falls?"

"Love it. It's just far enough from my hometown and my parents to be perfect."

He gave the expected chuckle. Funny how some kids wanted distance between themselves and their too-attentive parents, and some kids would do just about anything to be noticed.

"Is Owen in?"

"No. He's in Harrisville all day."

"Has he got a busy morning tomorrow?"

Ronnie sat and pulled up Owen's schedule on her computer. "Actually, his morning is free."

"What's his earliest appointment?"

"Nine."

"I'll take it."

A few clicks of the computer keys, then she smiled up at him. "Done. See you tomorrow."

"See you then," he said, with a wave.

The next morning Leo spent an hour with Owen Danielson discussing the contract, his options for buying the property, and how to handle the liens and back taxes. Owen was a couple of years older than Leo. After high school, he went to college on the East Coast, but instead of staying gone, he came back to Eden Falls, bought one of the three historic Victorians lined up in a tidy row, and opened the only law office in town.

After Leo left Owen's office, he took a shortcut through Town Square—a two-block park—in the center of Eden Falls. He pulled his ringing cell phone out of his pocket, expecting Phoebe, but the call was from an unknown number.

"Leo Sawyer."

"Leo! Greg Webb here."

Leo recognized his once-upon-a-time business partner's voice immediately. "Greg, it's been a long time. What's going on in your world?"

"Funny you should ask. Got some time to meet me for about an hour tonight?"

"Where are you?"

"On my way to Seattle. I'll rent a car when I get in and should be in Eden Falls around seven. If you're free, I'll buy dinner."

Leo's curiosity peeked its head out like a cautious turtle. Back in the day, Greg liked being in the limelight, while Leo preferred to stay in the background. Greg had been the face of the company Leo started, while Leo was the brains. Greg brought in investors, and Leo worked the problems. Greg had big ideas and was always happy to spend someone else's money to bring those ideas to fruition. So far, the investors had come out ahead.

Greg had a nose for making money and knowing what would work and when to pull the plug.

"Do you still like Chinese?" Leo asked.

"Love it."

"I'll meet you at East Winds. It's on the town square."

"Great. Does that town have a hotel and, if so, would they have a vacant room?"

"Sure, but you're welcome to stay with me."

"No. I have to get up before dawn to make it back to Seattle for my flight."

"I'll book something at The Dew Drop Inn. It's modest but nice, and right around the corner from the restaurant."

"Thanks, Leo. I'll see you tonight."

Leo backtracked half a block to the inn while wondering what Greg had been up to since they severed their partnership. Leo imagined the guy wanted him to invest in some venture. He doubted he'd be interested but was willing to hear what Greg had to say.

Eden falls only had one hotel, The Dew Drop Inn was old but clean and quaint. Usually packed with tourists and outdoor enthusiasts during the summer months, the inn typically had rooms available during the winter months.

The owner, Karen, smiled at him from behind the front desk.

"Hi, Leo."

"Hey, Karen. Do you have any rooms available for tonight?"

"I do."

"Can I have one in a quiet corner?"

Karen laughed. "This is Eden Falls, Leo. They're all quiet."

"Yeah, but the guy who'll be staying isn't."

"Ah, one of those." She stood up and pulled an old skeleton key off a rack behind her. "Just one night?"

"Yes. He has an early morning flight out of Seattle."

She pushed the key across the desk and turned to her computer. "Name?"

"Greg Webb."

She glanced up like she didn't believe him. "Greg Webb, as in the entrepreneur on the cover of *Seattle Today* magazine?"

Right. Leo forgot about last month's piece featuring Greg. "That's the one."

"Wow, I'm going to have a celebrity staying at the inn."

Not exactly a celebrity, but Greg had definitely made a name for himself. As far as Leo knew, Greg still lived in San Francisco, so to be traveling to Eden Falls meant he had something in the works. "I'll cover his stay," Leo said, pushing a credit card across the desk.

"The key is for room ten, the quietest corner we have."

Leo pocketed the key. When he reached the sidewalk, he texted Phoebe. **Where were you all day yesterday?**

Cleaning up Christmas decorations, then working.

Where are you now?

Home.

I'll be over in a few minutes, he texted.

"I won't be here long. I'm going to Harrisville with Gunner and Izzy.

For Tim's trial?

Yep.

Can I tag along?

Sure.

He went back to Owen's to get his truck. Phoebe's apartment was only a ten-minute walk, but the temperature hovered around thirty degrees and a wind suddenly whipped up, making the air feel even colder.

Minutes later Izzy opened Phoebe's apartment door when he knocked.

"Today's the day, huh?" he asked.

She glanced at her watch. "Yeah, we have to leave in about thirty minutes."

"Mind if I go with you?"

"Not at all. Gunner's on a job in Harrisville, so he's going to meet us there."

Leo took note that the Christmas tree had indeed been taken down. He offered to help Phoebe more than once, but she waved a dismissive hand with the excuse that she liked the lights at night. Leaving the decorations out past New Year's Day was completely out of character for Phoebe. He shed his coat and threw it over the back of a chair.

"I just made some hot chocolate," Izzy said, heading into the kitchen. "Want some?"

"Sure. Where's Phoebs?"

"Bedroom."

Leo walked down the hall and knocked on Phoebe's closed door.

"Come in."

Leo opened the door and stopped. Phoebe stood near her closet in red panties and bra.

"Hey, Iz, what do think—?"

"Not. Iz."

Phoebe turned, gasped, and grabbed a sweatshirt to cover

herself—but too late. What he just saw would be burned into his brain. Forever.

"Leo! Get out!"

He fought a smile. "You said come in."

"That's because I thought you were Izzy! Get out!" She rushed toward him and pushed him back over the threshold, slamming the door in his face.

Leo leaned against the wall and sucked in a deep breath. Seeing her like that wouldn't help with the feelings he'd been fighting. He tried to clean up his mind—a mental dusting and clean sweep. He'd seen Phoebe hundreds of times in bikinis and those little workout shorts she wore to baseball practice. No big deal. But he'd never, in all their years of friendship, seen her in bra and panties.

He reached up and knocked lightly. "Hey, Phoebs?"

"What?"

"You look real good in red."

"Shut up."

He chuckled all the way to the kitchen.

"What did you do, walk in on her?" Izzy asked, handing him a mug of hot chocolate.

"She told me to come in."

Izzy picked up a bag of mini marshmallows with a raised brow.

He held out his mug. "Marry me, Izzy."

"You're too late. Gunner asked me first."

"Thanks a bunch, Iz," Phoebe said, stomping into the kitchen wearing jeans and a sweater.

Leo tried to think of anything but the red bra and panties under her clothes. Nope. Even the delicate red lace that ran around the edges sat permanently engraved in his mind.

"Hey, don't blame me," Izzy said as she poured another mug of hot chocolate. "You're the one who invited him into your bedroom."

"You could have warned me he was here. I thought it was you," she said, taking the mug.

"Phoebe, I've seen you in a swimming suit hundreds of times," he said, trying to make light of the situation.

Except none of her bikinis had red lace.

~

*P*hoebe sat between Leo and Izzy on the hard bench of the courtroom while Gunner testified. Despite Izzy's testimony, it looked like Tim was going to get off with a slap on the wrist.

"Do I need to be scared?" Izzy whispered, taking Phoebe's hand.

Phoebe glanced at Tim. His back was ramrod straight. When Izzy took the stand, his eyes remained glued on her. Now, while Gunner sat up front, Tim stared at a legal pad in front of him, looking completely harmless…but so had Ted Bundy.

Phoebe squeezed Izzy's hand. "I can stay with you for a while if you want."

"Would you?"

She met Izzy's eyes. "Of course. Maybe we should spend a couple of nights at your place and then a couple of nights at mine to change things up."

"That's a good idea. Can we start at your place?"

Phoebe nodded. She could tell Gunner was frustrated by the questions Tim's attorney kept firing at him, trying to add a twist that made Gunner look like the guilty one.

The footage of Tim entering Izzy's house through the old bomb shelter tunnel that ran from Izzy's garage to the basement had been ruled inadmissible. In fact, it might have worked against them because it proved Tim hadn't broken anything to enter. He'd simply walked in, as free as you please.

"I have to work tonight," she whispered to Izzy. "But you can stay at my apartment. Tim won't be expecting that."

Leo leaned close. "She can stay at my place. I won't be there until about nine, but Willy will keep you safe. And Gunner can stay with you until I get home."

"Thanks, Leo," Izzy said.

With Leo's security system, Phoebe would be able to work without worrying about Izzy's safety.

Gunner stepped down from the stand and took a seat next to Izzy, putting his arm around her shoulders. "I don't see any reason to stay. He's going to walk."

Tim glanced over at them for the first time, his eyes settling on Izzy.

Leo took Phoebe's hand. "Let's get out of here."

They left without a backward glance at Tim.

*P*hoebe walked into the station a couple of hours later. They'd stopped for lunch on the way home from Harrisville, and, for the first time ever, she imagined she was on a double date with her sister, Gunner, and Leo. She knew it wasn't so, but it could have been.

At least her apartment wouldn't be lonely if Izzy stayed for a while.

She passed Layne in the hall, and he tossed the cruiser keys to her.

"I just filled her up."

"Don't you mean you filled *him* up? His name is Mr. Darcy, and he has a charming British accent."

Layne turned back to her with raised brows. "I have known you your whole life and have never seen your romantic side."

"I can be romantic."

"Really?" He looked down into her eyes with a slow smirk. "Then why sound so defensive?"

"I don't." *Do I?* Truth be told, naming the cruiser was probably as romantic as she got.

Her high school class had been mostly boys, and she fit right in the middle of them, just one of the guys, trying to best them every chance she got, more tomboy than girly-girl.

"Yeah, you do." Layne waved and walked out the back door of the station.

Phoebe blew out a breath. Yep. Her tone totally came off as defensive. But why? So what if she wasn't romantic? No one she dated had ever complained.

Or maybe they did, and she just hadn't paid attention.

But she could be romantic if she wanted to be. She just never felt the need.

Tugging her phone out of her pocket, she scrolled to Leo's name.

"Hey, pretty in red," he said by way of an answer.

"Shut up. Am I romantic?"

Leo chuckled. "Well, before today, I would have said no, but after seeing you in—"

"All right, I get it." She disconnected the call.

Once outside, she dared Madam Venus to walk past so she could arrest her. None of this stuff ever mattered to her before. Now everything mattered.

Back to truth be told…she'd never been in love, and she dated some really great guys. Another truth, even before Madam Venus opened her big mouth, Phoebe always compared the men she went out with to Leo Sawyer. And they always came up short.

Phoebe walked around the square, stopping at Patsy's Pastries to say hi to JT's wife, Carolyn, who stood behind the counter filling napkin dispensers.

"Hi, Phoebe."

"Hey. I just stopped by to say thanks for the trophy cookie."

"You're welcome. JT said you took someone down single-handedly."

Phoebe was proud of her training as a cop, liked what she did, and didn't need kudos for doing her job. "The incident has been blown out of proportion."

She bought a Danish for dessert later, then ducked into Pretty Posies. The owner, Alex McCreed, was still on maternity leave after delivering her second son. Store manager Tatum Ellis stood behind the counter helping a customer.

Phoebe loved the shop Alex had inherited from her grandma. Like her grandmother, Alex supported local artists by displaying and selling their works of art as well as creating gorgeous and very unique bouquets.

Stopping in front of a display of rock art, she picked up a picture of birds sitting on a branch. People could be so imaginative. She hadn't been lucky enough to inherit a creative gene. Leo would argue. He insisted she was a great cook, and very resourceful when throwing things together for dinner.

"Hi, Phoebe. Isn't that a great piece?"

Phoebe turned to greet Tatum. A few years ago, Tatum ran out of gas and money while driving through town. JT found her parked behind a vacant building and filled her tank and her belly. When he found her a second time—living in her car—he introduced her to Alex, who gave her a job in the flower shop. They also helped her find an over-a-garage apartment to rent, and Tatum settled in like she'd always lived here. She kept to herself but was friendly, and could create a bouquet almost as unique as Alex's.

Because Tatum dressed a little on the eccentric side, people were leery of her. She had pink hair today and wore a black leather skirt with one black knee-high stocking, the other pink-and-black striped, with platform combat boots. Her white shirt had a pink heart with *Messed Up* printed in the middle, and her black top hat sported a silver scorpion pinned to a pink rose.

Phoebe often wondered if Tatum dressed the way she did as a shield, a way to protect herself and possibly conceal her past. JT would have performed a background check on her, and he'd have let the force know if he found anything they should be aware of.

"It is great. Who's the artist?"

Tatum picked up a card from the display. "She has a small studio in Spokane."

Phoebe's mom and dad's anniversary was coming up, and her mom would love the piece. "Can you hold this for me? I'll come back tomorrow and get it when I'm off duty."

"Sure. I'll put it behind the counter."

"When is Alex coming back?"

"I'm not sure. She loves spending time at home with her little family."

A shadow of guilt fell over Phoebe. She hadn't been by to congratulate Alex or Noelle, barely admitting to herself that she worried seeing the new babies might make her want one even more. She'd sent a gift to both through other people—gift cards—because browsing through the little clothes and shoes and hats to find something special for her friends' newborns would have undone her.

"Is she thinking of selling?"

"No. At least I don't think so. She's just torn between leaving the baby with her mom every day and staying home."

With best-selling murder-mystery author Colton McCreed as her husband, Alex wouldn't have to work another day in her life. Though Alex juggled a full plate, Phoebe couldn't imagine Pretty Posies without her. Not only did she own this shop, but she was also mayor of Eden Falls and a mother of two. On top of that, she and Colton were building a home on the mountain near Leo's house. Colton wrote from home, so he was there to help, and adorable little Charlie was in school during the day. Still, Alex had a lot going on.

Phoebe turned for the door. "I'll be back tomorrow, Tatum."

"See you then. Have a nice night."

Back on the sidewalk, she called JT.

"Hey, Phoebs, what's up?"

"We didn't stay to hear the final judgement, but I'm pretty sure Tim is free. Can you have Helen print out mugshots that we can put in the cruisers so everyone can keep an eye out?"

"Done. Are you sure he's free?"

"The prosecutor didn't have enough evidence despite the scumbag being in Izzy's house."

"I'll tell everyone to watch for him."

"Thanks, JT."

Phoebe's next stop was the Roasted Bean for a cup of strong coffee to keep her going through the night.

After she made her rounds, she got in the cruiser and started driving a lazy grid so the citizens of Eden Falls would know their police department kept watch. She tapped the horn when she passed Mason and Patsy Douglas, out for a winter walk. A cute couple who'd found each other later in life. Patsy was a platinum-blonde, outspoken bombshell, and Mason a shy introvert, but like peanut butter and honey, she smoothed over his reserve and he sweetened her cringe-worthy personality.

She rounded the corner and passed Alex and Colton's house just in time to see Colton and Charlie wheeling the trash cans to the curb. She tapped her horn again, and Charlie broke into his sunshiny grin while waving madly. Alex learned she was pregnant with Charlie the same day she was told her husband had been killed overseas while he served his country. Colton came to town five years later, and Alex, along with her adorable son, won the bachelor-for-life's heart.

Eden Falls was full of love stories—old and new. Her parents had been married for almost forty years. Their story was old, but still full of love. Izzy and Gunner, with their wedding just around the corner, were one of the new.

Who would fall in love next? She ran a list of singles through her mind. Who would leave to find love, and who would stay? One of the great advantages about living in a small town, she had a front-row seat.

~

*L*eo walked into East Winds ten minutes early. Pretty Juliette showed him to a table by the front window and took his order for tea and a couple of appetizers to tide him over, since Greg was always late, anywhere from ten minutes to thirty on a good day. Leo sat back and watched the intermittent traffic travel around the square. Foot traffic was minimal because of the freezing temperatures.

He pulled out his phone and called Phoebe.

"I'm not talking to you," she said after two rings.

"Why?"

"You said I'm not romantic."

"Why are you so worried about being romantic all of a sudden?"

"I can be romantic when I want," she said after a pause.

What had triggered Phoebe's preoccupation with being romantic? "Where are you?"

"Just pulling up to Mrs. Wallace's house. She heard a noise."

The image of the man in Harrisville pointing a gun at Phoebe's chest popped into his mind. "Don't go barreling in with guns blazing."

"Leo," she said, an edge in her tone.

He blew out a breath. "Okay. Be careful."

"I always am. What are you doing tonight?"

"I'm having dinner with Greg Webb."

"What? Where are you?"

"East Winds. He's meeting me here."

"Why's he in Eden Falls?"

"I'll let you know when I find out." He looked up when the door opened. "Greg just walked in. I'll call you tomorrow."

"Okay. Thanks for letting Izzy stay the night," she said before she disconnected the call.

He pocketed his phone, stood, and shook hands with his old friend when Greg reached the table.

"Good thing I didn't blink or I would have missed this town."

Leo didn't like when people dismissed Eden Falls because of its size. He loved this town and the residents. So many people had a hand in his growing up years, and he owed many of them for his survival, for molding him into the man he was today.

"Hi," Juliette said, coming to his aid without knowing it. "Can I get you something to drink?"

"Why is a beautiful girl like you wasting your time in a town like this?"

Juliette glanced at Leo.

"Ignore him, Juliette. He doesn't get out in public often."

"I'll have a beer," Greg said after taking his seat. He watched Juliette walk away then turned to Leo. "So, how's life?"

"Good." Leo leaned back. "I keep myself busy."

"How's Phoebe?"

The thought of her in red popped into his mind. For the gazillionth time. "Great. I was just talking to her when you walked in."

"I don't get you two. You're like a married couple without the license."

Which worked well for us until Madam Venus butted into our business. "There's nothing to get. We're friends. What's new with you?" he asked, trying to move on to another topic.

"All kinds of good stuff. That's why I wanted to see you. Were you able to get a hotel room for me?"

"Yep. At The Dew Drop Inn just around the corner." He pulled the key out of his pocket and slid it across the table.

Greg barked out a laugh. "The Dew Drop Inn? Perfect name for a town like this." He picked up the key. "What do I owe you?"

"My treat. You can buy dinner."

After they ordered, Greg propped his elbows on the table. "I have a proposition for you, a new business. I need a consultant. You say yes and I'll get you out of this tiny town."

"I might not want to leave this tiny town."

"You will after I tell you what I've got brewing," Greg said with a grin.

"What kind of business?"

Two hours later, Leo walked out of East Winds with a job offer.

CHAPTER 6

"Why couldn't Lara have her birthday party closer to home?" Leo asked, turning into the parking lot of a restaurant.

Phoebe smiled patiently. Leo had been snitty all week—not that she minded. She knew he was having a hard time because his parents were selling the farm and moving to California. "Seattle *is* her home, Leo. She's lived here since college."

"The parking lot is packed. Why can't she just throw a party for close friends like normal people?"

"Number one, thirty-five is a big birthday. Number two, if this party was just for *close friends*, we probably wouldn't be here, since social media is the only way we've stayed in touch with Lara for years."

"Fine by me," Leo grumbled.

"And three," Phoebe continued, "this is Lara. When has she ever done anything like a normal person?"

Lara Burk came from money. Her parents had always thrown extravagant parties. When the Burks lived in Eden Falls, all the kids coveted invitations to Lara's parties because they always included a huge surprise, like camel rides and hot air balloons. One year the theme, summer camp, involved tents and canoes and s'mores. Her parents spared no expense when it came to celebrating their only daughter's birthday.

"I can't even find a parking space."

"There's one," Phoebe said, pointing to the left. She shifted in her seat. "What's our safe word?"

"Fiddle."

She snorted. "How am I going to work fiddle into a conversation?"

"Be creative."

"Did you know Leo took up the fiddle? Leo loves to fiddle around in his garage. Or should that be tinker? Do you fiddle or tinker in the garage?"

"Doesn't matter," he said. "What is our *but I want to stay* word?"

She and Leo came up with safe words for almost every event they attended. They didn't use them often but always had a fun discussion beforehand. "Let's go with dimple."

"Cheek or butt?"

She rolled her eyes, which he didn't see because he was maneuvering into a parking space. "To keep the conversation clean, let's go with cheek."

"Dimple it is." He shifted into park and unbuckled his seat belt. "How far away is the hotel?"

Since the party didn't end until midnight—Lara's actual birthday was tomorrow—and the return drive to Eden Falls took two and a half hours, they'd be spending the night in Seattle. "Ten minutes."

He turned in his seat, frowning. "Sorry about my mood lately."

"Don't worry about it, Leo." He'd mentioned that he was thinking of buying the farm but didn't dare tell his dad for fear Rock would have Owen add a stipulation to the contract that locked him out. "I know you're worried about Rock and Sage. Have you picked up the contract yet?"

"Monday. And thanks for understanding."

"Anytime." She patted Leo's knee before climbing out of his Ferrari.

He held out his arm so she could hold on while walking through the parking lot in heels. "I really do like your haircut, Phoebs."

Her reflection still surprised her every time she passed a mirror, but she had to admit she liked it too. "Thank you."

When they stepped inside, they were met by two smiling women sitting at a table. "Uh-oh," he said, just loud enough for her to hear. "This doesn't look like a simple party."

She scoffed. "You thought it would be simple? This is Lara Burk's birthday party." She stepped up to the table. "We're here for—"

"The lock and key party," said a bubbly redhead.

"Name?" asked an equally bubbly blonde.

Phoebe agreed with Leo on this one. Why couldn't Lara just have a normal cake and ice cream party? Phoebe could actually go for some cake right now.

"A what?" Leo asked.

"It's a getting-to-know-you party." The redhead handed Leo a key on a lanyard. "Meet as many women as you can. If your key opens their lock, come back here to be entered into a drawing for some fabulous prizes," she said.

The blonde leaned closer, lowering her voice. "Lara really went all-out with the prizes," she whispered with a just-between-us nod.

The redhead handed Phoebe a lanyard holding a lock. "Once you enter the drawing, we give you another lock or key and you go back in to find another match for more opportunities to win."

Phoebe looked at Leo and they both laughed. This party was completely over the top, even for Lara.

"Coat check is just inside the door," the blonde said.

Once inside, Phoebe slipped out of her coat and put the lanyard over her head while she scanned the packed room.

"Remember fiddle to leave and dimple to stay," Leo said.

Phoebe nodded. She didn't think either of them would want to leave. The concept seemed like a fun way to meet new people. And receiving a new lock after you made a match gave you the excuse to move on to someone else, so you didn't have to spend the whole evening with one person. "I'm going to find the restroom."

Leo took her hand. "I'll join you. That was a long ride."

She liked the feel of his fingers laced with hers. She'd been standoffish this week, trying to get her feelings under control. Although Leo probably hadn't noticed because he was so worried about his parents.

When Phoebe exited the bathroom minutes later, she spotted Leo already working the room. Outgoing Leo made friends easily, especially female friends, so this kind of party would be right up his alley. She spotted Lara near the bar and headed that direction. She hadn't seen her high school friend in person since this time last year.

Before she made it across the room, a guy who looked half her age—which would mean he was too young to be drinking the beer in his hand—stepped in front of her.

"I don't think I've tried my key in your lock yet," he said, then snickered like he'd said something dirty.

Phoebe held up her lock.

His key didn't work. "Aw, too bad. Still, we can get to know each other. What's your name?"

"Phoebe."

"I'm Troy."

In Eden Falls, she would've pulled out her badge and asked for his ID. "Hi, Troy."

"So, what do you do, Phoebe?" he asked after taking a swig of his beer.

"I'm a police officer."

He lowered his beer, his confidence fizzling instantly. "Oh."

"What do you do, Troy?"

"I…uh, work for a bank."

While finishing your freshman year of college. She'd bet his legit ID for twenty-seven-year-old Troy was really nineteen-year-old Travis.

He pointed over her left shoulder. "I see a friend."

She smiled. "Nice to meet you, Troy. Don't drink and drive."

By the time he beat a hasty retreat, Lara had disappeared in the crowd. Two more men approached.

Here we go again. She pasted on a smile. "Hi."

The first guy to reach her held out his key. "You must have just gotten here. I think we've tried our keys in every lock."

It's not a race, boys. "I usually get a name before I share my lock."

A laugh burst out of guy number two, the Laurel of their Laurel and Hardy act. "I'm Sean and this is Gavin."

They both held out their keys, obviously not interested in the getting-to-know-you part of the lock and key game, since neither asked for her name.

When their keys didn't work, they moved along. "Okey-dokey. Nice to meet you," she said, turning back into the crowd.

Phoebe spotted Lara walking toward the bar again and headed that way. Ten minutes and several keys later, she finally reached her friend.

"Phoebe! I'm so glad you made it."

All of Lara's sentences should be followed by an exclamation mark. She was upbeat and energetic and did everything with volume and full-out enthusiasm.

"Hi, girlfriend. It's so great to see you. Happy birthday."

"Thanks!" After a hug, Lara held Phoebe at arm's length. "You look fabulous."

"So do you," Phoebe countered. And she did. Lara was a high-powered lawyer in Seattle and looked the part—a far cry from the pigtailed girl Phoebe knew in Eden Falls. Lara's gold dress fit like a glove and looked gorgeous against her olive skin tone.

"I heard Stella got married to Rowdy. So unexpected."

"Not that unexpected. The two of them have known each other all their lives and fought like a married couple half that time."

"I just can't see them together. And shy little Carolyn West with JT? I can't see them together either."

Phoebe didn't want to talk about all the couples that surrounded her everyday life. "It looks like Seattle is treating you well."

"Girl, you should change careers. I'll get you a job that'll quadruple your salary."

Yeah, no. She loved her job and loved her small town. "This is a great party. Huge turnout."

"It's a great idea, huh? I went to a crazy fun lock and key party in Tacoma last year. Too bad I could only invite single friends."

Phoebe glanced around again. Lara had this many single friends? She definitely knew more people than Phoebe—even when Phoebe counted married and single together.

"I ran into Leo earlier. He's still so adorable. And now that he's rich, he's even more so. Remember what a geek he used to be? But now...Wow!"

Distaste coated Phoebe's stomach at Lara's cunning smile and raised brows.

When they were in high school, Lara approached her one day after track practice and asked if she could ask Leo to a girl's choice dance.

"Why would I mind?"

"Well, because you two have been like…a couple."

"We've never been a couple."

"Really? So, you wouldn't mind?"

"No. Go for it."

Lara had studied her with squinted eyes. "So, you two have never…"

"Ew, no. Leo is like my brother."

"You won't get mad at me?"

"Nope."

Leo and Lara dated for a few months after the dance. Lara told everyone she broke things off, but Leo told Phoebe —and no one else—that it was the other way around.

"She was too controlling."

"Want me to spread the truth?"

"Naw. I don't care if people believe she broke up with me."

Geeky Leo graduated to second and third looks by the time he hit high school. He mowed lawns and shoveled snow to earn enough money so he could buy contacts, ridding him of his thick-lensed, black-frame glasses. After he sold his business he had eye surgery, because he hated wearing contacts.

By the time he cut his long hair and changed out his 60s style clothing, girls flocked like seagulls begging for crumbs at an outdoor seafood restaurant.

At twenty-seven, he became a billionaire when he sold his share in the dot-com business he built. If not for his multiple, high-end automobiles and beautiful mountain home, people would never know he had money. Leo was kind and compassionate, and he gave back to the community that supported him when his parents hadn't, donating time and ideas, and effort to numerous charities and giving generously. On top of that, he sponsored league sports in Eden Falls and surrounding areas and donated to the library and the schools in town.

"So, is Leo seeing anyone?" Lara asked.

Leo saved her from answering when he slung an arm around her neck. "Did you find a match for your lock?"

"Not yet."

"Did you try your key in Phoebe's lock?" Lara asked.

Surprise lit Leo's face. "I didn't think to try."

"Me either." Phoebe held up her lock and looked into his deep blue eyes. She'd been looking into those eyes for advice, for encouragement—for just about everything—since she was tiny. She knew everything about Leo, and he knew everything about her. There were no surprises left. None of those fun things you discover when starting a relationship.

She knew he hated beets and got angry when people took advantage of others. He loved the smell of cilantro and her shampoo and bonfires. They hadn't gone a day without talking in forever. Phoebe didn't want their friendship to change but was afraid it would when he finally found his someone. That *someone* was supposed to be her, according to Madam Venus.

Leo slipped his key into her lock, turned it, and her lock popped open.

Lara shook her head. "You say you're not a couple, but you two are together all the time."

Leo laughed. Phoebe would have joined in, but she didn't find it funny anymore.

Lara turned them toward the entrance. "Go put your

names in for the drawings. Dad went all-out this year. The prizes cost him a fortune!"

Phoebe felt Leo's hand on her back as he propelled her through the crowd. Before they reached the entry, she tugged him out of the crowd toward a dark corner.

"Phoebs, what are you doing?" he said with a chuckle.

She had to try. She needed to know if there was a chance. Needed to know if her feelings were real, or just her imagination after that psychic planted the thoughts in her head. She loved her best friend, but could her love for a friend grow into more?

Could his?

She believed a simple kiss would tell her all she needed to know.

Without giving him time to argue or push her away, she pulled his head down and kissed him.

For a moment he didn't respond. He just stood there and let her move her mouth against his. Then, like he'd been hit with defibrillation, he yanked her against his hard body and kissed her like she'd never been kissed before. A white-hot burn shot through her, knocking her heart into overdrive, pounding so hard it physically hurt. *Holy trout!*

She got up on tiptoes and wound her arms around his neck, and he deepened the kiss, pulling her even tighter against him. All background noise faded until it was just them, just this moment. And she knew. The answer was as clear as a sunny day on the lake. Madam Venus was right.

Just as suddenly as it began, he jerked his head away and took a step back.

She couldn't read his wide-eyed expression, but she knew by his heaving chest that he'd felt something too. He put the back of his hand to his mouth. "What was that?" he asked, his voice sounding like sandpaper over a rough piece of wood.

"Madam Venus—"

"Stop, Phoebe. Just stop." He held up his hand. "You can't seriously believe she predicted your future."

Phoebe's chest tightened, squeezing out all the air. She had her answer. But it wasn't the same as Leo's. "What if I do?"

He blew out a breath and ran fingers through his hair. "Well, do it with someone else."

Before he could turn away, she grabbed his arm. "Wait, Leo. Let's talk this through. We would skip all the awkward, getting-to-know-you stuff. I know every annoying habit you have, and you know mine. We already love each other. My family adores you, and your parents like me. Everyone already thinks we're a couple, so moving into a relationship would be so easy. And you can't tell me you didn't feel that —" she flapped her hand between them "—that connection just now."

Leo shook his head, looking angrier than she'd ever seen him. "I've told you I don't want to get married, and I don't want kids."

"Why?"

A look of pain crossed his face. "How can you ask that? You, more than anyone, should know why."

"You are nothing like your parents, Leo. I've seen you with kids. You'd be a fantastic dad."

"I'm not risking my relationship with your family because you believe some nutty psychic."

"My family would never—"

He held up his hand and backed away. "Just stop, Phoebs."

But she couldn't. "Unlike most women you date, you know I'm not after your money. I loved you way before you became a billionaire."

"No. You're worse than them. You only want me for my sperm."

Phoebe felt the verbal slap and sucked in a breath at the bitterness in his tone.

"I'm sorry." Leo rubbed his forehead. "I shouldn't have said that."

"But you did."

"Look, we're here to have fun. Let's go turn in our lock and key." He took her hand and led her to the table where he flashed a smile at the women. "We need a new lock and key."

"Great. Just fill these out with your name and email address, and you'll be entered in the raffle," one woman said, holding out two pieces of paper and pencils.

"You can have mine," she said to Leo. She accepted a new lock and walked back into the party. Leo called her name, but she ignored him. Her heart was racing, but with anger rather than the thrill of that incredible kiss they shared moments before.

She knew Leo felt the same thrill, the same explosive excitement she experienced. If he hadn't, he never would have kissed her back. And he definitely kissed her back.

Slipping the new lock lanyard over her neck, she disappeared into the crowd.

She and Leo didn't fight often, but when they did, they needed to retreat to their respective corners for a while. She went as far across the room as the crowd allowed, wishing Leo would accept the energy between them and recognize the possibilities.

Would he change his mind? Could she persuade him to change his mind *after* she stopped reeling from the kiss that left her breathless and wanting more?

This is crazy.

Madam Venus had turned her into a crazy woman. She just kissed her best friend. And it wasn't a kiss she'd forget anytime soon.

She glanced toward the door and spotted Leo slipping a

new lanyard over his head. The redhead who greeted them when they first arrived approached him, holding out her lock. He lifted his key with a wink. The redhead flipped her hair. Phoebe rolled her eyes. Yep, she'd officially and completely lost her mind.

She turned toward the bar and caught a man staring at her. He looked so much like Leo, she had to blink to make sure he was real. When she opened her eyes, he was still there. He smiled and her stomach dipped.

He pushed away from the bar, walked the few feet separating them, and stopped in front of her. "Hi, I'm Keaton."

"Nice to meet you, Keaton. I'm Phoebe," she said, shaking his hand. He had sandy blond hair and penetrating blue eyes. The resemblance to Leo was uncanny.

"Should we see if we're a match?" she asked, holding up her lock.

He inserted his key and turned it. Her lock popped open, and he grinned. "I had a feeling we'd be a match. Can I get you a drink?"

"Shouldn't we turn in our lock and key?"

"Is putting your name in a drawing important? I know I'd rather spend my time getting to know you."

She glanced toward Leo, who was still dazzling the redhead. "I'd love a drink."

While she found a small table nearby, Keaton went to the bar to get her a diet soda. When she looked again, Leo had disappeared.

"You don't drink alcohol?" Keaton asked as he set a drink in front of her and sat on the other side of the table.

"One of my grandmas was an alcoholic. One night she drove off the road, and neither she nor my grandpa survived. Her mother was also an alcoholic. Since addiction runs in my family, my sisters and I decided we wouldn't take the chance." She'd noticed he also chose a soft drink. "What about you?"

"Alcoholism runs in my family, too. So, I steer clear."

Something they had in common.

"How do you know Lara?" she asked.

"The Burks are old family friends. How about you?"

"Lara and I went to high school together."

He smiled and Phoebe couldn't pull her eyes away. "Do you still live in Eden Falls?"

"Yes."

"I live in Harrisville," he said resting his forearms on the table.

Just fifteen minutes apart. "What do you do, Keaton?"

"I'm a pediatrician."

A children's doctor. Which meant he must like children.

"What do you do, Phoebe?"

Her profession tended to intimidate men, but she'd never been shy about sharing what she did with others. Plus, it was a great way to weed out the ineligibles. "I'm a police officer."

"Interesting profession, and we live just down the road from each other."

She smiled. No shock, and not a negative word about her being a cop. "A hop, skip, and a jump."

Phoebe lost track of time while they talked. Keaton was funny, and she loved it when he said her name. While their conversation flowed into getting-to-know-you comments and questions, she decided she liked his smile and his ability to laugh at himself.

Maybe Madam Venus got it wrong after all. She said Leo was having twins, but maybe she meant someone who *looked* like Leo. And Keaton sure fit the bill.

CHAPTER 7

*L*ara stepped onto a small platform, microphone in hand. "Hi, everyone! Thanks for coming to celebrate my birthday!"

The party crowd cheered.

"Since it's almost midnight, and *almost* my official birthday, let's give away some prizes. I hope everyone entered their name multiple times, so you have more chances to win."

Leo had been looking around for Phoebe ever since she walked back into the party. He felt bad for pushing her away so harshly while he fought the tsunami of desire triggered by that incredible kiss.

He'd wondered how easy it would be to move into a relationship with her. Now he had his answer. She lit him up like a Roman candle with that kiss, and it took him more than an hour to settle his emotions.

But Phoebe needed to understand that because of the way he was raised, he never wanted to get married or bring children into the world. He could never imagine his parents with grandkids, and he would never leave kids with Rock and Sage.

Great. Now, Phoebe had him imagining little blonde twins running around the farm.

He shook his head to get rid of the fantasies.

Phoebe would find someone one day, and sure, their friendship would take a hit. He'd miss her more than she could ever understand, but he couldn't allow what they had to become more.

Walking past the bar, he finally spotted Phoebe at a table with a man. They were both smiling and looked pretty engrossed in conversation.

"Okay, the first prize is a gift certificate for a full-body massage, which goes to…" Lara reached into the big glass jar that used to be on the welcome table. "…Gina Winters!"

While Leo clapped, he watched Phoebe lean back in her chair and laugh. He'd been trying to extinguish the runaway feeling she inflamed with her kiss by meeting as many women as he could. None of them captured his attention for more than a few minutes, but he'd ended up putting his name in the raffle jar eight times.

"The next prize is two tickets to the Chihuly Garden and Glass Museum. And the winner is…Justin Waite!"

Another round of applause.

Lara droned on. She'd always loved being the center of attention in high school and sought mic-in-hand moments as often as possible. Apparently, that hadn't changed over the years.

"Leo Sawyer!"

Surprised to hear his name, he turned from Phoebe-watching and looked toward the stage, where Lara was waving a gift certificate of some kind.

"And for the record, I'd be happy to accompany you on that little weekend trip," she said, to a round of laughter, as he made his way forward.

A weekend trip? He looked at the coupon, which was good

for a two-night stay on a Seattle houseboat. "Thank you, Lara. This is quite a prize."

"You're welcome, and remember my offer," she said with a wink.

Leo turned away from the platform. He'd never stayed on a houseboat before. Might be kind of fun. Phoebe would love every minute.

Very aware his first thoughts were of Phoebe, he walked toward her. She was still so occupied with her conversation companion she hadn't heard that he won a prize. Or if she did, she didn't glance his way.

The guy she was talking to reached across the table and touched her hand. Leo didn't like his stomach-churning reaction, but the fact that she'd met someone she clearly enjoyed was good news—no, great news. Anything to get her mind off what that crazy medium predicted. For Phoebe to take what Madam Venus said to heart was so unlike her.

Phoebe leaned closer and pushed her hair back. He did a double-take every time he saw her, still not used to her shorter hair. The cut made her look younger than her thirty-four years.

Thirty-four.

He wondered if Phoebe remembered the night they made a pact to marry each other if they were still single at thirty-five. Back then he was naïve enough to believe his parents would change, and since his best friend was gorgeous, of course, he'd marry her. They even shook hands to seal the deal.

"And that's it. Congratulations to the winners! Thank you for coming to help me celebrate what is going to be the best year yet!" Lara said with a smile and a wave.

Phoebe and the guy were still deep in conversation. People started heading for the door, and Leo grew agitated. Ready to leave, he walked over to their table.

Phoebe must have sensed when he was near because she looked up. "Hey, Leo. This is Keaton Roe. Keaton, this is my friend Leo Sawyer."

Keaton stood and they shook hands while mumbling the perfunctory nice-to-meet-yous.

"The party is breaking up. Are you ready to go, Phoebs?"

She glanced around with wide eyes, then looked at the time on her phone. "I had no idea it was so late. Or early," she added with a laugh.

"I better get out of here too," Keaton said when Phoebe stood. "I'll call you Sunday."

Phoebe flashed her flirty smile. "Drive carefully."

Keaton smiled back at her. "I don't have far to drive. My uncle is out of town and letting me use his place."

"We don't have far to drive either," Leo said. "Phoebe got us a hotel room just down the road."

Keaton's eyebrows rose.

"Rooms—plural. I got hotel rooms." Phoebe shot Leo a frown.

"I'll be in the car." Leo turned for the door. He wasn't sure why he said that. Probably because Phoebe kissed him like her life depended on it just a couple of hours earlier and now, he was nothing more than an afterthought.

Grabbing his coat, he walked out into the frigid air. Would spring never get here? He was ready for something new.

From the car he watched Phoebe say goodbye to Keaton, who leaned forward and kissed her cheek. She waved and walked across the parking lot. When she neared his car, Leo jumped out and opened the passenger door, which was crazy. He'd never opened the door for her before.

She looked up at him. "What are you doing?"

He shook his head and shut the door after she slid into the passenger seat. Then he ran around and got behind the wheel. Phoebe took so long getting outside that the car had time to warm up. She snuggled into the seat and yawned. "Sorry. I hope you weren't waiting for me for too long. I lost all track of time."

"Nope."

She smiled and waved when they passed Keaton, who stood next to an SUV.

"Which way?" Leo asked, before pulling onto the street.

She tapped the screen on her phone a few times. "Turn left here. Then take a right at the first light. It's about five miles down on the right."

Leo didn't know why he felt so irritated, almost to the point of anger. "I won a prize in the raffle."

"Oh, yeah?" she asked, without turning her head his way. "That's great."

His irritation swelled when she didn't even ask what he won. "You were too busy to even hear if Lara called your name."

"Did I win something?"

"No."

"Then it doesn't matter, does it?" She pointed. "There's the hotel."

He turned into the overhang near the front desk. "What name did you—"

"I'll take care of it," she said, opening the door and sliding out.

He tugged out his wallet. "Here's my credit card."

"I've got it, Leo." She shut the door.

She was independent enough that she wouldn't let him pay for her room, but he wouldn't let her pay for his either, so he climbed out and followed her inside. She'd just pulled out her credit card.

"Put them both on this," he said, handing the clerk his card.

"Put one room on each card," Phoebe said, sliding hers across the desk.

Independent *and* stubborn.

While the clerk handled the transactions, Leo went out, parked the car, and grabbed their overnight bags.

On the elevator ride to the sixth floor, Leo studied her reflection in the metal door. She was looking down with a smile on her face. "I think we should talk about what happened."

She glanced at him with a dreamy expression. "What happened?"

"The kiss, Phoebs. You couldn't have forgotten."

"Oh." She did that bunny-nose-wrinkle. "Sorry about that. I don't know what got into me. It was a stupid, impulsive moment." She flashed a quick smile. "Forget it happened."

He would never forget. That moment had left him a little discombobulated and a lot shaken, and she described it as stupid and impulsive?

The elevator doors opened, and she exited. He followed her down the hall until she stopped at a room.

"This is me."

His room was across the hall. "What time do you want to leave in the morning?"

"Whenever. Just give me a call when you wake up."

He nodded." Good night."

"'Night, Leo." She went inside and closed the door.

Any other night she would have come into his room and kept him up until dawn watching scary movies or chick flicks. Then she would have fallen asleep on his bed, and he would have ended up sleeping in her room.

～

*P*hoebe woke up feeling fabulous. She hadn't wanted to drive all the way to Seattle for Lara's overindulgent party any more than Leo did, but she was so glad they did. Meeting Keaton eased her mind as far as Madam Venus's prediction went. There were hundreds of men out in the world who looked like Leo. The psychic simply experienced a brain blitz because she was used to seeing Phoebe and Leo together around town and assumed they were a couple.

She opened the curtains and looked out at the dreary day. Spring couldn't come soon enough for her. It was past time for sunshine and temperatures warm enough that she didn't have to wear a coat.

Carrying her overnight bag into the bathroom, she took a quick shower, put on a little makeup, and dried her hair. She slipped into some comfortable leggings and a heavy sweater for the ride home then checked her phone. Leo still hadn't called and she was starving.

Getting her bag packed, she shouldered that and her purse and left the room. She'd get a table in the hotel restaurant and order some breakfast. When Leo called, she could order his so it would be at the table when he arrived.

In the lobby, she followed the wonderful smell of pancakes and bacon to the restaurant entrance and spotted Leo already at a table.

"Just one?" the hostess asked.

She pointed to Leo. "Actually, I'm with him."

"Here's a menu, and I'll have the waitress bring you a glass of water."

"Thank you." Phoebe carried her bag over and dropped it near his chair. "Why didn't you call me?" she asked, sitting across from him.

"After your late night, I thought you'd need your sleep."

"You had just as late a night as I did."

"I just assumed you'd stayed up late talking on the phone."

"To whom?"

"Your new boyfriend."

Okay, Leo definitely rolled off the wrong side of the bed this morning and seemed determined to start a fight. She, on the other hand, felt carefree for the first time in months, so she let his comment roll off her back. "Have you ordered?"

"Yes."

A waitress set a glass of water in front of her. "Would you like a cup of coffee?"

"No, thanks. I'll take a glass of orange juice, please." She studied the menu for a moment. When the waitress came back with the orange juice, she ordered walnut French toast made with brioche and a side of bacon.

"Since when does French toast win over pancakes?"

She shrugged. "I feel like something different. Did you wake up as hungry as I did?"

"Nope." Leo pulled out his phone and started texting someone, ending their short conversation.

Okay. Her phone pinged a message and Keaton's name appeared on her screen along with a notification. She touched the screen.

Good morning. Hope I didn't wake you. Just wanted to tell you I had a great time last night.

She texted, **Me too.**

Are you on your way back to Eden Falls yet?

No. Grabbing breakfast first.

"What are you smiling about?"

Phoebe looked up and met Leo's scowl. "I didn't realize I was smiling."

"You are."

"Look, Mr. Grumpy Pants, I'm not letting your bad mood rub off on me."

"I'm not in a bad mood."

She snorted to let him know exactly what she thought of that silly declaration.

I'll call you when I get home. Keaton texted.

Okay. Drive carefully.

You too. Talk to you soon.

She sent a smiley face and tucked her phone away, then glanced up to see Leo still scowling. "Do you want to talk about what's wrong? Is it your parents' potential move?"

"They listed the farm with your dad, so I wouldn't call their move potential."

This was the side of Leo she didn't understand. His parents disappointed him time after time, year after year. Nothing he did made a difference. He had been a straight-A student, built a dot-com business that sold for more than a billion dollars, and everyone liked him. He was friendly and kind. And still Rock and Sage were too busy with their own agenda, or too stoned, to pay much attention to their only son, who loved them more than they would ever deserve.

"Have you considered moving with them?"

He looked at her like she'd grown an extra eye in the middle of her forehead.

Luckily the waitress chose that moment to set their breakfasts in front of them. Her French toast looked divine and smelled even better. "Thank you."

"Anything else I can get you?"

"No, thank you," Leo said.

She poured the rich maple syrup over one of three pieces and cut a bite. The French toast tasted as good as it smelled. Delicious.

Cutting another bite, she held it out. "You have to taste this."

"I don't want any."

"One bite, Leo. It's amazing."

"I don't want—"

She touched the French toast to his lips, tempting his wrath. "One bite. You can wash it down with milk if you don't like it."

He opened his mouth, closed his lips around the bite, and pulled back, scowling the whole time. She could tell he liked it, though he'd never admit it. He was too angry. About what, she didn't know. Maybe just the world in general.

Or maybe because she'd kissed him. That was a really stupid move on her part, but she wasn't sorry. She wanted to know if she'd feel anything, and she did. So did he, but if he wanted to deny it or be snitty about it, that was his problem.

"You made my lips sticky."

For a split second, she thought about teasing him with, *I could lick the sticky off*, but he was in such an ornery mood, a comment like that would only make him angrier. "No, you did, by not opening your mouth in the first place."

She ate half her breakfast, and he ate the rest. On their ride home, they barely spoke…unusual for them, but if Leo wanted quiet, she'd oblige. She half-turned in her seat and watched the rain and buildings of Seattle turn to snow and evergreens.

"You never told me what you won last night."

"Two nights on a Seattle houseboat."

She turned to look at him. "That's cool."

"I know." He smiled for the first time that morning.

"You also never told me what Greg Webb came to see you about."

"A job."

"Really?"

He took a deep breath and stared at the road ahead. "A job that will require me to move."

Her stomach dropped. She'd hated the years when he lived in Northern California. Despite talking to him every day and the occasional visit, she'd missed her best friend desperately.

"Since my parents are selling the farm, there really isn't anything keeping me in Eden Falls."

Ouch. That stung like a slap. So he wouldn't see her sudden tears, she turned to face the side window and watched the snow drift down. "You've already decided?" she asked once she trusted her voice to not give her tender feelings away. She'd been closer to tears more times in the past few weeks than she had her whole life.

"Pretty much."

And you didn't think to talk to me at all? That hurt, too—not that talking to her was a requirement, but he'd been doing just that for almost thirty years. "Where?"

"San Fran."

"At least it's a city you know. What about Willy and your house?"

"I want you to move into my house—rent-free, of course —and take care of Willy."

She looked at him. "I'll be happy to take care of your house and Willy, but not rent-free."

"I don't need your money."

"I know you don't, Leo, and I don't need your charity."

"I could find any number of people who'd be happy to move in rent-free."

Well, he certainly managed to settle a dark cloud over her happy day. *Mission accomplished, Leo.*

"Then ask them," she snapped, completely aware of how snarky she sounded.

"Willy knows you."

"Willy knows a lot of people. He's a friendly dog."

She realized as she stared out at the passing trees, that an important element in the dynamic of their friendship had shifted overnight. Ever since their kiss. Had he decided to take this job beforehand, or was the kiss the deciding factor for him? She hated to think she'd pushed him into leaving.

Actually, she should go farther back. To the day Madam Venus included Leo in her twin prediction. Ever since then she'd looked at her best friend differently. And she wasn't sure she could go back. Which made everything her fault. Leo wanted to keep things the way they were, but she'd pushed him until he decided to take a job in another state.

His moving might be the best thing for them, at least for a little while. They wouldn't see each other every day, but they'd stay in touch, just like before. Nothing would sever the friendship they'd shared forever. And distance might heal the rift she wedged between them with her stupid decision to explore their possibilities.

CHAPTER 8

*L*eo stopped in front of Phoebe's apartment and looked over at her. She'd been quiet for most of the trip, but he didn't blame her. He'd been off-kilter since she kissed him. And even before that. Madam Venus had managed to mess them both up with her crazy gibberish.

A sledgehammer to the head would have had less impact than Phoebe's kiss. He didn't sleep at all last night, and he wanted to blame Phoebe, but he was just as much at fault. He'd grabbed hold of her—his lifeline—and kissed her right back. Which hadn't been nearly enough to satisfy his longing to have someone in his life who would stay forever.

He shook himself from the inside out. "Forever" contradicted everything he wanted for himself.

"You don't need to get out," she said, opening her door. "Just pop the back for me."

"Are you staying with Izzy tonight?"

"She's going to stay here. We figured if Tim comes around, he'll go to the Victorian before he comes here."

"We'll talk later?" he asked, but she shut the door without answering.

He hit the button for the trunk, and she grabbed her bag. She held up a hand before going inside.

Leo drove to Gunner's house, surprised to see his truck in the driveway at noon on a Saturday. Gunner's dog started barking before he reached the porch.

The front door opened, and Gunner leaned out. "Hey, Leo."

"Hi, Gun. Do you have a minute?"

"Sure. Come in out of the cold," Gunner said, pushing the door wider.

Leo stepped inside and looked around. "You did a great remodel on this house. Are you planning to sell it after the wedding?"

"I think we'll either live here or buy something else and rent out Izzy's attic apartment."

"The attic is a great space, too. Izzy showed me around a couple of weeks ago." He bent to give Gunner's dog a good rub behind the ears. "Hey, Domino. How are you, boy?"

He glanced up at Gunner. "Why not live in the Victorian?"

"No room to expand when we have kids."

Kids? Gunner had as crappy a childhood as he did, and he wanted kids?

None of my business. "Seems crazy to own that beautiful Victorian and not live in it."

"I told Izzy the same thing when she first bought the place and told me she planned to live in the attic. But another business—or three, counting her event planning, the tea shop, and the real estate office—next to Owen Danielson's office makes sense." Gunner motioned toward the living room. "Have a seat. Can I get you anything to drink?"

"No, thank you." Leo sat on the sofa. The dog followed him.

"Domino, come over here," Gunner said when he took a

seat across from Leo. "Sorry. If you show him any attention, he's your friend for life."

"Willy's the same. Too friendly to be much of a watchdog." Leo patted Domino's side.

"Domino, come." The dog walked over and plopped down next to Gunner's chair. "So, what's going on?"

"Not sure if you've heard, but my parents are selling their farm."

"I hadn't heard. You okay with that?"

No, but he was trying to come to terms with it because he knew he couldn't change their minds. And they deserved to live in comfort.

"I don't have much choice." Leo rested his elbows on his knees and cupped his hands. "Anyway, I'm going to buy the place, and I need someone to do some renovations."

Interest lit Gunner's eyes. "What are you planning?"

"Maybe something completely crazy. I want to gut the main house and turn it into a restaurant, but I want to make sure the bones of the house are good enough. Rock and Sage haven't exactly taken care of the place. I'll hire someone to come in and get the fields in shape. I'm thinking a farm-to-table restaurant, community garden, and an events venue."

Gunner nodded. "Eden Falls could use a place like that."

"Neil told me the Hayes family next door have talked to him about selling too, so I'm thinking of buying their property and adding an orchard. Maybe a small vineyard."

"Wow. That's quite an endeavor," Gunner leaned forward and ruffled his dog's fur.

"The barn is falling in, but if I replace it, I thought Izzy could use the space for weddings and other large celebrations."

Gunner smiled. "She'd love that. She's always saying Eden Falls needs more party places. She'll be able to have smaller gatherings at the Victorian, but fifty people are the max until we get the screened-in porch fixed up."

"Inside the house, I'd like to knock down some walls to make a more open eating area. I thought about bumping out the back wall and adding two kitchens—one for the restaurant and one as a catering kitchen that would be available to service the events in the barn and other gatherings—if I can find someone interested in cooking."

"Have you talked to Iz about any of this?" Gunner asked.

"No. I plan to visit her next if she's home."

"She is. I was just headed over there."

"I'll follow you if you don't mind. I wanted to check with you first, to see if you'd be available to oversee the renovation."

"I'll be available as soon as I finish the Victorian's kitchen and back porch. Izzy would have my head if I put her renovation behind yours."

"I'm not in a huge rush to finish, but I am in a rush to get the plans set. I've got a job opportunity in Northern California and plan to leave soon."

"What? You're leaving Eden Falls?"

"An opportunity came up suddenly, and with my parents leaving, I don't see any reason to stay."

Gunner opened his mouth, then closed it without saying anything.

"If you're interested, I'll walk you through the house as soon as my parents move out."

"I'm more than interested." Gunner stood when Leo did. "How do your parents feel about you tearing up the house?"

"If Rock had any idea I was the buyer he probably wouldn't sell, so I'll have to wait until they leave or go through a third party. Once they leave, they'll never be back." Saying that still made his throat ache. "So they'll never know."

~

*I*zzy set a glass of ice and a can of fizzy water in front of Phoebe.

"Thanks."

"So, tell me about the party," Izzy said, pulling out a barstool next to Phoebe. "Lara's parents never held back when it came to entertaining."

Phoebe popped the top on the can and poured the water over ice. The scent of grapefruit tickled her nose. "It was an extravagant lock and key party. Once a guy matched his key to your lock, both your names were entered in a drawing. Then you got another lock or key for round two."

"I went to a lock and key party a few years ago in San Francisco. It was a great way to meet lots of people, and the prizes they gave out were pretty amazing."

"I can't begin to guess how much Lara's parents spent. Leo won a two-night stay on a Seattle houseboat."

Izzy's eyes grew wide. "That's a cool prize. Did you win anything?"

"No." Phoebe took a swallow of her drink. "I only put my name in the hat once, and guess whose key fit my lock?"

"Who?"

"Leo."

Izzy laughed. "He's the only match you made all night?"

Phoebe bit back a smile.

"Oh, tell me, tell me," Izzy said leaning forward. "You met someone, didn't you?"

"I did. He's a pediatrician in Harrisville. He was there because his family is friends with Lara's."

"A pediatrician?" Izzy asked, jumping off her stool when the teakettle she'd put on the stove started to whistle. "Cute?"

"Handsome. In an eerie, Leo Sawyer kind of way."

"What?" Her sister poured water over a teabag in a mug that said,

I want to ki _ _ you!
Options may vary.

"Where did you get that mug?"

Izzy looked down like she'd forgotten which one she was using, then grinned. "Gunner gave it to me after the particularly trying day when I had to decide on colors for the dining room."

"I guess it ended well since you're both still alive."

"It always ends well." Izzy poured a spoonful of honey into her tea and slid onto her stool. "So, this guy looks like Leo?"

"He's a couple of inches shorter, and the shape of his face is different, but they look so much alike. Actually, that's why I stopped by. You're still friends with that lunatic psychic, right?"

"Yes." Izzy blew on her tea and took a sip.

"Next time you see her, ask her a hypothetical question for me."

Izzy raised her brows. "A hypothetical question?"

"Yeah. Ask her if possibly someone who looks like Leo is having twins rather than Leo himself."

"Why?"

"Because this guy—his name is Keaton—looks so much like Leo, it's scary. I actually did a double-take when I first saw him."

"Maybe Leo has a brother."

"No, just a doppelganger. Their mannerisms and the way they talk are nothing alike."

"Do we get to meet him?"

"I invited him to family dinner tomorrow."

Izzy looked over the rim of her mug. "Your first date is family dinner? You're brave."

Looking back, that probably didn't qualify as the smartest idea she ever had. "So? Will you ask the kook? Maybe she made a mistake. What if, in her visions, or however she sees these things, she saw a man who looks like Leo, and then when she saw us together, she assumed."

"I don't think that's how it worked with Leo."

"How what worked with Leo?" Leo asked, following Gunner into the kitchen.

Gunner bent forward and shared such a sweet kiss with Izzy, Phoebe needed to look away. Why had this happened to her? She'd been completely happy with her life just the way it was before Madam Venus messed everything up—including her relationship with her best friend.

Leo leaned a hip against the counter. "What were you two talking about?"

"The day I went to Madam Venus's house—"

"Please, don't tell me you're still talking about that woman." Leo sighed.

"I'm with you there," Gunner added. "She creeps me out."

"She creeps you out because what she said came true," Izzy said, patting her fiancé's chest. "We found love in this house. Now, back to your question, Phoebe."

"What's the question?" Leo asked.

Phoebe had never believed in psychics, and she couldn't believe she was hanging on to Madam Venus's predictions so tightly. But as hard as she tried to let it go, she couldn't.

"She wants me to ask Madam Venus if she could possibly have meant someone who looks like you would father her twins."

"Wait. What's going on?" Gunner asked. "You're having twins?"

"No," Leo said with a snort.

"I remember when you said having twins would be like

getting two prizes in a box of Cracker Jacks," Izzy said to Leo.

"Yeah, two prizes for someone else." He looked at Phoebe. "Let's back up a step. Who looks like me? And if you're talking about the guy you just met last night, aren't you jumping the gun a little? You can't be thinking of having babies with a man you barely know because a psychic told you you're having twins."

"I just want Izzy to ask Madam Venus if it's possible. Maybe she got it wrong. Maybe she meant someone who looks like you."

"Can someone fill me in?" Gunner asked.

"Madam Venus said Leo and Phoebe are having twins. Together," Izzy told Gunner. She glanced at Phoebe. "The day Leo and I went to her house, Leo parked at the front corner. Madam Venus came into the living room through a black curtain from the back of the house. All the windows were covered in black fabric. There is no way she saw Leo, yet she said to tell him congratulations before she got to the door where she *could* see him." Izzy took a sip of tea. "If it's any consolation, she said you'd have pretty babies."

Gunner glanced from Leo to Phoebe with raised brows.

Leo looked like he might punch something. Or someone.

Izzy laughed. "Can I get you something to drink, Leo?"

"No thanks. I came to talk business, not babies."

"Business with me?" Izzy asked.

"Let's sit at the table to talk," Gunner said, pulling out a chair for Izzy.

While the others moved to the table, Phoebe stayed on the stool, listening to Leo spill out a plan to buy his parents' farm and renovate, surprised and hurt that he hadn't discussed any of his plans during their five-hour drive to and from Seattle.

Izzy squealed with excitement when he mentioned

rebuilding the barn so people could hold weddings and other events there. He also talked about turning the house into a restaurant and hiring a chef, building two kitchens, and hiring another cook to do the catering. She liked the idea of farm-to-table. He mentioned buying the adjoining farm for a vineyard and orchard. Leo detailed all the changes he wanted to make while she imagined the jobs he'd create and the people he could help with a community garden.

Her takeaway—Leo would make a great husband and a fantastic father. He was so kind and thoughtful of others, always trying to help their little town by growing the economy.

"Your plans will create quite a few jobs in the area," Gunner said.

"That's what I'm hoping."

Did Leo keep his plans from her because she kissed him? Well, one thing was certain—if he refused to acknowledge the spark that flared between them, he was living a lie.

She shouldn't have kissed him, because she knew how he felt about marriage and kids. No matter what Madam Venus predicted, Phoebe should have respected that.

Her cell phone vibrated with a call. She glanced at the screen and smiled when Keaton's name popped up. "Iz, can I take this call in your office?"

"Sure," Izzy said with a wave.

Phoebe connected the call. "Hi, Keaton."

"Hi. Hope I didn't catch you at a bad time."

"No, just visiting my sister, but she got pulled into shoptalk," Phoebe said, walking all the way to the huge front windows. "Did you make it home okay?"

"Yep. How about you?"

"After a hearty breakfast, we made it home just fine."

"So, that guy you were with…"

She pushed all emotions and predictions aside. "Leo and I are just friends."

~

*L*eo lost his train of thought when Phoebe walked out of the kitchen. Jealousy shot through him like a jolt of electricity. Based on her silly smile and quick exit, he guessed her caller was the guy she met in Seattle.

He had never before felt jealous of Phoebe and another guy. Never. This jealousy came about because of that stupid kiss they shared, the one that kept him up half the night, and put an uncomfortable wedge in their almost-lifelong friendship. Normally he would have walked into Izzy's kitchen and wrapped an arm around Phoebe's neck. Now he was afraid to go anywhere near because she might take any touch or sentiment the wrong way.

Why did she believe that stupid prediction? So much so that she thought a guy who might look a little like him—a guy she just met!—would fulfill a psychic's prediction?

The job offer and the move to San Francisco had come at just the right time. Distance would get his mind off Phoebe and babies. His attention would be diverted to busy work, which would also help him get past the feelings of rejection because of his parents leaving. He and Phoebe would talk on the phone, probably every day, same as now. But time would help them move back to their old norm.

Could there be such a thing as *old norm* after the intensity of emotion he experienced when her lips touched his?

Phoebe's laughter floated into the kitchen. "Anyway," he ground out. "I don't want you to think I'm trying to cut into your business, Iz."

"Oh, not at all. Do you have any idea how excited I am about this? Eden Falls has needed a place to hold events. I think an old barn will be so appealing. Brides will love it for the rustic charm, and grooms will love the relaxed vibe of the setting."

"After you leave, will you hire someone to manage the renovation and the schedule for events?" Gunner asked.

"Wait!" Izzy said. "Where are you going?"

"A business opportunity came up in the San Francisco area."

"You're moving?"

"Relax, Iz. I'm only going down the coast a ways."

"It's a thirteen-hour drive, Leo. I used to live there, remember?"

"I used to live there too. I know how far it is."

"But you've always said you love Eden Falls."

He sat back, uncomfortable with the conversation that would probably circle back to the parents who never wanted him in the first place. "I do, but with my parents leaving, I don't have any fam—"

"If you say you don't have family, I'll knock you right out of that chair, Leo Sawyer. You know you've always been part of our family." She stuck her finger in his face. "Don't you *ever* say that in front of Mom. You'll break her heart. And Dad just might never forgive you. Well, he would because he's a softy, but I might not."

Leo smiled. Izzy could be just as softhearted as her dad. "This is a great business opportunity."

"So what? You don't need the money."

"Let's circle back to Gunner's question. Yes, I plan to hire someone."

"I can manage the schedule for you." Izzy rolled her eyes —an Adams sisters thing.

"You have enough on your plate with your event planning business and the tea shop."

"I'm interviewing people for the tea shop manager's position next week. And I'll hire a receptionist to help me with event planning," Izzy said. "I can include the barn schedule in her list of responsibilities."

"I offered Phoebe my house rent-free and she refused. See if you can talk her into it. In fact, you can both stay there until your wedding. I have a security system and motion sensors. Since they've released Tim, you'll be much safer there."

"That's a great idea," Gunner said to Izzy.

"Also I need someone to…adopt Willy. Phoebe said she'd take care of him."

"You're leaving your dog? Why can't you take him?"

"I'll be working long hours to get this new business up and running, and I don't want to leave him alone all day in an apartment. Just see if you can talk Phoebs into staying at my house where Willy will have more room."

"She'd probably go for it if you charge her a minimal amount."

"She's my best friend, and I don't want or need her money." He stood up. "Also, see if you can get this crazy twins thing out of her head, and keep her away from Madam Venus. Phoebs just might hit the woman."

"Do you need a hug? You're sure ornery today." Izzy stood up and hugged him without giving him a choice. "Is it because of your parents, or something else?"

His parents leaving, Phoebe and her craziness, the move…which, truthfully, he didn't want to make. Living in a big city wasn't for him. He tried it once and had been relieved to sell his part in the company he built so he could move back and be near Phoebe again. "I'm not ornery. I just have a lot going on right now."

"Well, I for one am so excited about your new venture. Are you going to keep the vegetable stand out by the street? You should. Saunders' Orchards is the only one left around here. People love to buy fresh fruit and vegetables from stands. And it's a great way to connect with the community."

Izzy was right, but it would add one more item on his to-do list. "Possibly down the road."

"Hey, my friend Joanna keeps bees. Maybe she could set up a little stand nearby and sell her honey. She also makes candles and soap."

"One thing at a time, Iz. First I have to buy the property without Rock finding out."

"How?" she asked.

"Owen and your dad are working something out for me. Please keep this quiet until the deal goes through or my parents leave town, whichever happens first."

Izzy mimed zipping her lip.

He grabbed his coat off the back of his chair. "I'll let you know what's happening as soon as I can, Gun. I'm looking at a March or April timeline."

Gunner nodded.

"Wait a minute," Izzy said, holding up her hand. "This renovation comes behind my renovations and our honeymoon."

"I'm not in a huge rush, Iz. Everything can wait until after your projects are done, and I'd never interrupt your honeymoon."

Leo glanced toward Izzy's office while trying to rein in another jolt of jealousy—something he'd have to analyze later—and anger. "If Phoebe ever emerges from her phone call, tell her I'll talk to her later."

CHAPTER 9

*L*eo walked into the church's chapel and started toward the Adams family's usual spot, then stopped short.

Phoebe's new buddy was sitting in Leo's place. He wasn't even gone yet and had already been replaced. Now he was the odd man out—the only single left—life just kept poking at him. Mr. and Mrs. A had each other. Stella and Rowdy were cuddled up close, Izzy sat next to Gunner, and Phoebe now had…Leo couldn't even remember the guy's name.

He guessed he should feel lucky they left enough room for him on the end.

And when had Phoebe ever brought a guy she just met to church? She usually waited until the sixth or seventh date—if they made it that far.

Before he met Phoebe, Leo had no idea what the word religion even meant. His parents meditated and chanted, but they never spoke of a higher power. The first time he went to church with his new best friend he'd literally quaked in fear. He didn't know what to expect, but everyone was so friendly and kind. They treated him like he mattered. He wasn't able to go to church with Phoebe every weekend but liked the sense of peace that came over him when he could.

Since then, he'd studied religion, and had many great talks with the preacher, Josh Brenner—a guy who loved fishing and Patsy's Pastries as much as Leo did—and finally, to his parents' disgust, joined the church as a full-fledged member when he turned eighteen.

Rowdy scooted closer to Stella to make a little more room. They seemed like an unlikely pair to him, yet they matched so effortlessly. Leo hadn't thought marriage was in Rowdy's DNA, but Stella came along—someone Rowdy had known his whole life—and captured his heart. Or he'd captured hers. Maybe both.

Preacher Brenner walked up to the podium and delivered a message about a person's power to heal from within.

At thirty-five, Leo knew his parents would never change, which meant it was time he learned to heal and move on. Rock and Sage would be fine. Once they settled in their little commune, they'd live happily ever after, which, in truth, was all he ever wanted for them.

The Adams always ate a big family dinner after church. And he felt like a third wheel when they needed to add an extra setting for him.

The job in California looked better by the minute.

Neil had a habit of going around the table asking about their lives. Stella told a funny story about one of her second graders, and Rowdy talked about how he'd joined a search party that located a couple of lost hikers. Izzy and Gunner discussed wedding plans and how the Victorian's renovations were progressing.

Phoebe told everyone about Lara's party and how she and Keaton met. She actually giggled. Giggled! So not like Phoebe. Although by the end of dinner, Leo had to admit the man seemed okay.

Still, Phoebe was attracted to Keaton for all the wrong reasons—seriously wrong on so many levels.

Should he step in? Tell Neil and Bev what Phoebe was thinking?

"What's new with you, Leo?" Neil asked, dragging him out of his disconnected thoughts.

Neil already knew about him buying the farm, and would have told Beverly by now, so he shared his other news. "I have a job offer in San Francisco."

"What?" Beverly asked. "Are you taking it?"

"Yes."

"I thought you were buying your parents' farm. Neil said you're making all kinds of plans."

"I am. Gunner will start on the renovations when he finishes working on the Victorian. I'll probably have to raze the barn because there's so much damage, but I'm hoping to keep the house."

"I had no idea you were planning to move, Leo," Neil said.

"He's not," Stella stated. "You can't move, Leo. I won't let you."

"San Fran isn't that far away, Stella. You and Rowdy can come visit anytime. I'll show you the city and take you to some great restaurants."

"I agree with Stella," Beverly said, blotting away tears with the tip of her napkin.

Phoebe poked her mashed potatoes with her fork. "Leo's already made up his mind."

"Tell him he can't go, Phoebe," Stella demanded, swiping fingers under her eyes. "Talk him out of it. If anyone can, it's you."

Phoebe glanced from Stella to him. "Leo's a big boy. I can't make him change his mind."

At least Beverly, Stella, and Izzy, who also dabbed under her eyes, would miss him.

He almost chuckled at his own drama. He had a lot of friends in Eden Falls, and he hoped to travel back and forth often—one of the reasons he wanted Phoebe would stay at his house, so he'd have a bed, be able to visit his dog, and see the person he'd miss the most.

"So I'll have two children to worry about," Beverly said. "What are we going to do about keeping Izzy safe?"

"I'll move into Leo's house, and she'll stay with me until the wedding," Phoebe said.

"Oh." Bev breathed out a sigh of relief. "Leo has all those wonderful security gadgets. That's a good idea, Phoebe. Having a dog around will also help."

Phoebe laughed. "Willy will only be a help if we need him to lick someone to death."

"So you *will* stay at my house?" Leo asked.

"If you charge me rent," Phoebe said without making eye contact.

She and Keaton shared a private smile, and unease rippled through Leo. Keaton just might be the guy to come between him and his best friend.

~

*P*hoebe couldn't believe Leo had actually decided to move. Did their kiss lead him to that final decision? To move because of a kiss would be a huge mistake. In fact, she'd go so far as to say he was making a mistake anyway.

He already tried big city life and came home after a few years. He loved Eden Falls and his mountain home that she'd give her eye teeth to live in. She could stand in his living room and enjoy the view out of his floor-to-ceiling windows all day, but she absolutely wouldn't live there for free. He should have known better than to even suggest such a thing.

The best thing about living at Leo's? Izzy would be safe. He'd installed all kinds of security.

She'd helped Leo plan and build his home and had been there every step of the way, so in a way, it was her idea of perfection. When she helped choose kitchen cupboards and appliances, she did it as a friend, trying to look at everything from Leo's future wife's perspective. She chose the long double-sink vanity in the master bath with his wife in mind. Even though he said he'd never marry, she believed he would.

Leo wasn't meant to be alone. He was warm and generous and fun to be around. He wore his heart on his sleeve, and it was bigger than almost anyone else's she knew. He hated his upbringing, and she couldn't blame him, but those hardships made him who he was…sweet, kind Leo. Those childhood years made him look at life differently than someone who'd known safety and security all along. Reaching for love and attention all his life helped him give it more freely than someone who'd known and taken that love and attention for granted.

When he finally chose a wife, she would be a very lucky woman.

After dinner and a yummy dessert, Phoebe walked Keaton to the front door of her parents' house.

"Are you sure you can get a ride home with one of your sisters?" he asked.

"Yes. Thanks for coming today."

"I had a great time." He slipped on his coat.

"Are you sure you have to leave so soon?"

"I have rounds tonight, and there's one little boy in particular that I need to check on. I also have to work a twelve-hour shift tomorrow, and I'm covering for someone on Tuesday night. Are you free for dinner on Wednesday?"

"I'm on duty. What about Thursday?"

"I have a business dinner that night. Friday?"

"Friday will work," she said.

"I'd hoped I wouldn't have to wait almost a full week to see you again." Keaton smiled. He had a beautiful smile. "I'll pick you up at six-thirty.

Phoebe couldn't wait. She had a nice time today. He held her hand during church and seemed comfortable around her family. She could tell Stella and Izzy liked him, and he'd talked easily with Rowdy and Gunner. Only Leo seemed to hold back a bit, but that might be her fault.

Why couldn't she have met Keaton before she kissed Leo? She hated the awkward tension she'd created between them.

Keaton kissed her cheek and left her to analyze why only her cheek got any action as she waved from the porch.

When she shut the door and turned, Izzy was standing behind her. "You were right. Keaton looks a lot like Leo."

They both plopped down on the sofa together. "I know. It's uncanny, don't you think?"

"Yep. But everything else is completely different, his mannerisms, the way he talks. It's pretty eerie, though."

"Now you can see why Madam Venus probably got it wrong."

Izzy was quiet, looking off somewhere over Phoebe's shoulder.

"Come on, Iz. She could be completely wrong. She could have meant someone who looks like Leo."

"I can't say everything that Vera predicts is true, because I don't know. And I'll admit I'm still a skeptic, but what she predicted for me, that I would find love in the Victorian, came true. She predicted Misty conceived back in October and that turned out to be true. She also knew I wanted to buy her house before I said a word. She knew you were my sister, and she talked about Oops—again without knowing we're sisters."

Phoebe sat forward slightly. "What did she say about Adelaide?"

"She gave her the 'you'll find love when you move home. The boy will have green eyes' spiel that psychics tend to give to teenagers," Izzy said, using finger quotes.

"Oopsie is moving home?"

Adelaide—or Oops, as they called her—came along after Neil and Bev thought they had all the blessings they were supposed to receive. Now Oopsie attended college on the East Coast and was due to graduate this spring.

"According to Vera, she will."

Phoebe fell back against the sofa cushions. "I like it when you call her Vera. It humanizes her."

Izzy laughed. "She's not a divine being, Phoebs. She's human and makes mistakes. Maybe she did mean someone who looks like Leo will have twins."

"But that's not what you said."

Izzy shrugged. "Maybe what she told you is completely wrong. You shouldn't try to live your life by her predictions. *And* you also shouldn't try to fit Keaton into a place that he doesn't belong just because he looks like Leo."

"I'm not."

Izzy looked at her with raised brows.

"Did you believe her when she said you'd fall in love in the Victorian?"

"No. Well…I'm not sure. But I never thought if I did find love that it would be with Gunner." Izzy reached over and set her hand on Phoebe's knee. "If you like Keaton, go for it because *you* like *him*, not because he looks like Leo or because Vera told you."

Phoebe turned on the sofa so her back was to the arm and pulled her knees up. "I hate this, and I hate her."

"Hate is a strong word, Phoebe." Izzy leaned sideways and propped her elbow on Phoebe's knees. "You don't hate her.

She just made you think about things you've never considered before—an intimate relationship with your best friend, and children. Moving into the relationship with Leo would be easy. Everyone in Eden Falls already thinks you're more than just friends."

Phoebe rested her forehead on her sister's arm so Izzy wouldn't see her tears.

Izzy twirled Phoebe's hair around her finger. "Did I hit a nerve?"

"Oh, Iz. I did something so stupid."

"What?"

She lifted her head and wiped under both eyes.

"Phoebe, what happened?"

Phoebe looked over Izzy's shoulder to make sure they were the only ones in the room. "I kissed Leo at Lara's party," she whispered.

Izzy's eyes widened to huge. "You did?"

"I wanted to see if I felt anything. To see if he responded."

"And?"

"I did. He didn't."

Izzy frowned. "Are you sure?"

"He kissed me back." Just the memory made her heart take off like a runaway train. She knew Leo felt something because of the way he acted—was still acting—but she'd keep that to herself. "Then he pushed me away and asked what I was doing."

"You probably just surprised him."

Phoebe lifted a shoulder. "I surprised him so much he immediately went off to flirt with a redhead."

"You know Leo. He flirts with any female. Ever since his geek-to-chic transformation, everyone with double X chromosomes looks twice." Izzy reached out and rubbed the outside corner of one of Phoebe's eyes. "I'm worried that the only reason you're attracted to Keaton is because he looks like Leo."

"I wouldn't do that."

"Are you sure? You may be doing it without realizing."

Phoebe didn't answer, because maybe Izzy was right. Other than the party, she and Keaton were only together once, and they'd been surrounded by her family. It usually took several dates before she felt much attraction, but something was different with Keaton. Was she rushing things, trying to convince herself that she felt something when she really didn't?

"You've never brought a first date to church or family dinner," Izzy said as if reading her mind. "You wanted Mom and Dad's approval. You wanted to make sure Keaton fit in before you even took the time to get to know him."

"No."

"Come on, Phoebs."

"What are you two talking about in here?" Stella walked into the room and nudged Izzy aside with her hip so she could sit between them. She glanced at Phoebe and her eyebrows shot up. "Are you crying?"

"She choked a second ago and it made her eyes tear up," Izzy said.

Stella looked at Izzy. "Liar. What's going on? Did Keaton make you cry?"

"No. Nothing's going on," Phoebe said. "We were just talking about first dates."

"Are you ready to go, Iz? I didn't get a chance to feed Domino before we left," Gunner said from the kitchen door.

"I'm ready. Want a ride home, Phoebs?"

"Yes, please," Phoebe pushed to her feet. Since Izzy was spending the night at her house, she'd be in the bedroom while Iz and Gunner made out on her sofa.

"Wait. Tell me what's going on," Stella called.

"Later," Phoebe heard Izzy say as she left the room.

In the kitchen, Phoebe gave her mom and dad cheek kisses. "Thanks for dinner. It was delicious as always."

"Are you leaving already, sweetie?" her mom asked.

"Yeah, I told Gianna I'd work the phones for her in the morning before my shift."

Leo got up from the table. "Want a ride?"

"No, thanks. You stay. Izzy's staying with me, so I'll catch a ride with her and Gunner."

Phoebe watched a shadow cross Leo's face. "I drive right past your apartment."

"We're going *to* her place," Izzy said, coming to her rescue. "And we brought my car, so there's plenty of room."

Phoebe pushed her feet into her boots and shrugged into her coat. "I'll wait outside," she said before she slipped out of the back door.

~

*P*hoebe was pulling away from him, the same thing she did before he moved to San Francisco the first time.

After Izzy and Gunner left, followed by Stella and Rowdy, Leo said his goodbyes since he'd be flying to California on Thursday to find a place to live.

Yesterday Owen texted that the contract laying out the terms for his loan to his dad for moving money was ready. Leo would pick it up in the morning and give a copy to his dad to read over. If Rock agreed, he could stop by Owen's office, sign the contract, and Leo would hand over the money.

Next Leo would work through another real estate agent, tell the agent he wanted to keep the transaction anonymous and offer more than the listed price for the farm. The agent would tell his dad the buyer offered more to avoid a bidding war. The profit would give Rock and Sage enough money to pay him back for moving costs and still leave them plenty to live on for the rest of their lives. Underhanded? Yes. But he didn't see any other way to handle the transaction and help his parents at the same time.

He stopped at the curb across the street from Phoebe's apartment. Gunner's truck was at the curb. Her blinds were closed, but the living room lamps were on. Any other time he would have given her a ride home and followed her inside. After popping corn, they would watch a movie together, because Sunday nights had always been their night. No boyfriends or girlfriends allowed—just him and Phoebs if she was off duty.

He wished he could go in but pulled back onto the street and drove home instead.

The next morning Leo and Willy took a drive into Eden Falls. First stop, Owen's office to pick up the silly contract. Owen wasn't in, but Ronnie had everything ready to go.

She pulled the contract out of the manilla envelope. "Owen marked the spots where your dad will need to initial. If you have your driver's license, I can certify your signature right now."

He pulled his license out of his wallet and handed it to her.

After signing, she stamped the contract and slipped it back into the envelope. "There you go. Once your dad has read over it, he can bring his license by and I can certify his signature too."

"Will do. I'm going to be out of town, so can you email me the bill. Owen should have my email address."

"It's in the file. I'll get it to you."

"Thanks, Ronnie. Tell Owen thank you for me." He headed for the door.

Second stop, Patsy's Pastries. The wonderful scents of cinnamon, citrus, and sugar assaulted him before he even stepped inside. JT's wife smiled from behind the counter.

"Hi, Leo."

"Morning, Carolyn. How are you?" He stopped in front of the case displaying delectable-looking refined carbs and empty calories.

"Good. What can I get for you this morning?"

"What are these? They look fabulous."

"Raspberry cream cheese bites."

"And these?"

"Caramel pecan cinnamon rolls."

"I'll take two of each, plus a doggy treat and two coffees. Oh, and will you add a half dozen assorted donuts boxed separately?"

"How are your parents?" she asked.

He always ordered the assorted donuts for them before a visit. "They're selling the farm."

She turned to look at him. "Really?"

"They're moving to a commune near LA."

"Good news or bad?" she asked, with a compassionate expression.

Carolyn didn't have the greatest childhood. In fact, he and Carolyn were kindred spirits in that sense. She'd been raised by a spiteful sister after her parents were both killed in a car accident. Other than her estranged sister, she didn't have any family except for JT, and here Leo was, whining about his life.

He glanced around while she poured two cups of coffee. "Patsy isn't here today?"

"She and Mason took off for the coast."

"She's been doing that a lot, hasn't she?"

"Now that she's a happily married lady, she and Mason take lots of little three- and four-day trips."

"Good for them. She was never able to do that before you came home."

"Coming back to Eden Falls is the best decision I ever made."

After high school, Carolyn moved to San Francisco to attend culinary school and later escaped an abusive husband by coming home. Now she managed Patsy's Pastries and was happily married to Eden Falls' police chief.

"Funny that three of Eden Falls' finest all moved to Northern California but found their way back."

"I know," Carolyn said with a smile. "I was shocked when Izzy left her job at the art gallery to move back to Eden Falls. She loved that place."

"I think she loves her Victorian and, apparently, Gunner even more."

"It's nice to see Gunner smile again. He was pretty broken up after his wife divorced him a couple of years ago."

Izzy and Gunner did seem happy. They were constantly holding hands and grinning at each other during dinner last night. Same with Stella and Rowdy.

He took the two cups of coffee Carolyn handed him to the end of the counter and doctored one for Phoebe. She was a cream and sugar girl.

"Is Phoebe on duty this morning?"

"She's filling in for Gianna."

"Oh, that's right. This morning's when she and Layne find out whether they're having a boy or girl."

"I didn't know they were having a baby." Leo capped Phoebe's cup and pulled out his wallet.

"Seems that half the town is either about to have a baby or just had a baby."

He glanced at her. "Except us."

Carolyn blushed bright pink. "Except you."

"What? You and JT are pregnant?"

"Well, I am."

Leo walked around the counter and pulled Carolyn into a hug. "Congratulations. I didn't know."

"Thanks. We just found out Friday, so it's still very new."

His first thought—*this is just what Phoebe doesn't need to hear.* "I'm really happy for you both, Care. Tell JT congrats for me."

"I will," Carolyn said, her smile radiant.

He walked out to his truck and dropped Willy's doggy treat on the seat. "Be right back, boy." Then he crossed the square to Town Hall, turned to the right, and went down a short hall to the small dispatch room where Phoebe sat behind a desk with a headset on. She looked tired this morning.

His chest tightened at her smile. He would miss these moments.

"Why are you out and about so early?"

"I picked up the contract from Owen so I can take it out to the farm." He held out the cup of coffee and bag of treats.

"Oh, thank you."

"You only get one of each. The others are mine."

She peeked inside. "Yum. These look wonderful. Pull up a chair."

He grabbed a chair from the police station's break room and tugged out the napkins he stuffed in his pocket at Patsy's. They sat close in the tiny room, their knees occasionally touching, and devoured the sweet treats Carolyn probably made at four this morning.

Phoebe seemed like her old self, chatty and happy, so he kept Carolyn and JT's news to himself. She'd find out soon enough.

CHAPTER 10

While Leo maneuvered around the deep ruts and potholes in his parents' driveway, he wondered why his dad wouldn't let him grade, which was ridiculous. He parked near the back door and stared at the van his parents planned to drive to California. That pile of junk probably wouldn't make it out of Washington.

He grabbed his phone and did a quick internet search. A car dealer in Montana was selling a 1974 white over chrome yellow Volkswagen van with a new engine that had 35,000 miles on it. The van looked like it was in great condition, so he made the call.

Ten minutes later he knocked on the back door, then knocked again before pushing it open to see his mom making her way into the kitchen. "Leo! Rock, Leo's here."

"I brought you some donuts." He set the box on the table.

"You know the way to my heart. Is that cute girl still working for Patsy?"

Sage looked remarkably drug-free and alert this morning. "Yep. Carolyn is still there. She asked how you and Rock are doing."

"She's been sweet since she was a little girl. Does she still blush?"

Leo remembered Carolyn's pink cheeks when she told him her and JT's news. "Yep. She still blushes. She and JT are expecting their first baby."

"Oh, Alice and Denny Garrett must be thrilled. This will be their third grandchild, right?" She cozied up to him. "When are you going to give me a grandbaby?"

Leo almost scoffed aloud. She hadn't been a mom, so whatever gave her the idea she could be a grandma? "I'm not."

"Leo, you don't want to have children?"

"Not in the cards for me." *Tarot or otherwise.*

"Speaking of cards, didn't one of the Adams sisters buy that psychic's house?"

"Izzy did. She turned the main level into a tea house-slash-events planning office. Neil has his offices in the second level, and she lives in an apartment in the attic."

Rock strolled into the kitchen, his long hair looking like an unkept bush sitting on his head. The smile on his dad's face brought Leo's thoughts to a screeching halt. He couldn't remember the last time he saw his dad smile.

"Morning, Leo. Did you bring the contract?"

"I did." Leo held out the manilla envelope. "You need to initial and sign it in front of a notary to make it official. I put twenty thousand dollars down. Do you think that amount will be enough to make the move?"

"Twenty thousand," his mom screeched. "We need like two hundred dollars."

"It'll cost you more than two hundred in gas alone, Mom."

"Well, you can tear the thing up. I just got off the phone with Neil. We have an offer for twenty thousand dollars more than the farm is listed for." He picked Sage up and twirled her around, a laugh bursting from both. "I told you we'd sell this place fast."

Leo told Neil to make the offer last night after dinner, hoping his dad wouldn't want details about the buyer. He really didn't want to go through a third-party, quitclaim ordeal.

Leo leaned back against the table and enjoyed his parents' happiness. Time to stop thinking about himself and let his selfishness go. This move might be just what they needed. Sunshine, similar people living a similar lifestyle, and an easier routine. They wouldn't have to worry about money, food, or necessities ever again, which should give them a sense of peace. All he'd ask is that they keep in touch.

When Rock set Sage down, he held out his hand. "Here. I'll tear it up, but not before I say—" his dad swallowed and looked down at the manilla envelope "—thank you for your offer. I know I've been hard on you for what you did, but when Neil came out to list the farm, he told me about some of the good you've done around town with your money. Some of the charities you've helped and the money you've donated to the library and the homeless shelter."

Rock finally met what Leo could only assume was his stunned gaze. "Why didn't you ever tell me?"

"I don't go around talking about it, Dad. I'm not sure how Neil knows."

What did his parents think he did with his money? If nothing else, they'd raised him to be mindful of those less fortunate.

Sage threaded her arm through Leo's. "Word gets around in a small town."

Pulling the contract out of the envelope, Rock ripped it in half, then ripped it again and again. "Selling this farm will give us more money than we'll ever need."

Sage took the pieces, threw them in the air, and danced as they rained down.

Leo tugged out his phone, pulled up the website with the VW van, and held it out for his dad to see. "I found this 1974 van with a new engine. I can go pick it up tomorrow or the next day. Or I can get you something newer if you'd like."

Rock took Leo's phone. "Look at this, Sage. What do think?"

"I love it."

"Where is it? I'll go pick it up myself," Rock said, handing Leo's phone back.

"I'd like to do this for you as a going-away present." Leo didn't dare tell them he was the person buying the farm, but he could be upfront about the van.

"It's really in nice condition, Rock. Why can't we let Leo do this one thing for us?" Sage smiled at Leo.

"Okay." Rock gave a shrug, like the issue of money had never come up before. "Thank you."

"I'll try to get the van here by tomorrow night."

Back in his truck fifteen minutes later, he bumped down the driveway and turned toward town. He passed the high school, fire station, and post office. Flipping a U-turn, he parked in front of Eden Falls Hardware and Lumber.

Mason Douglas used to give Leo odd jobs here when he was a kid, little things he could do like sweeping up sawdust and unpacking boxes, jobs that gave him enough money to buy new tennis shoes or food. Mason ended up selling the store to his son-in-law, Beam.

Leo walked through the front door and breathed in the scent of cedar and the tang of metal.

"Hey, Leo."

Beam Garrett stood behind the counter grinning.

"Just the man I need to see."

"Yeah?"

"You still fly?"

"When I can. I don't get the chance very often."

"Can you get your hands on a plane?"

"I have a buddy in Harrisville who owns a twin-engine Cessna. He lets me take her out every couple of months."

"Think you could take it out tomorrow?"

Beam's eyes lit up like a flare. The big man got his nickname from a football coach who said he blocked like an I-beam. He stood around six-five, with huge biceps, and a heart that was even bigger. "Mason's been out of town but will be back in here tomorrow. Where are we going?"

"Kalispell, but if things work out, it'll only be a one-way trip for me. Are you okay with that?"

"I'm a big boy. I've flown alone many times." Beam waved to another customer who walked in. "The flight will cost you."

"You get the plane and let me worry about the cost."

"What time do you want to leave?"

"Since I'm driving back, the earlier the better."

"Eight?" Beam asked.

"Sounds great. Text me if you run into any problems."

"If you don't hear from me, I'll pick you up at your place at seven-thirty."

"You don't mind driving?"

Beam laughed. "Not if I get to fly. You have no idea how much I miss being in the air."

Before Beam got married and bought the hardware store, he flew tourists around the Seattle area in seaplanes.

"Thanks, Beam. Hope to see you tomorrow."

Leo walked outside and paused, looking over Eden Falls, hoping to spot Phoebe circling the square or driving past in one of the patrol cars. Instead, he spotted Maude Stapleton, bundled up against the cold, chipping away at a sheet of ice in front of Pages Bookstore. He crossed the street and walked the half-block between them.

Maude looked up before he reached her. "I hope you're coming to help."

"You know I am." He took the shovel from her. Maude also gave him odd jobs around her shop when he was a kid. He'd unpacked books, swept floors, and dusted shelves, "Don't you have any high school kids who can do this for you?"

"Yeah, but they're in school."

Right. It was only nine-thirty.

"I heard you're moving," she said, looking up at him.

"You heard right."

"Who's going to shovel the walk?"

"You don't know a kid who can help around here? Gunner and I can't be the only ones."

"Yeah, I've got someone." She pulled up the collar of her coat. "Didn't you already try leaving Eden Falls once and decide you didn't like being away?"

"This is a business opportunity doing something I love."

"Can't you do something you love right here?"

He stopped shoveling as her suggestion hit him right between the eyes. A consulting job could possibly be done from Eden Falls. He'd have to mull that idea over. The ice broke apart when he hit it with the corner of the shovel.

She stepped in front of him. "I saw a for sale sign in front of your parents' farm."

He shoveled around her. "They're going back to commune life."

"Does your move have to do with Phoebe and Madam Venus's predictions, or your parents leaving?"

"Neither."

"Or both."

"Let it go, Maude."

She moved in front of him again. "You know, you're nothing like your parents."

He straightened and rested his elbow on the shovel handle. "Doesn't matter. I'm not meant to be a dad. I wouldn't know where to start."

"You have the perfect role model."

"Rock was not—"

"I'm not talking about Rock. I'm talking about the man who raised you. The man who picked you up every time your parents disappeared. The man who still calls you *son* in public."

Neil Adams *was* the perfect role model. Five kids already, and he took Leo in and treated him like one of his own. He and Beverly both were the best parenting role models any kid could ask for, and he'd benefited from their caring, generous ways.

Still, he couldn't chance what would most likely happen if a relationship with Phoebe didn't work out. They'd choose Phoebe—as they should—and he'd be alone again.

Leo nodded while he scooped the last of the ice off the curb and handed the shovel back to Maude. "Not sure I'll see you again before I leave, but I'll stop by when I'm in town for Izzy's wedding."

"You're going to lose her, Leo."

"Who?"

"Don't play dumb with me. You know who." She shook her head like he was a hopeless cause.

"Phoebe and I are—"

"Just friends," she finished for him. "You keep telling yourself that, and you'll die sad and alone."

"You're just a ray of sunshine today."

"I'm always a ray of sunshine," she said, adding a smirk. "Just ask my husband."

After Maude went back into the bookstore, he looked

around for Phoebe again. Still no patrol car, so he pulled out his phone and scrolled to her number.

She connected the call immediately. "Hey." He could hear panting breath and the rustle of something. "Now's not a good time."

"Where are you? Or shouldn't I ask?"

"Chasing Mr. Polanski's Bigfoot."

Leo laughed. Mr. Polanski regularly reported that Sasquatch was stealing his chickens, and the kids responsible were tricky enough to get away every time. "Be careful. I hear Bigfoot likes to harass pretty blondes in red."

"Shut up. Oh! Gotta go. Mr. Polanski's pulled out his gun."

"Be—"

He didn't get the "safe" out before she disconnected the call.

He'd been hoping to arrange a time when they could sit down together and discuss his plans for the farm, like when she helped him plan his house. Her opinion and ideas were important to him.

~

*P*hoebe and Eli finally got Mr. Polanski settled down and back in his house. He usually called the police when a chicken went missing, but they were all present and accounted for this time. And yes, she knew every chicken intimately, including their names. She and Eli climbed behind the wheels of their patrol cars, and she followed him down the mountain road that ran along the river toward Eden Falls.

Snow started falling when she got halfway back to town. The fat, white flakes floating down through the trees looked so beautiful. For some reason, a memory of making snow angels with Leo when they were in second grade popped into her mind. Leo didn't know how to make a snow angel, didn't even understand what an angel was, so she plopped down in some fresh white powder and made one. Amazed by how real it looked, Leo plopped down next to her to make his own. They'd each made a half dozen angels before walking to her house for some hot chocolate and dry clothes.

Almost every memory she had included Leo. And she might have ruined everything by being so stupidly impetuous. She'd sort of apologized, but she could do better.

Her phone pinged with a message, so she pulled to the side of the road.

Meet for dinner at East Winds???

She stuck her index finger between her teeth and pulled her glove off. **Yes**, she texted back.

Six-thirty. Want me to pick you up?

I'll meet you.

The message bubbles bounced along her screen and then disappeared twice before **See you tonight** appeared.

She set her phone aside, slid on her glove, and pulled onto the road, her patrol car skidding a little to the right.

Once she hit Eden Falls, she circled the square and parked behind the police station. She'd missed lunch while chasing Bigfoot and was starving. Going in the back door, she walked through the break room, found a plate of cookies, and picked up two.

"Hey," Mac Johnson said, entering the room.

"Are you on duty tonight?" she asked, taking a bite of the gingerbread cookie with the perfect cookie/frosting ratio.

"Yeah. Lucky me. The streets are getting slippery."

She held out the patrol car keys. "I'm going to take a walk around the square before I clock out."

"Okay. Have a good night, Phoebs."

"You too." She gave a little wave as she left the room.

The sun had already disappeared behind the buildings

around the town square, and the snow was coming down even harder than before. Mac and Layne would be busy with accidents tonight. The lights came on inside One Scoop or Two. In passing, she spotted two high school boys flirting with the two girls behind the counter.

Ah, to be young again.

Seemed like only yesterday she'd been one of those girls enjoying that pulse-pounding moment of meeting a new guy. She wanted to go back there, to that simpler life, when things seemed so hard but in hindsight were so very easy. Geez, she'd settle for going back to the day before Madam Venus's prediction, except keeping the knowledge of what would happen so Phoebe could avoid her.

Ha! Here she was, wishing she had the same psychic ability as that crazy woman.

Mac's dad waved from the front window of The Fly Shop when she walked by. Crossing the street, she glanced at Pretty Posies and smiled at the display window full of touches of spring while the snow fell heavy and silent around her. She already had the picture she bought for her parents' anniversary wrapped and ready to go. Patsy's Pastries was already closed for the day, the windows dark.

Phoebe stopped at the corner. Town Square looked like a winter wonderland. Very few cars were out, and the snow-covered sidewalks and pine trees were pristine and bright under the streetlights.

She glanced at her cell phone. She was off duty as of five minutes ago. If she clocked out now, she'd have enough time for a quick shower before meeting Leo for dinner.

~

*L*eo got a table for two near the window and ordered tea and lettuce wraps to tide him over while he waited.

He'd had a productive day. His parents not only accepted the offer on the farm, but they were also okay with him buying them a van—two checkmarks in the *Finally!* column. Plus, Beam had arranged for the plane, and the weather was supposed to clear up by midnight, so they'd be leaving for Montana early tomorrow morning. If everything went as planned, he'd be driving back into Eden Falls about this time tomorrow.

The next day he planned to meet with the same realtor he worked with the first time he moved to San Francisco. After Leo emailed some specifics, Gabriel said he had a dozen condos or houses ready to show. Again, if everything went smoothly, he'd be back in Eden Falls by Saturday afternoon.

After tonight he wouldn't see Phoebe for almost a week. He'd planned to invite her along on this trip to San Francisco but decided against it after Lara's party.

She walked through the door and headed toward him, unwrapping the scarf around her neck, the scarf he gave her for Christmas two years ago.

"Hey," she said. "Sorry I'm late."

The first thing that struck him was her scent…light, but still surrounding him as soon as she shrugged out of her coat. He'd never been able to pinpoint why it steadied him. Phoebe possessed the ability to ease his worries, make him smile, chase away doubts and fears. Despite Rock and Sage moving away, he knew that, if possible, Phoebe would be around for him. Just as he would always be around for her.

A small voice whispered *How?* in the back of his mind. How would he be around if he moved two states away? How would he be able to help if she got into trouble?

He glanced at his watch. "You're not late, I just got here a little early. Did you catch Bigfoot?"

She snorted and slid into the seat opposite him. "He eluded us again. Good news, though. Mr. Polanski didn't lose any chickens this time."

Leo chuckled.

While he poured her a cup of tea, she spooned some of the chicken concoction onto a bib lettuce leaf and rolled it up. "Remind me to breathe and chew tonight. I haven't eaten anything since our pastries this morning."

The waiter stopped next to their table.

"Hi, Patrick."

"Hey, Phoebe. Are you both ready to order?"

"Yes, I'd like the chicken and vegetables with crunchy noodles instead of rice, an eggroll, and a salad."

"Whoa, you're changing things up tonight," Patrick said with lifted brows. "Salad instead of soup?"

"Just a little."

"And you, Leo?"

"I'll take the Szechwan chili chicken with rice, two egg rolls, and egg drop instead of wonton soup."

"You're changing things up tonight, too," Patrick said.

"That's right. I'm going wild with my soup choice."

"Should be about fifteen minutes," Patrick said, turning toward the kitchen.

"What did you do today?" Phoebe asked.

"My dad accepted my offer for the farm."

She smiled. "Congratulations."

"And Beam is flying me to Montana in the morning so I can buy Rock and Sage a van that will actually get them to California."

"You had a busy day."

"Come with me," he asked before he could think it through. Beam would be in the plane with them, then Leo would be at the wheel for the drive back—he wanted to shut down his thoughts when they turned in this direction. He'd never been afraid to be alone with Phoebe before. But that kiss changed everything.

"What time are you leaving?"

"Beam is picking me up at the house at seven-thirty."

"I work, but maybe someone would be willing to swap shifts with me. I'll go look at the schedule after we eat."

"It would be great to spend the day together. I fly to San Francisco the following day to look for a house."

Phoebe looked out the window and took a sip of her tea. "Things are moving fast."

He leaned forward and rested his elbows on the table. "Are you going to stay at my house?"

"I'll rent your house," she said, picking up her phone when it vibrated.

"Phoebs—"

"Give me a number or drop the subject, Leo. We've been disagreeing about *your* money for years. It's getting old. I'll be happy to rent your house and take care of Willy. The end. If you can't accept that, find someone else." She pushed away from the table. "I have to take this."

Leo watched her stop near the hall leading to the restrooms. Based on her smile, Leo would bet the caller was Keaton.

Okay, Leo would have to come up with a reasonable price for rent. Since she worked for Eden Falls police, she didn't make enough to cover his mortgage and buy groceries too, but the amount he gave her would have to be believable or she'd never stay.

Pulling out his own phone, he quickly texted Neil, asking what he considered a reasonable amount to be.

Is Phoebe being stubborn?

What do you think?

LOL was Neil's reply. **Give me until tomorrow. Bev and I are just sitting down to dinner.**

Thanks. He tucked his phone back in his pocket just as Phoebe returned to their table. Long ago they'd agreed to not let phones interrupt their dinners. Guess she forgot the rule *she* insisted on.

"Keaton?" he asked as she slid into her chair.

"Hmm?"

Patrick appeared with his soup, her salad, and egg rolls. He set an extra bowl on the table. "Lin made too much fried rice, so he sent some out."

"Yum, tell him thank you," Phoebe said.

"Want more tea?"

Leo picked up the teapot and held it out. "Yes, please."

"What's going on at work?" Leo asked after Patrick walked away.

"Nothing new. Gianna—"

He waited, but she suddenly became very interested in her salad. "What about Gianna?"

"What?"

"You started to say something about Gianna."

"Oh…uh, she told me a joke, but I can't remember the punchline."

He studied her a moment, an egg roll halfway to his mouth. "That's not what you were going to say."

She shoved a bite in her mouth and nodded.

"You know I'm going to bug you until you tell me the truth."

"It has to do with babies," she said around her mouthful.

This was the moment when he would normally bring up Carolyn and JT expecting a baby, but times had changed. Their relationship had changed. "Never mind."

An expression he didn't want to try to decipher passed over her face before she looked away.

"I want to discuss the farm with you. I'm going to need your help."

"I don't know anything about farming."

"No, but you can read blueprints and know-how to design efficient kitchens." He divided the fried rice into two small bowls.

"You're not going to be here."

"That's why I'd like your help. Can you sit down with me on Saturday night and help draw up some plans?"

"I'm on duty."

"Sunday?"

"Keaton's coming to church and family dinner again."

He could see by her expression that she was getting frustrated. Because he asked for help? Or because he was leaving? "After dinner?"

She blew out a breath. "Okay. After dinner."

"At my place."

Phoebe nodded before meeting his gaze. "I can't pay you rent until the first of next month."

He bit off the first response that came to him. "We can work something out."

She was quiet through the rest of their dinner. At least until she opened her fortune cookie.

"What?" he asked when she frowned.

"Trade me."

"You can't trade fortunes," he said with a laugh.

"Who says?"

"It's an unwritten rule."

"There is no rule." She held out her hand. "Here. Trade me."

"What does yours say?" he asked.

"The window of opportunity won't open itself." She glared when he chuckled. "What does yours say?"

"You can open doors with your charm."

"Of course, it does," she said, dropping hers in her teacup.

Phoebe grabbed the bill before Leo could. She usually just gave him her share, which he complained about and she ignored.

"No, Phoebe," Leo said, reaching for her hand.

She pulled away. "Consider this a going-away dinner and an I'm-sorry dinner rolled into one."

"I'm not moving yet, and what are you sorry for?"

She busied herself with opening her wallet and pulling out a few bills. "For *opening a window of opportunity*. I shouldn't have, and I'm sorry."

"I'm not sure what—"

"The kiss, Leo. I know it made you uncomfortable and made things between us awkward, and I'm sorry."

She set the money on the table and slipped on her coat. He turned toward the window at the squeal of brakes, and the screech of metal on metal sent a shiver up his spine.

Phoebe dropped everything and sprinted for the door.

CHAPTER 11

Phoebe faintly registered Leo calling her name as she ran out of East Winds' front door. A small SUV had jumped the curb kitty corner to the restaurant, and a truck sat wedged against the driver's side of the SUV.

She yanked her phone out of her pocket and called dispatch. "Gianna, we need Brandt and possibly an ambulance at the northwest corner of the square." The SUV looked familiar, but she couldn't place it until she saw Mac's wife slumped over in the driver's seat. "Gianna, tell Mac it's Noelle."

The door of the truck popped open, and a young girl stumbled out. Phoebe grabbed her arm to steady her. "Are you okay?"

"I-I think so," the girl said between sobs. "I couldn't stop. My brakes—"

"Nothing hurts?" Phoebe asked.

The girl shook her head.

Leo skidded to a stop next to them.

"Take her into East Winds to stay warm and call her

parents," Phoebe said over her shoulder as she rounded the SUV. "Brandt is on his way."

Beck, Mac's ten-year-old son, looked at her with wide, terror-filled eyes when she reached the front passenger door. She looked past him. Noelle's head was down, her hair covering her face. In the back, the baby was screaming.

"Noelle won't wake up," Beck said through the window, his voice shaking.

She tried the handle. "Can you unlock your door, Beck?"

He did and she leaned in. "Are you okay? Does anything hurt?"

"I bumped my head."

She leaned closer to take a look. He had a nice-sized goose egg growing, but the skin wasn't broken. "What about your arms or legs? Your tummy? Does anything else hurt?"

"No. Can you make Noelle wake up?"

"Your dad and an ambulance are on the way. They'll take care of her." She reached over him and unbuckled his seat belt.

Brandt Smith appeared next to her. He must have run the two blocks from the fire station rather than wait for the truck to warm up. "What we got?"

"Beck has a bump on the head but says nothing else hurts. Noelle is unconscious. Leo took the girl from the truck into East Winds. She said she wasn't hurt, but she might be in shock."

"Let me check the baby." Brandt opened the back door. "The car seat is secure, and the neck and head bumpers are in place."

"His name is Lucas. I got to name him."

"Lucas is a good name, Beck," Brandt said. He unbuckled the baby and lifted him out of the car. "Hey, little guy. You're okay. Just a little shaken up." Brandt held the baby out. "Can you hold Lucas, Phoebe? I want to take a look at Beck's head."

For a split second, Phoebe stood immobile. She'd never held a baby before, but she knew she needed to support infants' heads, so she took Lucas and held him against her shoulder. He was bundled against the cold in a one-piece puffer with a warm beanie on his head, but Brandt still handed her a blanket from the back seat, and she wrapped it around Lucas, protecting his head and face from the falling snow. She followed Brandt's lead and swayed with Lucas while whispering, "you're okay" again and again until he calmed down.

Skidding tires made her duck into a doorway to shield the baby in case it was another out-of-control car, but it stopped in time, and Mac jumped out. A fire engine pulled in behind them, and several men swarmed into action.

Mac fell to his knees next to Beck and looked him over, running hands down his son's arms, and studying the lump growing on Beck's forehead. "Are you okay?"

Beck had been so brave, but the tears welled at his dad's question. "Noelle w-won't wake up."

A lump tightened Phoebe's throat when Mac pulled his son into his arms and held on tight.

Brandt had crawled into the passenger seat to examine Noelle. "Phoebe, tell one of the crew I need a neck brace."

She turned toward the fire truck, but a fireman was already jogging over, holding one out.

Mac stood up and lifted the baby's blanket so he could see his other son.

"Brandt thinks he's okay. Just angry," Phoebe said, trying to relieve some of Mac's fears.

"Mac, can you give me a hand?" Brandt called.

The baby finally stopped crying, so Phoebe put her arm around Beck's shoulder and pulled him into her side. "Noelle will be okay, Beck. Brandt and your dad will take good care of her."

Beck nodded while trying to blink away his tears.

After a still-unconscious Noelle was freed, Brandt and Mac lifted her out and strapped her to a backboard, then carefully carried her over the snowbank to the stretcher near the ambulance, and the EMTs loaded her into the back.

"I'll ride with Noelle," Brandt said. "You can follow. I think a doctor should look at the bump on Beck's head and check Lucas, just to be on the safe side."

"I'll drive you," Phoebe said without a hint of reservation. She'd seen Mac's shaking hands and knew he was scared for his family.

"Thank you, Phoebs. I'll put Lucas's seat in your car."

"I can do that while you take care of the stuff in Noelle's car," Leo said, suddenly next to them. "The tow truck just pulled up."

"How's the girl?" Phoebe asked.

"Shaken up, but an EMT checked her over and said she's okay. Her parents should be here any minute."

Leo took the car seat from Mac and held out his other hand for Phoebe's keys. "I'll get it started so it'll be warm."

"Is my dad coming too?" Beck asked after Leo walked away.

"We're all going to follow Noelle to the hospital."

Layne pulled up in another patrol car. "Everybody okay? I just saw the ambulance pull away."

"They're taking Noelle to the hospital," Mac said. "Will you see if JT or Eli can cover my shift for the rest of the night?"

"Yeah. You need a ride to the hospital?"

"Phoebe's taking us."

Layne nodded. "If you're not back in time for your shift tomorrow, I can pick it up," he said to Phoebe.

"Thanks. I'll let you know."

She crossed the street with Lucas and waited while Leo fought with the car seat, growling a curse word every thirty seconds, which was so unlike him. She glanced through the back window. "You're putting it in wrong."

He leaned out. "What?"

"Babies are supposed to face backward. You have to flip the seat around."

"You could have told me," he said, a scowl wrinkling his brow.

"Here. Hold Lucas and I'll put the seat in."

He glanced from her to the bundle she held close and went back to work on the car seat.

She lifted the blanket and breathed in Lucas and his sweet, powdery softness. He felt cozy against her chest. So tiny. So fragile.

Two minutes later, Leo straightened and glared at her. "What are you doing?"

She startled at his harsh growl. "What do you mean?"

"This isn't going to change my mind about having kids, Phoebe."

"Are you being serious right now? I'm helping Mac because he has his hands full. Have you forgotten that's what friends do for each other?" *Un-believable.*

"I think you have an ulterior motive."

"And I think you're an idiot." She pushed past him and buckled the baby into the car seat.

He planted one hand on the car and the other on the door, hemming her in. "What about tomorrow? You said you'd come to Montana with me."

She tried to make sense of his ludicrous question before ducking under his arm. He wasn't acting like the helpful Leo she knew so well. "This is a little more important than flying off to buy a van. Mac needs help."

Mac and Beck crossed the street, and the three of them climbed into her car. She watched Leo disappear in her rearview mirror as she drove away. Insulted and hurt that he thought she would use Noelle's accident to try and change his mind, she fought back another round of tears. Leo had always been first in line when anyone needed help. What changed?

Phoebe tried to keep their conversation light during the fifteen-minute drive to Harrisville Regional Hospital. Beck answered her questions about school and even laughed at a silly joke Stella told her a few weeks ago.

When she stopped at the emergency entrance, Mac told her she could leave. "Not yet. You might need help."

An hour after she sat down in the waiting room, Mac walked out with a hand on Beck's shoulder and baby Lucas in the crook of his arm. "Thanks for staying."

"Of course. How're you feeling, Beck?" she asked.

"I have a headache."

"They gave him something, said he may be a little stiff in the morning," Mac said. "Little Lucas came out without a scratch."

"How's Noelle?"

"She's going to be okay. Since she was unconscious when she arrived, the doctor on call wants to keep her overnight." He gave her a tight-lipped smile. "I know this is a lot to ask, Phoebs, but—"

"Give me the code to your house and tell me what to do," she said. Because how could she not?

"I'd call my mom and dad, but they're in Idaho visiting an aunt."

"Don't bother them. I'm here."

"Beck knows the code. Noelle keeps breast milk in the freezer. Just warm it up in hot water and pour it into a bottle. The bottles are in a drawer under the silverware." Mac rubbed his forehead. "Geez, I'm not sure Lucas will take a bottle. He's been with Noelle since he was born and has never needed a bottle until now."

"Don't worry, we'll figure it out. Won't we, Beck?"

"Yep. I can help," he said with a confidence she loved. She wished he could share a little with her.

"Good, I'll need all the help I can get. How much and how often should I feed Lucas?"

"About two ounces every two hours. Diapers are in the baby's room. Beck can show you."

Phoebe held out her hand. "If you'll give me your keys, I'll get someone to drop your car off here in the morning."

Mac handed over his keys, then hugged Beck and kissed Lucas on the forehead. "Thank you, Phoebs. I'll owe you."

"You don't owe me anything, Mac," she said, taking Lucas in her arms and throwing a blanket over his head.

Being this far out of her element scared her, but surely, she could figure out how to change a diaper and fix a bottle. Mothers around the world did it every day. Still...just the words "breast milk in the freezer" threw her. She didn't want to imagine how it got from mother to fridge, but of course, her mind tried to conjure up an image. Guess she'd find out when she got to Mac's house.

If she needed help, she could always call her mom. Beverly would love to get her hands on a baby, since none of her five daughters had delivered a grandchild yet.

The roads were still slippery, but the snow had finally stopped, which would be good for Leo and Beam's flight to Montana. Plus, the temperatures were supposed to warm up over the next few days.

At Mac's house, Beck got out and opened the garage door with the code and she drove inside. Luckily, she'd been in Mac's house many times before he married Noelle, so she knew the lay of the land.

"Are you hungry, Beck?"

"I like ice cream."

"I think the situation calls for ice cream. Let's have a look in the freezer."

She lay Lucas on the sofa, unzipped his little one-piece coat, and pulled off his beanie to reveal his dark hair standing on end. He was fussing, but not really crying.

"Before ice cream, let's change this cutie's diaper."

Beck led the way down the hall and into a bedroom. She spotted a cushy pad on a low dresser and diapers stacked at the end—everything but a flashing neon sign telling her that's where she was supposed to change the baby. She unsnapped the legs of his one-piece outfit and wiggled his feet out. His toes were so tiny and cute. "You might have to help me, Beck. I've never changed a diaper before."

"You haven't?" Beck said a little too wide-eyed, like changing a baby's diaper should be an everyday occurrence for everyone. "You just take one off and put another one on."

Sounded too easy to Phoebe. She pulled the two tabs and then picked up a clean diaper to see exactly how it worked. "Okay. We can do this. This side down, just like microwave popcorn."

She opened the diaper and gagged. "Oh, baby, you didn't tell me you pooped."

Beck giggled and handed her a plastic pack of wipes. "Dad uses like a hundred of these when Lucas poops."

"I might need two hundred."

She pulled out six and went to work, cleaning all the cracks and crevices, then pulled out another three to make sure she got everything. Lifting the baby's feet, she slipped the clean diaper under his bum. As soon as she did, he pooped again—all over the clean diaper and her hand.

Beck literally rolled on the floor in a fit of laughter.

"Gross," she groaned. "Lucas, you could have warned me

with a smile or a wink. No need for such a drastic initiation of the newbie."

She started the process all over again. "Beck, where does Noelle keep the baby's pajamas? I think we're going to need a clean pair."

Beck came back with a white onesie covered with monkeys. "These are the ones I got for him."

"I love monkeys."

Beck nodded with bright eyes. "Lucas likes them too."

After she changed and dressed Lucas, she put him in the crib. "I need to wash my hands. Where does Noelle put the dirty diapers?"

"In that diaper pail."

"Ah, handy-dandy." She threw the diaper out—along with two dozen wipes—and went into the bathroom to wash her hands. Meanwhile, Lucas started to cry. Mac said he usually ate every two hours and it must be way past time.

Back in the bedroom, she picked up Lucas and followed Beck down the hall for ice cream. Beck dug in the freezer and came up with vanilla. "We have chocolate sauce too."

"Yum, my favorite way to eat ice cream," she said bouncing the baby, whose cries were getting more insistent. "Where's the baby's milk?"

Beck pulled out a frozen plastic bag and handed it to her. She couldn't imagine how the milk went from mother to bag but wasn't about to ask Beck to satisfy her curiosity.

The date and a sweet little message to Lucas were written in sharpie. "Cute." She turned on the water until it ran hot, then filled a pan and dropped in the plastic bag. She opened every cupboard in the kitchen before she found the bottles.

"You can put Lucas in his bouncy seat. He likes that."

Good. Phoebe was pretty sure she couldn't hold a baby and pour milk into the tiny top of a bottle without dumping half of it on the countertop.

She strapped Lucas in the seat, then dished ice cream for Beck while bouncing the seat. She could use a little sweet fortification, so she dished a scoop for herself, then went back to the sink to refresh the hot water because the crying was escalating.

When she turned back toward the table, she noticed Beck stabbing at the ice cream. She put a hand on his shoulder. "Are you okay? You seem quiet. Does your head still hurt?"

"No, I'm just afraid about Noelle."

"Noelle is tough. She's going to be just fine."

He put a spoonful of ice cream in his mouth then looked up at her. "Are you going to spend the night?"

"Yep."

"Do I have to go to school tomorrow?"

Oh, boy. Talk about being out of her element. Left up to her, getting him ready for school while dealing with a newborn would be a big *No.* "Let's see how you feel in the morning."

"I don't think I'm going to feel very good." He put the hand holding the ice cream bowl on his forehead. "I might have a fever."

She snorted. "Do you have a test you didn't study for?"

"I don't have a test until Friday," he said on a yawn. "I could stay here and help you with Lucas."

"We'll see."

"It's past my bedtime. I won't get my healthy eight hours of sleep."

Phoebe laughed and went to the sink. Lucas was done waiting for his dinner, and she didn't blame him. Both kids had a crazy night.

She tested a drop of milk on the inside of her wrist—because she'd seen it done in a movie—and it felt warm, but not hot. She poured the milk into the bottle, hoping the temperature was right and unbuckled Lucas. "Do you need to take a shower tonight, Beck?"

He yawned. "I take one in the morning."

"If you're finished, put your bowl in the sink and get ready for bed, okay?"

He did as she asked and headed down the hall.

"Don't forget to brush your teeth!" He wasn't going to get a cavity on her watch.

"I won't."

Now, what happened at bedtime? Beck could read, so he was probably too big for a bedtime story, but she could make sure he was tucked in. "Let me know when you're in bed."

"Okay," he called, disappearing into his room.

She bounced Lucas, who was really squawking now. "Just a few more minutes, buddy. It's almost your turn. Let me get your brother settled."

Lucas stopped crying and looked at her. Would he be able to tell she wasn't his mom? Could he see clearly, or feel scared? Inadequacy wasn't something she felt very often, but the feeling bore down on her heavily tonight. "Everything's going to be okay. Mommy will be here tomorrow," she said as much for herself as for Lucas.

"I'm ready!"

She propped Lucas against her shoulder and walked down the hall. Tucked under his covers, Beck's eyes were already at half-mast. She ran a finger along his forehead, pushing his hair aside, careful of his bump. "Do you say prayers before bed?"

"I already did. I asked for Noelle to be okay."

"Don't worry about Noelle, Beck. The doctors only want to keep her overnight to be safe. Your dad will bring her home tomorrow."

He nodded. "Can you leave the door open a little?"

"Sure. Sleep well. If you need anything, just call. I'll be in the living room, okay?"

He nodded and his eyes drifted shut.

She left the door ajar and went to the living room. "It's finally all you, cutie. I know you don't understand what I'm saying, but I feel silly just looking at you and not talking. You're a lucky kid to have such great parents, and your big brother will always be around to help you. That's what big brothers do. Or so I've heard. I always wanted a big brother. Leo, he's my best friend…at least until I screwed things up. He and I, we go way back."

She remembered Leo's angry look earlier. "I think you scared him tonight. But sometimes being scared is good. Or bad. I guess fear can push you both ways. But it really doesn't matter since he's moving."

Lucas puffed out his bottom lip in the most adorable pout, then opened his mouth for a full-fledged scream.

Phoebe laughed. "I guess we're done with the chitchat portion of this evening."

Sitting in a rocking chair, she cradled the baby close and touched the bottle to his lips. He whipped his head back and forth a few times as a drop of milk slid into his mouth. It took a couple of tries and some mother's milk bribery, but Lucas finally latched on to the nipple and started to suck.

She leaned close and took a deep breath of his sweet baby smell. "I'm going to miss Leo terribly. The first time he left, I knew deep down that he'd come back. This time I'm not so sure, and that scares me, Lucas. Even if we're talking on the phone and emailing and texting, it won't be the same. This move just might change everything."

The tiny swallowing sounds Lucas made tightened her chest and brought tears to her eyes. This tiny human had only been on earth for a short time, but he'd already made such a huge impact on so many lives. Mac was over the moon happy when he learned Noelle was pregnant. Initially, his marriage of convenience with Noelle was to help him keep custody of Beck, who he'd raised almost since birth. It wasn't supposed to last, but they fell in love and were now living their happily-ever-after—the kind of fairy-tale story Phoebe used to believe only happened in books.

~

After Phoebe drove away with Mac and his sons tonight, Leo went home with her words ringing in his ears. He spent an hour or longer just standing in his too-quiet house, embarrassed and angry at his reaction to Phoebe helping a friend.

She was right. He was an idiot.

The image of Phoebe cuddling the baby close while keeping a comforting hand on Beck's shoulder clouded his mind as he looked out at the lights of Eden Falls from his front windows. She'd looked so beautiful. So...motherly. Phoebe with a baby—something he hadn't been able to picture before—was now in the forefront of his mind, and he wasn't sure how to process any of it.

Or why he felt the need to.

Yet the longing to see Phoebe made his heart beat so hard, so fast, he could barely breathe.

He stayed where he was because his fear of wanting to hold the baby and comfort Beck continued to swamp him in waves of overwhelming proportions until he couldn't stand it any longer. His urge to see Phoebe was suddenly stronger than his urge to bolt. He jumped in his truck and drove to her apartment, but she didn't answer the door. On a whim, he drove to Mac and Noelle's and spotted her through the living room blinds.

Leo sat at the curb, his truck's heater turned to high and

watched Phoebe pacing back and forth with Lucas on her shoulder. He tried to imagine his mom or dad doing the same with him when he was a baby and couldn't. Who had fed him or changed his diaper?

He'd retained very few memories of life before his family moved to Eden Falls, and even fewer pictures. The ones he did have, were of him barefoot and filthy. In one, he was playing with a rusted metal truck on a pile of dirt and weeds —probably not even taken by Rock or Sage. In a way, he was glad he remembered so little about their commune days.

Aching desire kept him from driving away.

Fear of that aching desire kept him from going inside.

CHAPTER 12

The next morning, Leo was waiting outside when Beam drove up to his house. The weather prediction for today was for clear skies and warmer temperatures. Perfect for flying.

He'd been up with Beam several times over the years, but Beam didn't fly much anymore. Once his daughter Sophia was born, he sold his plane, bought his father-in-law's hardware store with the money, and became a respectable and permanent businessman in Eden Falls. Not that flying tourists around Puget Sound hadn't been respectable, but now he'd set down roots, started building a home, and was expecting his second child.

Beam and Misty probably wanted Madam Venus to move to the South Pole as much as he did.

Leo remembered his shock when he received Beam's wedding invitation. Beam—like his brother Rowdy—were the two of his friends least likely to get married. And to marry Misty Douglas and then have a baby was one for Ripley's Believe It or Not. The two weathered a bumpy start, but they seemed happy now.

"Sorry I'm late," Beam said when Leo slid into the front seat. "Sophia wanted a story before I could leave."

"Not a problem. I'm not on a strict timeline." He just wished he'd spent the extra ten minutes in bed trying to catch up on the zero amount of sleep he got last night.

"So why are we going to Montana this morning?" Beam pulled onto the mountain road that would lead them onto the highway.

"I'm buying a van for my parents and driving it back."

"You couldn't find a van closer to home?"

Leo gave him a side-eye. "I'm pretty sure you've met my parents. Do you think they'd accept just any van? This is a 1970s VW with a new engine."

Beam chuckled. "How are Rock and Sage?"

"The same. Stoned more often than not. They're heading to LA, moving into another commune."

"Selling the farm?" Beam asked, slowing as he drove through Eden Falls.

Leo scanned the site of the accident as they passed.

"I can't imagine anyone else living out there," Beam added.

"I bought it."

Beam scoffed. "What are you going to do with a farm?"

Leo spent the fifteen-minute drive to the Harrisville airpark telling Beam about his plans. When Beam floated a few ideas his way, Leo made notes on his phone.

"I'm excited to see these developments happen," Beam said, turning into the airpark. "That's a pretty piece of land that's been neglected for too long."

Leo didn't have any problem imagining how beautiful the place could be with a little TLC. He just wished the grandmother he'd never met was still around to see the main house turned into a homey restaurant and the gardens flourishing again. When they moved in, the little stand by the road was already there but had fallen in since his parents took over. He liked the idea of restoring that tradition to honor his grandmother.

The possibilities for the farm were endless, making him wish for the thousandth time that his parents had allowed him to help. Beam suggested adding a greenhouse where Alex could start flowers for Pretty Posies. A hen house for fresh eggs, beehives, an orchard, a community garden…so many ways Eden Falls residents could benefit from all that land.

The flight was smooth, and they arrived in Montana ahead of schedule. Once Beam fueled up, he'd be on his way home.

Leo held out his hand. "Thanks for the ride, Beam. It's been a while."

"You're the one who deserves the thanks. I love owning the hardware store, but man, I miss flying."

And the next idea popped into Leo's mind. If he bought a small Cessna and kept it in Eden Falls, Beam might be willing to ferry him back and forth between San Fran and home. The plane could also be used by others or in emergencies. He'd have to do a little research on maintenance and fuel. Since Beam owned a business, he couldn't be at Leo's beck and call, but maybe if he prearranged the days. He'd have to table that idea until the ink dried on the purchase of the farm.

"Well, I appreciate you taking the morning off to bring me." He handed Beam the cost to cover everything. "Be safe on the flight home."

"Always. You got a ride from here?"

Leo held up his phone. "Yeah, I've got a car coming."

He stood off to the side of the runway and watched Beam take off. Being back in the air with his buddy had felt good and brought back fun memories.

His car pulled up minutes later and drove him through town to the car dealership, where the van sat out front, all cleaned up and looking pretty. He got out and circled the van. The exterior was in pristine condition. He hoped this small gesture would please his parents.

"That's a beauty, isn't it?" asked the man emerging from a side door of the dealership.

"Yeah, it is."

"I have a guy on his way from Washington to look at it."

"I'm the guy. Leo Sawyer."

The man grinned and shook his hand. "I didn't expect you so early."

"Yeah, we made good time. Can I take a look inside?"

"You bet. Be right back with the keys."

After checking the interior, Leo took the van for a spin. It drove rough and noisy like every VW van he'd ever seen, so his parents should feel right at home in it.

"Okay. Let's get this done," he said when they got back to the dealership. "I've got a long drive home."

Six long hours of open road and time to think about Phoebe, remember the image of her walking back and forth comforting an unhappy baby, tucking a scared boy against her side while he watched his unconscious stepmom being lifted out of a wrecked car. And he'd accused her of trying to trick him.

Yep, it's going to be a long ride.

~

*P*hoebe was completely exhausted but in the best kind of way. She'd gotten zero sleep last night, opting to hold a snuggly baby instead.

She also let Beck sleep in this morning after clearing a

no-school day with Mac. She suspected he'd stayed in bed even after he woke up, afraid she'd make him go.

Mac said Noelle was conscious and doing well, and his dad would drive in from Idaho to pick them up around noon.

Beck finally stumbled into the kitchen at nine. Lucas was fast asleep in his bouncy seat, which she set on the table while she made Beck a pancake breakfast. Since Noelle was a restaurant owner and an excellent cook, Phoebe's pancakes probably didn't come close to what Noelle made, but Beck didn't complain while he downed every bite.

After breakfast she fed Lucas, then she and Beck sat on the floor and played a couple of board games. With lots of giggling from both, Beck trounced her twice.

"Phoebe?

The tone of Beck's voice made her look up after moving her piece around the Sorry board. "Hmm?"

"Are you letting me win because I was in an accident?"

"Ha! I wish I could say yes." Phoebe ruffled his hair. "You're winning because I haven't played board games in years and I'm rusty. Plus, you're pretty good at this."

"What games are you good at?"

"Poker." She'd been playing with Leo and the guys for years.

"Will you teach me?"

Phoebe laughed. "Not on your life. That's a game your dad will have to teach you."

The baby mewed like a kitten and blinked sleepy eyes a few times.

"I'd better get a bottle ready and a diaper changed. Can we finish after I feed Lucas?"

"Can I play video games instead?"

"Sure. Let's pick this up real fast and then I'll watch you while I feed Lucas."

His eyes lit. "Okay."

They made fast work of packing up the board game, then she went into the kitchen to warm a bottle with Lucas tucked into the crook of her arm.

Her phone beeped a message with a picture of the van Leo would be driving home. **What do you think?**

She considered not answering after his accusations last night, but that wasn't her way. Very seldom did their arguments last overnight.

Sweet. Your mom and dad are going to love it! She grabbed a plastic bag of milk from the freezer and put it into a bowl of hot water.

I think so. Headed home now. How is everything?

Still at Mac and Noelle's. Beck is killing me at board games.

Any idea when Noelle gets home?

Mac called a while ago. He's expecting to be home around noon.

How is Noelle?

Phoebe refreshed the water that had gotten cold from the frozen milk. **Mac says she's doing well.**

That's good to hear. Want to go to Renaldo's for dinner when I get back to town?

Renaldo's offered two pizzas for the price of one tonight. Leo usually ordered two, then took one home to eat for lunches for three or four days. Except he wouldn't be home to eat them this week. He'd be in San Francisco looking for a place to live. **Raincheck. I see a bed and twelve hours of sleep in my future.**

While Phoebe carried Lucas down the hall for a diaper change her phone pinged another message.

You have to eat, Phoebs.

I'll grab a can of soup if I wake up. Gotta change a diaper. Drive carefully.

She pushed her phone into her back pocket, changed

Lucas, and headed to the kitchen for the bottle. She'd finally gotten the hang of pouring the milk into a bottle without spilling a drop, much improved after a pretty dismal start.

Sitting on the sofa next to Beck, she watched him play video games while Lucas made his little swallowing noises. If Leo could hear—

Nope, she wouldn't go there. But holding this baby while watching Beck was nice. Surreal, but nice. She'd never even imagined herself in this position with nieces and nephews, but here she was, falling more in love every second with the idea of being a mother. She didn't want to, but she could do it on her own if it came to that.

Marrying someone like Keaton because he looked like Leo wasn't the answer. Other options were available, and if adoption didn't fit with Madam Venus and her visions, that would be her problem, not Phoebe's.

When Beck changed games, she out Lucas on her shoulder for a burp. Luckily, Mac remembered to text her about the burping part since that was a tidbit she hadn't known. In fact, her knowledge of babies—and kids—had grown exponentially over the past sixteen hours.

She heard a car door moments before the back door opened. Beck turned to her with wide eyes before jumping off the sofa. "Dad and Noelle are home!"

While he dashed off in his excitement, Phoebe tucked her nose against Lucas' soft, milky-smelling neck and breathed deeply. Her time was up, and she wanted a baby—a whole family—even more now than she did yesterday.

~

*L*eo took his time driving back to Eden Falls, enjoying the ride and the scenery. His parents never took him along on their mini-vacations to follow the Grateful Dead around the country, instead, leaving him at home to fend for himself. The farthest he'd ever traveled with Rock and Sage was their move from the Northern California commune to Eden Falls.

He never even had a chance to meet either set of grandparents. His mom was an only child, and his dad refused to tell him anything about his side of the family. Leo suspected if Rock did have extended family somewhere out in the world, they didn't even know Leo existed.

Once he had a school assignment to construct a family tree on poster board. He'd fretted over that assignment until he had a stomach ache. He didn't want to be the kid with only three leaves on his tree.

Finally, he turned to Phoebe's mom for help, and Beverly told him he was a part of their family, so he could add their names to his poster. He ended up with a huge tree and even added Sage and Rock to the mix. In the end, he decided to keep that tree in his bedroom at the Adams house. Proud of his work, yet afraid of his parents' reaction, he'd never shown them the project.

How could he even consider fatherhood after his neglectful upbringing? Yet that's where his mind went after seeing Phoebe with Mac's two sons. The sight stirred something inside him that he'd never experienced before. Something that terrified him at the same time.

Leo wasn't sure putting his fears aside to give these new feelings room to grow was right for him. His instinct to run had always been stronger than his willingness to risk failure, but now, a desire to find what he'd so desperately missed out on fired through him like a spark of electricity.

Neil and Beverly taught him, along with their daughters, to dream big and reach for the stars. He'd done both. He hadn't changed the world, but he was trying to make the little corner he lived in better for everyone. Could he do that with a family? Bev and Neil did.

He pulled into the farm after dark. His parents were in another universe or realm, wherever they tripped off to when chemically stimulated. He roused them enough to bundle up and come outside. Sage jumped up and down like a kid when she saw the van.

Rock circled it. "Sweet ride, Leo. Whose van?"

"It's yours, Dad. I showed you the picture on my phone, remember?"

"Right on. This is ours, baby." He grinned at Leo. "Where'd you get it?"

"In Montana."

"Montana?" Sage hugged Leo's waist. "You drove all the way to Montana and back?"

They remembered absolutely nothing of the conversation in the kitchen yesterday. "Beam Garrett took me to Kalispell in a plane this morning. I bought the van and drove back."

"Beam? The big guy who owns the hardware store?" his dad asked.

"Yes." He'd hoped his dad could give him a ride home, but he was too messed up to get behind the wheel. Normally, he'd call Phoebe, but she said she'd be sleeping, so he texted Neil. **Any chance you could pick me up at my parents' house?**

Sure. Be there in 10.

Leo handed his dad the title, the bill of sale, and the keys. "When are you leaving for California?"

Sage looked from him to his dad and shrugged. "Tomorrow?"

Oh, brother. "You haven't packed yet. Are you renting a moving truck?"

She flapped a hand. "My mom left us the furniture, so

we're leaving it as a gift for the new owners. I never liked that early American stuff anyway."

Looked like he'd be renting a dumpster.

"Neil can mail everything we need to sign," Rock said.

"You already have a mailing address?"

"I'll write it down for you." Sage danced her way into the house, touching her thumb and middle fingers together like she was playing finger cymbals to a song only she could hear. Snow and mud caked her 1960's galoshes. It was a wonder she could even lift her feet.

"The van is cool, Leo. It'll get us to California, right?"

"It should. The new engine only has thirty-five thousand miles."

"Right on. Thanks."

Leo turned to his dad. "I have some news. I got a job in San Francisco."

Rock scoffed. "Selling out again."

"Not selling out. Helping a startup company, working for an honest wage."

"Same thing."

Why did they have to repeat this conversation over and over? Nothing he did would ever be right according to his dad.

"I'll be closer to LA…so I can visit you and Sage." He heard the hope in his voice.

"Right on," Rock said.

A car turned into the driveway, the headlights flashing across them. Leo held up an index finger to let Neil know he'd be right there. Then he went inside to get the address from his mom, who'd forgotten why she went inside.

"I have to go out of town, but I'll be back Saturday to help you pack."

"Sure, honey. See you then." Sage waved him out.

Outside, Rock was standing near the driver's side

window talking to Neil. Owen Danielson and Neil were probably the only two men in town Rock trusted.

"I told Sage I'd come by on Saturday to help you pack up the van," Leo said.

"See you then." His dad patted Neil's shoulder. "Take care of the kid after we leave."

That short sentence was as close to "I love you" as Leo would ever get. But it was more than enough to tighten his chest and put a lump in his throat.

That short sentence let Leo know that, despite everything, his dad cared.

"Leo always has a place with us," Neil said.

After Rock backed away from the car, Neil rolled up the window and turned around in the rutted drive. "Your dad said you bought that van for them today."

"They need something more reliable than what they've got. The one around back needs to be towed to a junkyard."

"Have they packed?"

"I didn't see any boxes inside, so my guess is no."

Neil pulled onto the road. "Call if Bev and I can help in any way."

"They're leaving everything here and buying new. And to be honest, they deserve new. The furniture was here when we moved in thirty years ago. The couch has been sitting on cinder blocks since I was in high school. What they do pack won't be organized. They'll just throw what they plan to keep in boxes and fold the flaps over."

He was almost afraid of what he'd find when he went through the closets. Just the thought of the basement gave him the heebie-jeebies. The smart decision would be to bulldoze the whole place and start from scratch. Building a restaurant from the ground up would probably be easier anyway. But then he'd lose the small part of his parents and any other family member the house still contained.

"Well, they'll have more money than they'll ever need living in a commune," Neil said.

"Right, which means I won't have to worry whether they have food in the cupboards."

"You'll still worry."

Yes, he would. "Did Phoebe call about Noelle? Did she get out of the hospital?"

"Mac brought Noelle home a little before noon. Phoebe said she seemed to be okay."

Leo glanced at Phoebe's apartment as Neil drove past. "Mac, Beck, and the baby were all upset last night, but Phoebe and Brandt calmed them down."

"She has that way about her, doesn't she?"

"Yes, though on the outside you'd never guess."

Neil laughed. "No, you wouldn't. That girl of mine is one tough cookie, but she's got the softest of hearts. She's going to miss you. We'll all miss you." Neil cleared his throat, a sure sign he was going to say something that made him uncomfortable. "I wish you'd reconsider this job offer and stay."

Neil had a way of choking Leo up with emotions ever since he was a little kid. He was the kindest man Leo knew, which was saying a lot since Eden Falls was full of kind men and women. "It's a great offer."

"And I'd understand you taking it if you needed the money. Taking it when you don't need it makes me think you're running. But from what? Are you leaving because of your parents? Or is it Phoebe?"

"Phoebe?"

"This is a small town, Leo. I've heard about Madam Venus and what's going on."

Leo talked to this man about everything. Why not this? If Neil was going to take sides, Leo might as well find out now. "She kissed me. *We* kissed."

Neil turned onto the road that led to Leo's house. "And you felt nothing."

Leo wished that were true. He wished he could go back to that night and…and what?

To not kiss Phoebe back would have been a lie.

"No, I did feel something," Leo said. "That's the problem. Phoebe knows me better than anyone. She knows I wouldn't have kissed her back if I didn't feel anything. I was the first to break away, and ever since…"

"Things are different."

"Yes. I already love Phoebe, and I think falling *in* love with her would be like slipping on a comfortable pair of jeans." *But if things go wrong, I don't want to lose the Adams family.* "I don't want to get married, Neil. I don't want kids. Phoebe more than anyone knows this and the reason why."

"What is the reason?"

Leo looked at him in astonishment. "You're kidding, right? You saw how I was raised. You saw—"

"You aren't your parents, Leo. You may have your dad's blue eyes and your mom's nose, but you are your own person."

"How do you know? How would I know? What happens if I have kids and decide I don't—"

"You won't." Neil pulled up in front of Leo's house and put his car in park. "You're nothing like your parents, and never will be. Their blood runs through you, but you were raised differently. You know what it feels like to be left, and you'd never put your child through that. In fact, I believe you'd react the complete opposite way because of your parents. And you're smart enough to know that."

"So you think Phoebe and I—"

"No, that's not what I'm saying. That decision is between you and Phoebe. What I'm saying is *don't* let the way your parents behaved influence the rest of your life in a negative way. *Don't* make decisions based on your fear of doing what they did. You get to choose, Leo. This is your life. You should live it the way you feel is right. If you want that job in San Francisco, then you should grab it with both hands. But make sure you're grabbing for the right reasons and not because you're trying to outrun your feelings."

Leo tried to swallow around the lump in his throat, so close to tears he needed to look away.

"Bev and I love you like a son, Leo. And if you and Phoebe decide to date and things don't work out, our feelings for *you* won't change. I may not like the decisions my kids make, but that doesn't change my love for them. And that includes you."

Leo rubbed his eyes with both fists. This wasn't the first time he'd cried in front of Neil, and it probably wouldn't be the last. "Thank you for the ride. My dad wasn't..."

"You know you can call me anytime. If you need to talk, I'm here."

Leo climbed out of the car and watched Neil's taillights disappear into the darkness.

His surrogate father just gave him a lot to think about and now his mind felt more cluttered than ever.

CHAPTER 13

After his very early morning drive to the Seattle airport, and the two-and-a-half-hour flight to San Francisco, Leo was ready to find a place to live and get back to Eden Falls, which should tell him something.

He'd believed distance between him and Phoebe would be for the best, but after his talk with Neil, he wasn't so sure. To deny he felt something when Phoebe kissed him would be an obvious lie because he'd kissed her back like the touch of her lips was as necessary as air.

He walked into Gabriel's San Francisco real estate office just after noon. The man helped him find his first condo as a twenty-year-old kid and then helped him sell it before he moved back to Eden Falls a few years later, and Leo was confident he'd come through again.

"Gabriel, it's good to see you."

"Hey, Leo. Moving back for a second go-around?" Gabriel was tall, built like an offensive tackle, and one of the most personable men Leo ever met. After only minutes, he made people feel like they'd been friends forever.

"I think the saying goes, third time's a charm, but we can shoot for two. How are Lyla and the girls?"

"Wife is doing great. Girls are teenagers and rabid about boys. How's Phoebe?"

Leo wished he could unload everything that was going on. "She scared me to death a couple of weeks ago disarming a nut who was trying to hold up a diner."

"A scare like that can take a few years off your life."

"Agreed."

"She's not married yet? I figured when you didn't snap her up someone else would," Gabe said.

He, along with everyone else, loved to tease them about being together when they weren't. "Nope. She's still single."

Minutes later, he and Gabe hit the ground running, seeing eight places before six o'clock. By the time Gabriel stopped in front of his hotel, Leo was having strong second thoughts about this move. "How easy is it to find a place that's month-to-month?"

"As transient as this area is, not hard to find, but you'll pay a pretty price."

"Think you can line up a few in the financial district tomorrow?"

"Sure. I'll pick you up here at ten."

"Thanks, Gabe."

In his hotel room, he ordered room service, showered, and fell into bed. Where he tossed and turned for over an hour. He finally grabbed his cell phone and texted Phoebe. **Are you awake?**

He'd called her this morning, but the call rolled to voice-mail, and he didn't leave a message.

His ringing phone startled him. He hadn't expected her to call.

"Hope I didn't wake you," he said by way of answering. He propped himself up against the headboard.

"No," she said, her voice, floating to him as soft as a feather on a breeze. "I slept all day yesterday, so now I'm wide awake. Dad said you got the van. Did Rock and Sage love it?"

Love was probably a little too strong a word. "They liked it. Sage was excited."

"Good. Congrats on getting them to accept a gift."

"A first, right? I'm going over on Saturday afternoon when I get back to help them pack. Sage said they were leaving most of the furniture, so I doubt they'll rent a trailer. They'll probably just load up the van with whatever fits and leave everything else behind."

"I can come by and help," she said.

Just what he'd hoped. "You don't have to."

"You know I will. Besides, I want to tell Rock and Sage goodbye."

"I won't argue. Maybe if you're there I won't get too emotional."

She laughed. Something she didn't seem to do much anymore. "Yes, you will. As you should. Did you find a place to live?"

"Gabriel showed me some great places. By the way, he said to tell you hello."

"Aww, how's he doing?"

"Great. Says the girls are teenagers and boy-crazy."

Phoebe laughed again.

I could live with that sound ringing through my house all the time. That thought stopped him for a minute. But it was true. "Anyway, I'm thinking of looking for a place that's month-to-month rather than buying."

"Why?"

I'm not sure yet. "I'll be back and forth a lot while building the restaurant. Once it's done, I can find something more permanent."

He wasn't sure what he wanted from her, but it was more than her silence. "What do you think?" he finally asked.

"Makes sense."

"That's it? You're usually full of opinions and more than happy to throw them around, whether I want to hear or not."

"I don't know what you want me to say, Leo. You accepted this job without saying a word to me. Now you want my input?"

He *had* taken this job without talking to her, and usually, they discussed almost everything. He wasn't being fair. "You're right. I'm sorry." He seemed to be saying that a lot lately.

"Apology accepted."

And she'd been saying *that* a lot lately. "I better let you get to sleep. Talk tomorrow?"

"Yep. Good night, Leo."

"'Night, Phoebs."

Leo set his phone aside and closed his eyes. Phoebe usually made everything right in his world. She calmed his nerves and settled his mind. Reaching out to her was like taking a sleeping pill, but not tonight. He stared at the ceiling for a long time after they hung up.

The first condo Gabriel showed Leo the next morning was perfect. Month-to-month, within walking distance of work, and three bedrooms would give him office space and a guest room for Phoebe's visits.

After signing the lease, he headed to the new office, which was located on the sixteenth floor of a high-rise in the business district. It was still in the throes of assembly, with men from a moving company carrying furniture into offices, and employees scurrying about with boxes of files and computer equipment.

He walked through the chaos and eventually found Greg Webb's office. After Greg's sales pitch, Leo believed the company could make money hand over fist. While grabbing a bagel this morning, he wondered if he could possibly accomplish this consulting gig through emails and video chats from Eden Falls. He didn't need to be in the city to work through a problem, and if something came up, he could hop on a plane and be here in hours.

Greg looked up from his computer screen. "Hey, Leo. You made it. Did you find a place to live yet?"

Leo shook Greg's extended hand, then dropped into a modern, truly uncomfortable chair. "Just signed a lease."

"What do you think of the place?"

"Bustling with activity."

"Have you seen your office?" Greg stood. "You're going to love it."

As he followed Greg through the maze that would be work cubicles, Leo decided to wait until after he got the lay of the land and saw firsthand how things would run before mentioning the idea of working from Eden Falls.

Greg stopped next to a glassed-in office with Leo's name on the door. A woman with short, spiky black hair and a nose ring was arranging a desk across the hall.

"Casey will be your assistant," Greg said. "Casey, this is Leo Sawyer."

Looked like it was too late to be included in the hiring process of *his* assistant. He held out his hand. "Nice to meet you, Casey."

"You too, Mr. Sawyer."

"Just Leo, please."

"Okay, Leo."

"I have to go to Washington tomorrow morning, but I'll be back on Tuesday and we can go over some things then."

She nodded. "Sounds good."

"We'll have your desk and some furniture moved into your office by then," Greg said. "I've scheduled an all-hands-on-deck meeting for Wednesday at nine."

"Good to know." Leo walked into the office. Phoebe would love his perfect view of Treasure Island. He wished she was here right now to help him set up his furniture and get organized.

Truthfully, he wished he was in Eden Falls instead of San Francisco.

~

*P*hoebe brought Willy to her apartment Friday morning. He could laze around while she cleaned, and packed up things she wouldn't need while living at Leo's. She felt excited to move into such a spacious house and not excited at the same time. Leo's house was beautiful, and the setting picturesque. She'd spent so many nights there and stored so many good memories that it would feel weird to invite a date over for dinner or to watch TV. She hadn't thought of that before she finally agreed.

For the first time, she wondered if Keaton would have a problem with her living at Leo's.

But staying at Leo's made more sense since she would be watching Willy. Leo had a fenced-in yard—not that Willy would run off. That dog was totally devoted to Leo—and Phoebe only had a tiny patio and no grass. At Leo's, Willy had plenty of room to roam. All her apartment offered was a living room, kitchen, and two bedrooms to wander around in when she wasn't home.

If Leo did the renovations on his parents' farm right—which he would, because he had the Midas touch—the restaurant and barn would be a dreamy place for dining and other events. He'd give half of everything he made to charity and half of everything he grew to shelters in the area while creating jobs in the community because that was what Leo did—he helped others.

She glanced around her living room. Leo wouldn't take any of his furniture, opting to buy new because it was easier. Which meant she'd have to do something with hers.

Ever since college graduation and scoring a job with the police department, she'd lived in the same apartment with the same hand-me-down furniture from her parents and things she'd picked up at yard sales. She spent so little time at home that she didn't need much. What she had was comfortable and cohesive and worked for her.

So, what to do with all this stuff? Neither of her sisters who lived in Eden Falls needed furniture.

Phoebe plopped down on the sofa and scrolled through her contacts, stopping on Amy Saunders. She and her husband owned an apple orchard just outside of town. They also helped organize and run the Eden Falls Shelter.

"Hi, Amy, this is Phoebe Adams," she said when Amy answered her phone.

"Hello, Phoebe. I haven't talked to you in ages."

Willy put his head in her lap, and she rubbed his soft ears. "It has been a while."

"How's life?" Amy asked.

Phoebe wasn't sure how to answer that question anymore. Her life was now divided into two sections—before Madam Venus and after. Idyllic and frustrating. Satisfying and unfulfilling. She decided a simple answer was best. "Good. Hope your family's well."

"Well as can be."

"That's good to hear. Are you busy with plans for Brandt and Jillian's wedding?"

Amy laughed. "Yes, and I'll be glad when it's over. Why

they decided on a long engagement is beyond me. They're both so eager to be together, I just can't make sense of it."

"To each their own."

"True. So what can I do for you?"

"I have some furniture that's still in good shape and wonder if you know anyone who could use any of it."

"What do you have?"

"A sofa and two chairs, end tables, lamps, kitchen table and chairs, a queen-size bed with headboard, a dresser, two nightstands, and a couple of bookshelves. I also have kitchenware—pots, pans, dishes, silverware."

"Wow, I know several families who could use most if not all of those things."

Phoebe owned very little that she was attached to. What did that say about her? That she was emotionally stunted?

How had she lived almost thirty-five years with nothing substantial to show for it?

She worked a job she loved, then went home to her little apartment which suited her just fine. She dated a guy for a few weeks or months, then moved on to the next, never getting serious or feeling like she wanted more.

And she'd been completely happy with that life until Madam Venus interfered.

"Is the furniture yours?" Amy asked.

"Yes. Leo is moving to San Francisco for a job, so I'm going to rent his place and take care of his dog."

"You don't need your furniture?"

"No." She could always buy what she needed if Leo took his things. She didn't make a lot of money, but she didn't spend a lot either. In fact, she had a nice little nest egg saved if she ever decided to buy a house. "Leo won't bother to take much with him."

"Does Leo leaving have anything to do with his parents selling their farm?"

"Maybe a little." *Or maybe I ran him off.* Phoebe ran her fingers under Willy's jaw, and he groaned with pleasure.

"Eden Falls will miss him."

Me too. "I'm sure he'll be back to visit."

"I hope so. When are you moving, Phoebe?"

Even though she couldn't give Leo any money until the first of next month, she could move tomorrow. She'd take the guest room she usually stayed in so Leo could have his room when he visited. He'd built the house so every room included its own bathroom, which she especially loved.

"I don't really have a date. Just let me know when you can pick it up. If I'm working, I can try to get someone here to let you in."

"Perfect. Thanks, Phoebe. You have no idea how much your donation will help."

"I'm glad. I'll see you soon, Amy."

After she disconnected the call, Phoebe slumped onto the sofa. She could store the few things she planned to keep in a corner of Leo's basement. He talked about finishing the space one day, but—

What if he never came back? She'd never considered that. But what if he met someone in San Francisco or decided that he loved the city this time? His move suddenly felt more real to her, more permanent. More forever.

A loneliness engulfed her, making her weak.

Other than her family, she had no attachments—except to Leo. She could pack up some clothes and leave this apartment, only taking along memories of time spent here with Leo or her sisters, and be perfectly happy.

No. Content was a better word. She'd be content to live at Leo's. She'd be content to continue in a job with no advancement. She'd be content to live out her life as the only single Adams. Well, Adelaide was still single, but she wouldn't stay that way.

If Madam Venus was right, Addie would come home, which didn't seem likely. She was majoring in journalism, and the only job around Eden Falls would be the once-a-week newspaper. Addie wouldn't settle for that after interning at *The New York Times*.

"You might have been right about Izzy falling in love, and you might have been right about Misty's pregnancy, but you're wrong about me and Leo, and you're wrong about Addie. One more strike and you're out!" she yelled to the walls of her empty apartment.

After cleaning out a couple of closets, and adding lots to her giveaway pile, Phoebe showered and dressed. She felt like she'd been waiting for this date with Keaton for months instead of five days.

When he knocked on her door, right on time, she jumped out of her kitchen chair and put a hand to her jumping heart. "Settle down, girl. It's just a date."

She forced herself to walk through the living room, taking slow, measured steps, and opened the door slowly rather than throwing it open.

"Hello." He flashed a beautiful smile, and she released the breath she'd been holding.

"Hi. Come in."

He stepped over the threshold and held out a red rose. "Happy Valentine's Day."

"Thank you. Same to you." With all that was going on, she'd completely forgotten Valentine's Day.

After she took the rose, Keaton shoved his hands in his coat pockets. His blue shirt enhanced the sky-blue of his eyes. "I don't know why I'm so nervous. You'd think this was my first date."

He looked so much like Leo, but the voice was all wrong. The wrong tone, the wrong pitch, the wrong cadence. "I'm a little nervous too." *And, if you knew me, you'd know I don't get nervous.* "It's not like the first time we've been together."

"But it's the first time we've been *alone* together."

She hadn't thought of that, but he was right.

He glanced around. "You have a nice place."

"No. I mean, it's just a cookie-cutter apartment that you could pick up and place anywhere in the country. Nothing special."

"Maybe it's who's standing in it that makes it so nice."

Cheesy, but sweet.

"Are you ready to go?"

Phoebe held up the rose. "Let me put this in water."

She disappeared into the kitchen for a moment. She didn't have a vase for a single rose, so she filled a glass with water and propped it up in the sink before going back out to the living room.

"You look really nice in blue," he said before helping her with her coat.

"Thank you. You look nice in blue, too." Okay, how many times could they say the word "nice" in five minutes? And why were they having so much trouble with conversation tonight? It just wasn't coming naturally. Everything she said felt forced.

"Where are we going?" she asked, as she pulled the door closed behind them.

He took her hand. "Do you like Italian?"

"I love it."

"Have you ever been to Donatello's in Harrisville?"

"No."

"You're in for a treat."

She liked the idea of going somewhere new. Somewhere she didn't have a memory with another man—especially Leo —which was hard to come by. She and Leo used to go everywhere together. Except Donatello's, so it could become her and Keaton's spot.

Leo would tease her mercilessly if he knew how silly she was being.

During the drive, she and Keaton discussed likes. He wasn't a reader, but she could overlook that fault because they enjoyed some of the same movies.

Donatello's was small and quaint and set up in an old house, which made her think of Leo and his restaurant adventure. Tomorrow she'd see him at the farm and would have a chance to tell Rock and Sage goodbye. She hadn't visited with them in months.

Leo would be brave while they packed, but his heart would be breaking. Again. Maybe this would be the last time his parents hurt him.

He'd been dealt a raw deal in the family department, but he'd done okay for himself. Okay—ha! He was a billionaire, and generous to a fault. His oversized heart would go through a gamut of emotions this weekend, and she would be there for him like always. Just as he'd always been there for her.

Her dinner was delicious, and she enjoyed her and Keaton's getting-to-know-you conversation. Keaton talked about his family, close and extended. His parents and two brothers owned and operated several dry cleaners around the area. Keaton was the only one not involved in the family business.

"Do you have siblings other than Izzy and Stella?"

"Two more sisters. Georgiana lives in Chicago with her doctor husband and Adelaide is going to college in New York."

"How did your dad handle five girls in the house?"

Phoebe tried not to take offense. Sure, they'd had their squabbles, but none of them got into any serious trouble.

And Keaton wasn't the first person to ask the same question—like girls were so much harder to raise than boys. "I guess the same way your mom handled three boys in the house."

She could tell her comment surprised him. Then he smiled. "Touché. Are there times when you've been scared while on the job as a police officer?"

"I live in Eden Falls. It's not exactly the metropolis of crime. The most we get are drunken brawls on weekends and the occasional break-in. I chase Bigfoot more often than I chase bad guys."

"Bigfoot?" he asked with a laugh.

"Long story, but we usually end up chasing the big guy through the woods a couple of times a year."

"Does this chase begin with a tourist sighting?"

She laughed. "No. It starts with teenagers getting into Mr. Polanski's chicken coop."

"Have you ever disarmed anyone?"

"Just once," she said, thinking back to her night with Leo. There was one other time, but the perp's gun wasn't loaded.

She waved her hand. "Enough about me. Tell me more about you."

"Your life is much more interesting than mine."

She didn't see her life as interesting, but it wasn't boring either. Although that might change once Leo moved.

When they returned to Eden Falls, they sat in Keaton's car talking. For some strange reason she didn't understand, she didn't want to invite him inside. Keaton was easy to talk with and could keep up an interesting conversation, but something wasn't right. She wondered if he felt it too.

He walked her to the door, and her whole body quivered in anticipation of their first kiss. Maybe what was wrong would right itself. She hoped so.

They stopped on the step and faced each other.

"Thank you again for dinner. Donatello's was great."

"You're welcome. Are we still on for church on Sunday?"

"I'll meet you there. Same place, same time."

He touched the tip of his index finger to her chin and leaned forward. She closed the distance when he hesitated, tired of waiting. She wanted to feel more than the touch of his finger. She wanted to feel his lips on hers. She wanted to feel what she felt with Leo last weekend. She needed to *feel*.

This kiss could be a game-changer. It could shift her universe, and she'd be sure to tell Madam Venus to her face that she was wrong.

Their lips met briefly before he leaned away and…nothing. No skipping heartbeat, no racing pulse. Nothing.

She fought the tears and the quake rattling her body until she said goodbye and went inside and closed the door. Then she couldn't stop either.

CHAPTER 14

The new van was missing when Leo's truck slid and bounced down his parents' driveway Saturday afternoon, warmer weather having turned the ruts into a muddy mess.

Forget the grading. First thing on his to-do list: pave the driveway. And the fence that ran along the road was barely standing. When they first moved in, he remembered wild yellow, red, and orange roses climbing through the rails and around the post in a profusion of vivid color. He wanted that nice, three-rail fence and those roses back.

He pulled to a stop near the kitchen door and climbed out. Glancing at the overgrown gardens, he waited for Willy to jump out of the truck before shutting the door. Piles of junk were heaped in various spots all over the yard. Random mounds of branches covered with dirty snow, a lone five-gallon bucket full of trash, brown vines, and weeds folded over a rusted lawnmower. A bike his mom used to ride leaned against a tree, the basket hanging by one strap on the handlebars containing an old bird's nest.

The whole place would require a lot of work—so much

that he wasn't quite sure where to start. He walked around the house, looking at the eaves and siding. The roof would have to be replaced soon. Tearing the place down would be a smarter choice, but he didn't want to lose that tiny piece of the grandma he never knew, and the house her husband built for her.

After rounding the exterior, he stopped on the back stoop, tried the knob, and the door swung open. He didn't like going into his parents' house when they weren't home. He'd told them he'd be here to help pack, so where'd they go?

"Come on, boy," he said opening the door wide so Willy could go inside.

Back at his truck, Leo pulled out a stack of small boxes that would easily stack in their van along with several rolls of packing tape—something he was sure his parents wouldn't think to get—and markers to label everything.

As he walked through the kitchen, he noticed most of the cupboard doors were open, the shelves bare. Good. They'd started packing. And the built-in shelf in the living room was empty. Another good sign that his irresponsible parents hadn't left everything until the last minute. He didn't see any stacked boxes. Maybe they'd decided to trash it all and start fresh.

Down the hall, his bedroom hadn't been touched since the day he left home seventeen years ago, and a thick layer of dust lay over everything. He'd tried repeatedly to clean the bedroom out, but both parents said they'd take care of it. Even Willy looked appalled by the mess, sneezing twice at the door and turning away.

The filthy mattress still lay on the floor, his clothes still folded neatly and stacked in the doorless closet because he didn't have hangers or a dresser. The books he bought as a kid with the money he made doing odd jobs at Patsy's

Pastries or the Bookshop still sat on the milk crates he found in an abandoned building.

He crossed the hall to the bathroom. Every surface was disgusting. Why did his parents live like this? He'd offered to clean, and he'd offered to pay for a maid service, but they turned him down every time. The house looked nothing like the quaint little home they moved into when he was five.

He still remembered the excitement low in his belly at the idea of having a permanent roof over his head and a table with chairs in the kitchen. Actual plates and silverware, items left in the house when his grandma died. A bedroom all his own that he didn't have to share with other kids he didn't know. Here his things wouldn't disappear. Not that he had much in the first place. One of the men at the commune carved a horse and gave it to him, but someone took the carving two days later and he never saw it again.

He walked down the hall to his parents' room and all the air whooshed out of his lungs as reality hit him in the gut. His parents were gone. They left while he was in California. Left without even saying goodbye.

"Leo?"

He leaned against the wall to keep from falling. Willy sidled up to him and whined.

"Leo? Are you in here?"

The contents in his stomach churned and he put a hand to his mouth.

Phoebe turned the corner. "Oh, there you are. Looks like Sage and Rock did some packing while you were in San Francisco." She reached out and patted Willy's head. "Hi, boy."

He swallowed, around the lump, around the rising bile.

"Leo? Are you okay? What's wrong?"

"They're gone."

"What?" She stepped past him and glanced around their

room. A tiny gasp escaped before she turned to him with wide eyes.

He swallowed again as tears burned his eyes before spilling over. He swore when he left home that he'd never cry over his parents again, and here he was, about to break down and bawl like a baby.

Without a word, Phoebe wrapped her arms around his middle and leaned against him. She didn't say anything, just held him.

She felt good. Felt like home. Comfortable and right. Everything with Phoebe was always right. He breathed in her scent, so familiar, so calming.

He didn't feel embarrassed in front of her, didn't try to stop the tears. Phoebe would never judge. She would never mention this moment again. And, by her shaking shoulders, he could tell she was crying along with him. She used to do that as a kid. Phoebe was tough, but she had a tender heart.

After a while, she pulled away and wiped her face. "I better call my parents. They planned to come and help."

He nodded and ran the back of his hand over his eyes. After he heard the front door open and shut, he walked into the bedroom and looked in the almost empty closet. Just like his parents to leave a mess for the new owner to deal with. Just like them to only think of themselves. Just like them to steal away in the night with zero thought of how their actions might affect their only son.

And just like that, his decision to level the house hit like another gut punch. He'd erase every bad memory he had of this place. He'd rebuild and make all new memories, good memories. Happy memories. The barn would hold birthday and wedding and anniversary parties. People would come to celebrate love. He would make the entire farm a beautiful place to visit.

He ripped the threadbare curtains off the window and

dust swirled through the air, making him sneeze. Rock and Sage's stained mattress still lay in its spot on the floor, but the sheets and blankets were gone. They probably didn't even use boxes. Just threw everything into the van and drove away.

A hand rubbed between his shoulder blades. "You okay?"

No. During his entire childhood Leo always felt like he was treading water—one little wave and down he'd go, never to be seen again. That feeling of struggle faded into the background when he moved out on his own, but his parents had a way of dumping him right back into the middle of a storm-tossed sea that never completely settled. "I will be."

"What do you want to do?"

Rant and rage and rip something apart— "I want to get out of here."

Phoebe smiled. "Where to?"

"Pancake Palooza. We haven't been there in a long time."

"Your car or mine?" she asked, taking his hand and leading the way down the hall.

"Mine. And my treat. No argument."

"Your treat, but we can't be too long," she said, glancing at her phone screen. "I have to work."

"We won't be long."

He couldn't believe she agreed. Once outside, he opened the door of his truck and she waited until Willy clambered inside before she took the passenger seat. He shut the door and walked around to the driver's side.

"Thanks, Phoebs," he said after he slid behind the wheel and closed his door.

"For?"

"For being you, for always being here for me." *For being such a force of happiness and good in my life.*

She reached across the console for his hand. "Just like you're always here for me."

He probably shouldn't, but he lifted her hand and kissed the back while watching her. An expression he couldn't identify crossed her face but disappeared in a flash. It was an expression he wanted to investigate, though. One he might want to see again.

Leo took a moment to notice his pounding heart, his quickened breath, the smell and texture of her skin, the look in her eyes.

He smiled. She returned the smile, but with a wary edge. After the way he'd been acting, he didn't blame her.

She had no idea how much he appreciated her. If she hadn't been with him today, he'd still be leaning against the wall, grieving for something that he never had to begin with. She saved him once again.

~

*P*hoebe's heart did a little dance while she watched Leo watching her. But for once she wasn't sure how to read his reaction. His emotions were probably still reeling because his parents up and left without even saying goodbye.

Watching Leo bounce back from such a crushing blow didn't surprise her, though, Time after time his parents decimated him. They missed every school event from elementary through high school, every science fair where he consistently placed either first or second. Leo was also a champion swimmer, but his mom and dad never attended a meet.

Her best friend's biggest flaw was his self-doubt, rooted deep and painfully by the many times his parents disappointed him. She'd seen firsthand what their self-absorbed carelessness did to shape their son's outlook on life and his concept of marriage and children.

She understood why Leo had made the decision to not

have a family, but she knew Leo, knew everything about him, and he was nothing like his parents. Never had been and never would be. He'd always go out of his way to be different because that's how Leo rolled.

She sat back and enjoyed the ride, mostly in silence. Long ago she and Leo reached the point where they could be together without talking. Despite the quiet, she knew where his thoughts traveled. He'd wonder why his parents did what they did, and try to analyze the situation, placing blame on himself rather than on them. After living with those thoughts for a few days he'd eventually reach the conclusion that there was nothing he could have done, but it would take him some time.

"Look at the way the sun is hitting that mountain peak," he said pointing to the left.

"Pretty. You're going to miss that view while living in a big city."

"The place I rented has a view of San Francisco Bay."

"Lucky you."

"My office window does too."

"You live an enviable life, Leo Sawyer."

He snorted, the exact reaction she'd expected. "I got a guest bedroom so you can visit."

"Lucky me. Maybe I live an enviable life. I get to enjoy but don't have to pay."

Leo skirted Harrisville and drove ten minutes south before they entered the small town of South Fork, about the size of Eden Falls. He parked in front of Pancake Palooza and they climbed out. A warm breeze blew, whispering more promises of spring, and although it was still weeks away, the sweet anticipation lifted Phoebe's spirits.

Almost as much as Leo kissing her knuckles.

Yep, she'd been thinking about that the whole ride. The

whole thing seesawed between really weird—from a best friend point of view—to heart-stoppingly romantic from…

She wasn't sure how to finish that thought.

Pancake Palooza, always busy, had one table left when they entered. The smell of bacon and pancakes hit her as soon as they walked in the door, making her stomach growl.

The cute kid who showed them to the table held out a menu, but Phoebe waved it away. She knew exactly what she wanted, starting with strawberry pancakes with a side of orange marmalade.

"Want to share some fries for an appetizer?" Leo asked, pulling out her chair.

"Sure."

He sat across from her. "And bacon?"

"Of course."

The server delivered glasses of water and took their order.

"Sorry about earlier," he said, watching the server walk away rather than make eye contact with Phoebe.

"You know you never have to apologize for showing emotions around me, Leo." That he thought he did, hurt— and proved to her that their friendship had morphed into something less than it once was.

She wished she could blame Rock and Sage, who lived in their own little euphoric world, barely able to take care of themselves, let alone a kid. But this was on her. "Actually, it's me who needs to apologize."

His frown appeared. "For what?"

"For blurring the lines between our friendship. I shouldn't have kissed you, Leo. I'm sorry."

"You don't have to keep apologizing for that, Phoebe. It was bound to happen at some point. There's only so long a female can resist this." He waved a hand down his torso.

And Leo was back. Phoebe hoped he bulldozed his

parents' house. Getting rid of that place might purge the bad memories that plagued him. Once he knew Rock and Sage were settled and he visited to make sure they were okay, he could let go of some of the past, shed some of the responsibility he'd been lugging around since he was tiny.

Leo would still worry, and probably visit LA more than he'd come back to Eden Falls. But Rock and Sage would be happy to get back into a community with like-minded people.

"How was your date last night?" he asked, again not looking her in the eye.

She took a moment to decide how much to tell. "Nice. Keaton took me to an Italian restaurant in Harrisville."

"Donatello's?"

"You know the place," she said, rather than asked. She should have known Leo took dates there. Dark and romantic, it was just his kind of restaurant.

"Yeah, they have great food. Did Keaton rent one of the private rooms?"

"Nope. We ate with all the other lowlifes."

"Phoebe," he said in a father-reprimanding-his-rebellious-daughter tone. "I didn't mean anything by the question. Just wondering."

They sat back when the fries and bacon were delivered to the table.

"So…your date was just nice?"

This was a normal, before-their-kiss conversation, so why did it feel weird talking to Leo about Keaton? "We had a good time, and he's meeting me for church tomorrow," she said, dredging a fry through the ketchup Leo had poured on the edge of the plate.

"You don't sound very excited."

She looked up to meet his eyes. "I sound the same as I always do."

"No," he said, shaking his head. "You don't."

She wasn't about to tell Leo that Keaton didn't set off any fireworks for her, something she wouldn't have thought twice about saying before. She considered tomorrow to be a let's-be-absolutely-sure date, but she already knew—and was only fighting the obvious to prove Madam Venus wrong. So why didn't she tell Leo the truth? "You're entitled to your opinion."

He nodded while studying her.

Searching for a quick exit to the conversation, she asked, "How did you know about Donatello's?"

"Remember Claire?"

"The chick with purple hair?"

"No, that was Erica. Claire was the one with the Doberman pinschers."

"Oh, right." Leo went through so many girlfriends it could be challenging to keep them straight.

"She used to work there."

They moved the bacon and fries aside so the waiter could set their pancakes on the table. Leo spent a minute buttering each layer of his stack.

"Is the condo within walking distance of your office?"

"About five blocks."

"How is the new office?"

"It takes up the sixteenth floor in a nice building in the business district. When I got there, a moving company was delivering desks and file cabinets." He cut into his pancakes. "Greg already hired an assistant for me."

She smeared orange marmalade on the top pancake. "They didn't ask for your input?"

He stopped what he was doing and frowned. "No. Kind of weird, huh? But that's how Greg works. He probably hired some HR company to do the hiring."

She wasn't a Greg fan. "Is she young?"

"Maybe a few years younger than us."

"Cute? Single?"

"Your idea of cute and mine are completely different. I consider a puppy cute, and she doesn't look anything like a puppy. As far as being single, I have no idea. We didn't chit-chat about our personal lives."

"What color is her hair?"

Leo looked at the ceiling like he was deep in thought…or maybe praying for relief. She couldn't tell which.

"Is everything okay?"

Phoebe smiled at the server. "Everything is perfect as always. Thank you."

"Here's your caramel sauce. When I put in your order, Joe said to tell you both you're weird."

"Tell him thank you. Can I also get a little cup of peanut butter? No rush." Phoebe speared a strawberry and popped it in her mouth.

Leo reached across the table and nabbed one of her strawberries while she poured some of his caramel sauce on a corner of her pancakes.

The server came back a moment later. "Joe had it ready for you before I could ask. Enjoy."

Phoebe looked across the table. Leo grinned, and everything was as right with her world as it could be, given the circumstances.

"How is Noelle?" he asked.

"Other than a nagging headache, Mac says she's okay."

"That's good. I bet he's relieved."

"He is. So is poor Beck. He was really worried about her the night of the accident."

Their conversation lagged while they both focused on their pancakes. She wondered what Leo was thinking in this quiet moment. Maybe about the new job since that's what they'd been discussing. Or where his parents might be.

Maybe his new assistant attracted enough of his attention to earn a thought or two.

"Hey, are you free the first weekend in March?"

She lifted a shoulder. "I guess I can be. I'll have to look at the schedule. Why?"

"I called about the houseboat, and that weekend is free. We can stay Friday and Saturday night."

"You want to take me?"

He sat back like she'd shocked him. "Who else would I take? You're my best friend."

His answer made her smile and hurt her heart at the same time. He'd never think of her as more than a friend, and she needed to get past hoping he ever might.

CHAPTER 15

*L*eo spent way too much time watching Phoebe and Keaton interact during family dinner at the Adams house. Out of all the boys and then men Phoebe had dated, why did Keaton bother him so much? The guy interacted well with Phoebe's family, and treated Phoebe like she should be treated, so why didn't he fit in as snugly as Gunner and Rowdy?

Because he wanted Phoebe for himself.

Yep, he finally admitted he wanted to see where their relationship might go. It was still too early to weigh in on kids, but not saying goodbye to Phoebe after a movie night… the idea energized him like the bunny beating the drum in those battery commercials.

He woke up breathing like a racehorse just finishing the Kentucky Derby after a dream this morning—he and Phoebe locking lips, hot and heavy. He'd never ever dreamed about Phoebe that way before, not so much as holding hands or hugging. But the image had been so real, he swore he could smell her perfume on his pillow.

Now Leo watched her trying to find loopholes to fit

Keaton into his place. And he didn't like it. He didn't want to be replaced.

Except he couldn't do anything now, especially since he was staying at The Dew Drop Inn for the weekend. Phoebe told him he was being ridiculous, but he didn't want to step on Keaton's toes. In fact, he decided never to reveal these new thoughts and feelings if Phoebe seemed interested in Keaton. And she certainly did tonight.

"Is everyone ready for some cherry pie?" Beverly asked.

Stella groaned and put a hand on her stomach. "I ate too much."

Neil pushed back from the table and stood. "I'm ready. Who else wants a piece?"

Gunner and Rowdy raised their hands.

"Oh, all right. I'll have a piece," Stella said, rolling her eyes.

Izzy laughed.

Leo put a hand on Bev's shoulder before she could stand. "You stay here and relax. I'll help Neil."

Phoebe met and held his gaze for a long moment.

He might have blown his entire future happiness because he was scared her family would shun him if things didn't work out. Now that he looked around the table at the people he already considered family, he knew they would never leave him out in the cold. They'd been there for him since he was five.

The only people who'd ever left him in the cold were on their way to California. Or were already there. Not that he would know. His parents wouldn't think to call him and let him know they made it safely. They didn't even own cell phones because that would be submitting to the ruling classes.

While Neil cut the pie into nine equal pieces—the odd number because Leo was the only single here tonight. He got out the dishes and set them next to Neil, then collected nine forks from the silverware drawer.

"How are you?" Neil asked, sounding more concerned than usual.

"You don't have to worry about me. I'm okay. I think I've finally resigned myself to the fact that Rock and Sage are never going to change. I need to accept them for who they are and just be happy that they're healthy and happy and together."

"I think that's a good attitude to take." He glanced up from the pie. "They do love you, Leo. In their own way."

The opening line of Preacher Brenner's sermon, *"All of us go through changes. Some come and go without much notice, but sometimes these changes completely alter the course of our lives."*

At the time he wondered how that statement affected Phoebe. Did it make her think about him? Keaton? He'd fought the urge to look their way, but only because he didn't want to see them holding hands.

Next, he weighed what the statement meant to him. His parents' move wouldn't change his life much because he only saw them once a week and had very little interaction with them when he did visit. Most of the time his dad didn't even acknowledge his presence. And his mom probably only noticed his visits because the fridge shelves weren't bare.

Buying the farm would alter the course of his life in many ways—he hoped for the good. As he made lists and plans, his excitement grew, and he was looking forward to sitting down with Phoebe tonight after Keaton left. He hoped she remembered her promise to look over his ideas.

While Neil dished up the pie, Leo carried two plates at a time into the dining room.

"Thank you, sweetie," Bev said when he set a plate in front of her while listening to the family interact with his replacement.

He told Phoebe the truth when he said she didn't seem very excited. Sure, she was smiling and talking with her family, but she wasn't herself. She wasn't happy. And yes, he knew her that well.

After everyone had been served, he and Neil took their seats again.

"Did you find a place to live in San Fran?" Rowdy asked Leo.

Leo didn't want to talk about his move, because he wasn't sure taking this job was the right decision anymore. "Yeah, I rented a condo," he said, cutting into his piece of pie.

Stella leaned past Rowdy. "Why are you renting?"

His decision to rent over buying was right. At least for now. Living in San Francisco was a notion he'd been trying to sell to himself, but he already knew he couldn't stay away from Eden Falls or Phoebe for long. "The place I decided on was rent only."

"You're going to come home often, Leo," Beverly stated.

"I'll fly home as often as I can," he said, cutting another bite.

Bev tapped the table with the tips of her fingers. "When do you have to go back?"

"Tuesday."

"And when will you be home again?"

"Probably not until I close on my parents' property." He glanced across the table at Gunner. "Can we set up a time to go over plans that weekend?"

"Just give me a date and I'll make it work."

After their pancake, bacon, and French fries dinner, Leo had spent the rest of last night drawing up more plans for the farm. He'd roughly plotted out the different spaces and made a sketch of the barn and the exterior of the restaurant. Though he was far from an artist, he still felt like he'd captured his dream with a pad and pencil. He hoped his plans were legible enough for Phoebe to make sense of his lines and scribbles.

"I've decided to demolish the house and the barn and start from scratch." He would find some small piece of his grandmother in that wreck of a house and keep that piece alive. The rest would go.

"Oh, Leo, are you sure?" Beverly asked.

After yesterday, he was positive. "Yes. That way I can get exactly what I want without trying to work around what's there."

Phoebe nodded her approval from across the table.

"Do you need contact numbers for some demolition crews?"

"I'll probably leave that completely up to you, Gunner. We can talk numbers the next time I'm in town. I can't do anything until after I close anyway. But I promise to make it all worth your while."

He and Phoebe used to have so much fun climbing trees and exploring around the farm's pond. He couldn't call them carefree days, because nothing about his childhood had been carefree, but those few hours every couple of weeks were as close to heaven as he imagined he'd ever get. They'd sit in the barn watching dust motes dancing in the light while discussing the important details of life, like who performed the best cannonball at the pool or what they wanted to be when they grew up. Even back then Phoebe wanted to be a cop and he just wanted to feel secure and loved.

Seemed he was still searching for both.

"So, Keaton, do you think you'll stay in Harrisville, or is there a possibility of moving?" Rowdy asked.

"Harrisville is home, but there's always the possibility I'll be offered a job in another city."

"What other cities?"

Leo heard the concern in Izzy's voice and felt sure the

others did too. He watched Phoebe's reaction while Keaton talked about the possibility of being offered a position at larger pediatric offices around Washington State. She met his gaze, then looked down at her plate, suddenly very interested in an edge of crust.

The move to a bigger city might be good for Phoebe's career since there wasn't anywhere to advance within Eden Falls' small police force. That never seemed to bother Phoebe, but perhaps the possibility of moving up in another area of the state was inducement enough for her to move—that and having a baby daddy.

Leo finished his dessert and gathered up the dishes for Bev. Since he'd be missing several family dinners, he'd take his turn doing dishes before his actual turn. The temptation to stick his head in the dining room and remind Phoebe of their plans to discuss the farm at his house tonight shot through his mind, but to say something in front of Keaton would be petty. He'd texted her earlier to make sure she still planned to meet him, and she replied with a yes.

He started rinsing and loading the dishwasher while listening to the mumbled conversation and occasional laughter that floated into the kitchen. He'd miss this.

But you don't have to, a little voice reminded him. *You have a choice.*

Neil's words played through his head. *If you want that job in San Francisco, then you should grab it with both hands. But make sure you're grabbing for the right reasons and not because you're trying to outrun your feelings.*

That's exactly what he'd been doing, trying to outrun his feelings for Phoebe. Madam Venus might have changed Phoebe's feelings toward him, but their kiss changed *every-thing* for him. Did he believe Madam Venus's prediction? Not really. But he believed in Phoebe, and if a silly prediction brought them together, why fight it? Instead, he should tell her before the one person who loved him unconditionally found her way into someone else's arms.

Rowdy walked in, picked up a dish towel, and started drying the couple of pots Leo had washed. "You okay? You're quiet tonight."

"I just have a lot going on. My mind is running in a million different directions."

"Sorry to hear about your parents leaving."

Leo gave an it-is-what-it-is shrug, then rinsed another pan. "They'll be happier around their own kind of people."

Rowdy took the pan from him. "Did you get my text about Stella's surprise birthday tomorrow night?"

Leo put both palms on the edge of the sink and dropped his head. Stella's birthday party completely slipped his mind. "Yes. Sorry, I forgot to RSVP. I'll be there."

~

*P*hoebe was very aware when Leo left the room, aware of the tension between them that wasn't there yesterday, and wondered what had changed.

"The pie is really good, Beverly."

"Thank you, Keaton."

Phoebe listened to the water running in the kitchen. Leo did the dishes on Sunday evenings more often than any of the rest of them. She usually wandered in to help but decided to stay where she was tonight. She wanted to kiss Rowdy's cheek when he got up a minute later and followed Leo.

She looked at Keaton, and he flashed a smile her way. She really wanted to feel something—anything! A flock of birds wasn't necessary. She'd be happy with just a flap of a fly's wing.

"Have you guys got plans for after dinner?" Stella asked her attention on Keaton.

He glanced at Phoebe. "Do we?"

"Not tonight. I told Leo I'd go to his house and look over the plans he's drawn up for the farm."

"What farm?" Keaton asked, taking her hand.

"He's buying his parents' farm just outside of town." She stared at Keaton's thumb rubbing over her knuckles. Nothing. Absolutely nothing. She remembered the look on Leo's face, the way he'd gazed at her so intently. Kissing her hand had left her breathless. Just thinking about him gave her the flutter she hoped for from Keaton.

"And the plans?" Keaton prompted.

Phoebe shook herself out of her reverie. "He's going to renovate."

"I thought he was moving to California."

"He is." Phoebe extracted her hand and picked up her glass of water, hoping Keaton wouldn't notice she could have used her other hand.

Thirty minutes later, she stood on the porch watching Keaton drive away. He'd kissed her. Twice. And she let him because she needed to be certain. Rowdy had invited him to Stella's surprise party tomorrow, so she didn't talk to him tonight. Maybe a bolt of love-lightning would hit her and she could be as excited about meeting him as she'd been the night of Lara's party just two short weeks ago.

"Hey," Stella said, sticking her head out the front door.

"Hey what?"

"Let's have a sister's night out sometime this week."

Phoebe turned to go inside. "I have to work day shifts all week, so I'm free any night."

Leo walked into the living room. "You ready to go, Phoebs?"

"Yes. Call me, Stella Bella." She gave her sister a hug.

After she made her goodbye rounds, she bundled up and

walked outside into the air heavy with wood smoke from someone's fireplace.

She climbed into Leo's car and shut the door. "I'm not sure I'm the one you should be consulting about your renovation, Leo. Izzy's better at this kind of stuff."

"I disagree." He started the engine and pulled away from the curb. "Your ideas for my house were perfect, and this won't be much different. I want this place to be the destination for first dates and anniversary dinners. I want it to be on the nicer side, but I also want the customers to feel comfortable."

"Rustic charm?"

He looked her way and grinned. "Exactly. With a hint of glam."

"Rustic charm I can do. Glam really isn't my forte, but I'll let that suggestion stew for a few days and see what I can come up with."

Phoebe stared out the passenger window as they drove up the mountain road. Since Eden Falls was in a sparsely populated, low-light area, the night sky was breathtaking. The dark mountains rose like sentries, their snow-covered peaks lit by a bazillion stars.

He pulled onto his driveway. Instead of parking in the garage, he pulled around to the kitchen door. "I didn't even think about Izzy. Where is she tonight?"

"Gunner's going to stay with her at my place until I get home."

Inside Leo's kitchen, Willy met them with his usual ecstatic greeting. Phoebe sat on the floor and let him crawl all over her while Leo filled his food dish and refreshed his water.

She loved this mountain home. Leo, JT, and Rowdy had all built on the mountain, but Rowdy's house burned down last year in a fire that almost took Stella's life. He and Stella were living in town while their house was being rebuilt.

Leo went over to the kitchen table and Phoebe followed when Willy decided he'd rather eat. The first sheet of paper Leo rolled out on the kitchen table was a rough draft of the plot of land. She'd roamed all over the farm with Leo for years, so she had a pretty good idea of where the property lines lay. Leo already outlined where he wanted to put a community garden with access from a side road. The drawing also showed the small river-fed pond with a dock running out on one side and a bridge to a walkway leading to what he'd labeled as an orchard. Closer to where the house now sat, he sketched four outbuildings, including a barn, a big garden area.

"You're going to have chickens?" she asked pointing to a rectangle close to the barn.

"And a place for beehives over in this corner." He reached past her to point at the spot and she took a deep, slow breath, savoring his woodsy scent.

"Beehives?"

"Izzy has a friend with beehives. I thought she might like to expand."

"What's out here?" She pointed to a rectangle beyond the property line.

"The neighbors are ready to sell, so I thought I'd build Alex a couple of greenhouses. We could add to their orchard over here. They already have a few cherry trees, but they're in pretty sad condition. I wouldn't want to grow apples because of the Saunders' place just down the road."

This had turned into a major project, and Leo wouldn't be in town for the majority of the work. "If Gunner is going to be the foreman, you should probably be going over these plans with him."

"I want your opinion first, Phoebs. I'll go over everything

with Gunner when I close on the farm, but I want to know what you think."

She dropped into a chair. "This is such a huge project, I'm having a hard time wrapping my head around everything."

"Okay, let's start smaller." He pushed the plans aside and unrolled another piece of paper. "Besides the yard, which needs major work, the restaurant is my first priority. Here's my initial idea for the building. What do you think?"

Phoebe pulled the plans closer.

"I want a big foyer so people don't feel cramped while they wait for a table. Do you think I put the hostess podium in the right spot?"

"Leo, this is really big."

He sat down beside her. "Go big or go home, right?"

"Let me rephrase. This is huge."

"Too huge?"

Phoebe was having a hard time concentrating on the question with him sitting so close. He had no idea how much he affected her, triggering everything from shortness of breath to tingly skin, making her *very* aware that being near Keaton didn't have the same impact. Which meant she'd have to talk to Keaton tomorrow night.

She shook her head. "I can't answer that because I don't have enough information. Do you really think little Eden Falls can support a restaurant this size?"

"No, but I think the surrounding area can."

"Have you done comparable studies?"

"I've hired a company to do that."

At least he was doing his homework before jumping in with both feet, arms, and eyes.

She did a rough count of the tables. "I think you could take this whole middle part out and it would still be big enough. Then I would turn this wall so the bar faces out this direction, which would make it longer. That way you can add more stools."

"I don't want to step on Rowdy's toes."

"What you're planning and his place aren't even in the same universe."

"I'd still feel better talking to Rowdy before I make that change."

She turned the plans. "I like how you've separated these two rooms for private parties."

"What do you think about an accordion wall between them? That way I can have either one large room or two smaller ones."

"Something besides accordion doors, but I like the idea of separating the two rooms if needed. Why two kitchens?"

"One for the restaurant and one for catering the events in the barn."

Phoebe nodded. "Both have plenty of room. Will they have separate walk-in freezers?"

He rubbed a hand over his jaw, and she heard the scrape of whiskers against his palm. "I haven't decided. What do you think?"

"It would keep the two businesses separated. Plus, it will be easier for taxes and keeping the peace between chefs."

He huffed out a laugh. "True. I've heard chefs can be pretty territorial."

"And if one freezer goes out, you have a backup right next door."

"Good point. That one hadn't occurred to me. I knew your opinion would be invaluable," he said, rubbing a hand over her shoulder, heating the skin under her sweater.

Oh, boy. Phoebe pulled the plot plans over and scanned them again. "It's smart to add a driveway over near the catering kitchen so a van can get close." She tapped the plans with a fingertip. "What is this separate building just off that driveway?"

When Leo didn't answer right away, she glanced at him. "Just trying to think ahead."

She couldn't read his expression. "Are you going to put this building in, or is it just on the plans for possible future growth?"

He tipped his head from side to side like he was weighing his answer. "If I put it in, it will happen after everything else is finished." Leo unrolled another piece of paper and spread it out on the table. "What do you think of the barn?"

The sketches were rough, but she got the general idea. To her, a barn was a barn, but Leo had extended one wall for a kitchen and added a set of stairs leading to a loft. "I think you have a lot of work ahead of you."

He covered her hand with his. "That's why I need your help."

She looked into his deep blue eyes and her heart jumped. *This is going to get complicated.*

CHAPTER 16

$\mathcal{L}$eo climbed out of his truck. The sun was up, and the day promised to be nice and on the warmer side. The simple farmhouse in front of him looked just as awful as it did the first time he came here with Izzy. The siding was painted black all the way around, where before the sides were green and the front door a deep red. Seemed to him that Madam Venus, Goddess of Love, would entice more customers with happy colors.

But what did he know about marketing for a psychic?

He made his way to the front door, which opened before he even raised his fist to knock. Madam Venus wore a gold scarf covering her long black hair, a turquoise sweater with multiple gold chains around her neck, and a flowing purple skirt.

"Hello, Leo Sawyer."

Her voice, soft and welcoming, didn't match her garish attire. "You know my name."

"As you know mine." She opened the door wider and beckoned him inside like a spider to her web. "Please, come in."

The interior was as dark as the exterior. Candles provided the only light in the room once she shut the door. Ceiling-to-floor black curtains covered all four walls. She couldn't have seen him waiting in the car the day he brought Izzy here without Izzy noticing or have seen him walk past the window just now.

"I hope I'm not interrupting a séance or anything."

"No. I've been expecting you."

"*Riiight*," he said.

Her smile appeared slowly, almost serene. "Would you like to have a seat?"

On the other side of the room sat a small table and two chairs. "After you."

She circled the table and sat down, her gold bracelets clinking together when she moved her arm.

He sat in the other chair.

"What can I do for you, Leo?" She folded her hands on the table. "Is it okay if I call you Leo?"

He mimicked her body language. "Leo is fine, and if you were expecting me, you should know why I'm here."

"It's unclear why. You have a request and a question, and I'm not sure which you'd like to talk about first."

That unnerved him. He *did* have a question and a request.

"I'm sorry about your parents. Hurting you wasn't their intention."

He sat back in his chair. *How—?* Oh, she was good. She'd heard through the Eden Falls grapevine that his parents left and was using the knowledge to throw him off. "I'm not here to talk about my parents."

"If it's any consolation, they arrived in LA safely."

He wished Izzy wouldn't discuss his family issues with this kook. Next on his to-do list: talk to Iz about being so free with the details of his private business.

Another slow smile appeared. "I haven't talked to Izzy in several weeks."

He held back a shiver when the hair on the back of his neck rose. But the psychic wasn't finished yet.

"Their old van would have broken down somewhere close to…Klamath Falls, Oregon. It was on its last leg when your mom came by last week."

"Wait," Leo said, his heart dropping into his stomach. His mom said goodbye to a psychic and not her son. "Sage came to see you before she moved?"

"Yes. She was a regular of mine. She said they were moving because your dad needed a change to warmer weather."

His mom came to see a psychic before she and Rock skulked away without so much as a *see you later, Leo*.

"Their move had nothing to do with you, Leo."

"Exactly. They've never taken me—their son—into consideration." *Shut up! Why am I telling this woman anything?*

"Actually, you were at the forefront of their decision. Besides the weather, they moved to relieve you of the responsibility you feel to take care of them. They were afraid that sense of duty or concern held you back from following your own dreams."

"Everyone feels concern for their parents."

"I told your mom you're buying the farm—"

"No."

"—and your dad is fine with that. So is your mom. She's happy the property is staying in the family."

An odd sense of peace settled over him and Madam Venus smiled.

"Did she tell you that?"

When Madam Venus nodded, her gold earring glinted in the candlelight. "Should we move on to why you're here?"

Right. They hadn't even touched on those subjects yet. "I

want you to talk to Phoebe. Tell her you were wrong. She's taken what you said to heart. She never wanted kids before, and now it's all she thinks about. You told Izzy I'd have twins too, so…" He didn't want to tell the psychic about the kiss they shared and his rejection. "So, right now, she's dating a guy because he resembles me."

"Not after tonight."

"What?"

"She won't be dating…" She closed her eyes. "His name isn't clear, but they won't be dating anymore after tonight."

Leo leaned forward again. "You're wrong. Again. They went to church together yesterday. I ate dinner across the table from them last night."

"You can choose not to believe or you can choose to change your destiny, Leo. You can let things play out and be happy or you can change the course. You're afraid if things don't work out for you and Phoebe, her family will reject you, which will never happen. They love you. You need to learn the difference between your parents' love and Phoebe's family's love. Love comes in many different forms. You are like a son to Phoebe's parents."

This woman freaked him out. "Exactly," he said again. "A son doesn't marry and have kids with someone who's like a sister."

"They love you *like* a son, but you're not related. There's a difference." She lifted a shoulder. "As I said, the choice is yours. You can find happiness in San Francisco, but you'll *always* wonder."

Another shiver worked its way up his spine. He couldn't listen anymore, so he pushed up from his chair and strode toward the door.

"Leo. You didn't ask your question."

When he turned back, she was standing near the table, fingering a long gold chain holding a purple amulet.

He looked down at the floor—black like everything else in the room, then met her gaze. "Will Phoebe be happy if she marries someone else?"

"Yes."

He decided to ask one more. "Can she have twins with someone else?"

Madam Venus closed her eyes, tipped her head back, and swayed in a slight circle. Slowly she lowered her head, and her eyes came open with a look so intense he took a step back. "We are all able to make choices that change our destiny, Leo."

"That isn't a choice she can make, so you really didn't answer my question."

"Anything is possible."

Okay, he was done. He pulled out his wallet.

"The first visit is free."

First and only—he didn't plan to ever come back. He walked out onto the porch and took a deep, cleansing breath of fresh air, trying to clear his mind of the jumble Madam Venus created.

Scenery and fresh air wouldn't do it. He needed to talk to Izzy.

Climbing behind the wheel of his truck, he headed back into town. After rounding the square, he took a right and turned into Izzy's place. Her car was parked around back as well as Gunner's truck. He knocked on the back door.

"It's open."

Other than Gunner on a ladder cutting in the new wall color just under the crown molding, the kitchen was bare.

Gunner glanced over his shoulder. "Hey, Leo."

"Hey. Is Izzy around?"

"She's in her office with a client."

Even as unsettled as he felt, Leo wouldn't interrupt a

business meeting. Physical labor always helped when his thoughts were on overload. "Got another paintbrush?"

"There's one in the laundry room along with another can of paint. Help is welcome."

He opened a can and stirred the paint until well mixed. "Where do you want me to start?"

"Mind painting around the doors? There's a stepladder in the mudroom."

Leo had been blessed with his father's height, but he wasn't tall enough to paint above the nine-foot doors. He popped the stepladder open and got to work. "I take it you needed to prime."

"To cover the garish color, yes. I thought it would take two coats, but one did it. Not sure what that woman was thinking when she chose the paint colors in this house." Gunner turned on his ladder. "I remember the first time I walked in here with Izzy and thought, *the poor guy who has to fix this place up.*"

Leo dipped his brush in the can of paint and slowly dragged the new color above the doorframe. "And that poor guy is you."

"Yep. You saw this wreck of a place before Izzy bought it. I thought she was crazy."

"Turns out she's business smart. If she wasn't already busy as an events planner and opening the tea shop, I'd get her to manage the restaurant and events for the barn at the farm."

"Why don't you stay and manage it yourself?" Gunner asked. "Correct me if I'm wrong, but you hated working in San Francisco the first time."

"True, but I'm not a kid anymore." Leo moved to the side of the door. "Actually, I think the San Francisco job can be done remotely."

Gunner glanced at him. "So you won't be moving after all?"

"I haven't talked to the CEO about it yet. I'll see how things play out." He dipped his paintbrush and wiped the excess on the lip of the can. "Hey, Gun? Don't say anything yet about me working remotely."

Gunner held up a hand. "Say no more."

They painted in silence for a while. With the gentle back and forth motion of the brush, the tingling energy he'd felt after leaving Madam Venus's faded, and his anger receded.

"Not to bring up bad memories, but what makes you want to get married again?"

Gunner climbed down to move his ladder, then took a sip from a thermos on the floor. "My parents went their own ways long ago. I'm sure I have some of their traits and mannerisms, but I'm not them. After my divorce, I thought I'd never want to get married again, thought I'd never find a woman I'd want to marry, wasn't even looking, but Izzy changed my mind."

"What about her made *you* change your mind, though?"

A puzzled look crossed his face. "Her determination, her positivity, her sweet nature, her attention to detail, her love of family, her—"

"Got it," Leo said, cutting off Gunner before he launched into a detailed description of Izzy's every virtue.

"How can you want kids after the way you had to struggle through your own childhood?"

"I've always wanted kids. My mom loved me and Ariel in her own way. I like to think I learned from my parents' mistakes. And Izzy will be a great mom." He paused for a long moment. "I'm determined not to be like my parents. Sure, I might look like them and have the same mannerisms, but the resemblance can stop there. I'm me, and 'me' wants to be married to Izzy forever and have as many kids as we can be blessed with."

Leo ruminated on that until Izzy walked into the kitchen.

She blew Gunner a kiss, then smiled at Leo. "Hey, what brings you over here?"

"Madam Venus."

"Really," she said, without the question mark.

"When was the last time you saw her?"

Izzy walked into the laundry room and carried a calendar back into the kitchen. "January twenty-sixth I went by her house to drop off a birthday present."

So, she couldn't have told Madam Venus about his parents leaving. "Has she ever mentioned my mom going to see her?"

"No. She doesn't discuss her clients with me."

"When did you tell her I was buying the farm?" Leo got off the stepstool and balanced his brush on the lip of the can

Izzy raised a brow. "I didn't."

"How else would she know?" Leo grabbed a paper towel and wiped at a few paint spots on his hands.

"Not from me. The only time you've ever come up in our conversation was when she told me to tell you congratulations."

"What about Phoebe? Does she talk about her?"

"No, Leo. We don't discuss my family either. We talk about the weather and the town and our businesses."

"That woman creeps me out," Gunner said.

"She said Phoebe and Keaton were going to break up. Tonight."

"No," Izzy said, concern etching her features. "What's going to happen?"

"I have no idea, Izzy. The information came from someone who professes to be a psychic."

"Oh, no. Phoebe was hoping he—" She pressed her lips together and looked away from him.

"Phoebe was hoping he what?" Gunner asked, looking from her to Leo.

Izzy flapped a hand. "Not important. I have to…do something that's not in this room."

After she left the kitchen, Gunner turned to him. "What's that about?"

Leo rubbed the back of his neck. He knew exactly what Izzy was about to say. Phoebe was hoping Keaton would be the father of her twins. Instead of finishing her sentence for her, he picked up the brush and finished painting around the door, then moved on to the next one.

A few hours later Leo walked into Rowdy's Bar and Grill a little early to see if he could help set up for Stella's party. The first thing he noticed—Phoebe on a ladder hanging streamers. The second—Keaton holding the ladder for her.

It took a lot of willpower not to kiss Phoebe when he took her home last night, just to see if what he'd felt the night of Lara's party was real. He needed time to come to terms with his feelings, to make absolutely sure before he approached Phoebe about anything.

And he needed to see how things played out between her and Keaton. Despite what Madam Venus said about their imminent breakup, he'd never mess that up if they had a chance.

He walked toward the back wall where buffet tables were set up. The closer he got to the kitchen, the more tantalizing the smells. Izzy and Beverly were dumping chips and pretzels into bowls while Neil stacked napkins at the end of the table.

"Hey, ladies. Need some help?"

"Yes," Izzy said, sounding frazzled.

"Whatcha' need me to do?" He squeezed her shoulders.

"Will you go out back to my car and bring in the balloons?" She pulled a set of keys out of her pants pocket.

"Sure." He headed through the kitchen, but stopped next to Rowdy's cook. "Whatever you're making smells delicious, Juan."

"Stella's favorite, chicken enchiladas."

"They may just become my favorite tonight," he said, opening the back door.

He stared at Izzy's car, the interior completely obscured by colorful balloons. How did she manage to drive here? He opened the back hatch and started gathering the weights holding the balloons while some tried to escape. Four weights holding seven balloons each was enough for the first trip. Even then, he had to untangle a few before he could get the hatch pushed back down.

He went through the kitchen. Juan chuckled when he passed.

"Oh, thank you, thank you, thank you," Izzy said, hugging his waist.

"Why'd you get so many?"

"'Cause they're festive. This isn't all of them, is it?" she asked, taking the weights from him. "Why didn't you bring them all in?"

"I didn't want to pop any trying to get them out of your car."

"Can you get the others? Quick like a bunny? People are starting to arrive."

By his third trip, he got all the balloons inside and Rowdy's was crowded.

"Hey, I didn't see you come in," Phoebe said, walking toward him with Keaton hot on her heels.

That the guy was even here irked Leo. Keaton barely knew Stella.

"How long have you been here?" Phoebe asked.

"Long enough to bring in a million balloons."

"Yeah, I think Izzy went a little overboard with the decorations."

Keaton's cell rang. He looked at the screen. "I have to take this, Phoebe. I'll be right back."

"Go out the back so Stella doesn't see you," she said.

"Right." He headed for the kitchen door.

"When do you plan to move into my house?" Leo asked Phoebe.

"I guess next weekend. I'll take the guest room and I'll put Izzy in the other bedroom so you'll have your room when you visit."

"Since my condo is furnished, I'm not taking any of my stuff. I can come back next weekend and help you move your furniture in and mine into the basement," he said because he didn't want to wait longer than a week to see her again.

She fiddled with her bracelet. "I'm not keeping my furniture. Amy Saunders knows several families who can use it."

"You're giving everything away?"

She shrugged one shoulder. "I've had most of my things since college. I'll just buy new for my next place."

He slipped his hands into the front pockets of his jeans, hating that their exchange felt so unnatural. Even though they talked quite a bit last night, their conversation was stilted then, too. "Your next place?"

"Since I gave up my apartment, I'll have to find another place when you come back to Eden Falls. Maybe I'll put on my big-girl panties and actually buy a house all my own."

"What if I don't come back?" Leo asked, watching Izzy place bundles of balloons around the room.

"You think you'll be happy in San Francisco this time?"

"Everyone seems to think I'll come back because I did the first time, but I was a lot younger then."

"What about your house? And your dog?"

"They're yours."

She snorted

"Okay, you can pay me for them. Though I don't understand why you can't just accept a gift."

"Oh, I don't know. Maybe because your house is worth three million dollars. That's not a gift, Leo. A gift is a candy bar or blender."

Leo smiled at Phoebe's dramatic response. "I'll tie a balloon to the mailbox."

"You're a dork," Phoebe said, rolling her eyes.

"Well, this dork has a favor to ask. Will you stay at my place tonight or take Willy to stay with you? My flight changed so I'm going to have to drive to Seattle tonight."

"Sure."

Mac stopped next to her. "Sorry to interrupt."

"Hi, Mac," both he and Phoebe said in unison.

"You're not interrupting," Phoebe added. "How's Noelle?"

"Much better. She stayed home tonight because Lucas has a fever."

"Ah, hope he feels better soon."

"Thanks. Uh, I have a huge favor to ask, Phoebs."

She glanced between Leo and Mac. "Second one tonight. Ask away."

"Is there any way you could watch the kids the last Friday of the month? Mom and Dad want to take Noelle and me out to dinner, and every babysitter we know is going to the high school dance. If it's not convenient, we can make it another night."

Phoebe pulled her phone out of her pocket and tapped on the calendar app. "I don't have anything, so absolutely. I would love to watch the kids."

"Is six okay? We'll be gone about three hours."

"I'll be there at six."

"Great!" Mac chuckled. "Just so you know, you were specifically requested by Beck."

"Tell him I can't wait for him to beat me at Monopoly again."

"Thanks, Phoebs," Mac said, before walking away.

"You're going to start babysitting now?"

Phebe turned to Leo. "Why are you saying it like that? You heard him. They can't find a babysitter. In a way, I'm babysitting a dog for you."

"It just seems like— Never mind."

"No. Tell me what's bugging you."

"I just don't understand why you're taking what Madam Venus said so seriously. You've never believed in that stuff before. So why now?"

"Me watching Mac's kids has nothing to do with Madam Venus," she said, shaking her head. "Like before, I'm helping friends."

Why couldn't he accept that? She was helping a friend. Under different circumstances, he would have probably offered to help. When did his life get so complicated?

"Have you heard from your parents?"

Leo scoffed. "You know my parents. When have they ever gotten in touch with me?"

"I thought they might let you know when they arrived."

"They made it safely."

Phoebe raised an eyebrow. "So they did call."

"No. I…uh." He couldn't tell Phoebe he'd gone to see Madam Venus or she'd ask why. "I heard the news from someone else."

"I'm glad they made it."

"Yeah."

Gunner whistled loud enough to stop all the chatter. "Rowdy just pulled into the parking lot with Stella. Pretty sure you all know what to do when someone walks into their surprise party."

Leo went over to the side wall near the bar with a straight shot of sight to the door. Bev and Neil would appreciate a good picture of Stella's face.

The Adams girls threw him a surprise party on his sixth birthday, and another on his sixteenth. On his sixth, he cried. Not because everyone scared him when they yelled surprise, but because no one had ever celebrated his birthday before. The decorations, the presents stacked on the table, and the cake ordered just for him were so overwhelming, he broke down in tears. Neil had hustled him out of the room while Beverly started a game for the other kids. While Neil mopped his face, and told Leo that sometimes he got over-whelmed too and it was okay to cry.

The door opened and Stella walked in, followed by Rowdy, and the room exploded with shouts of "Surprise!!!" Stella stumbled backward and Rowdy caught her before she hit the floor. Leo kept his cell phone trained on the door and caught the whole thing in a burst of photos.

After Rowdy righted her, she slugged him in the chest before she was swallowed by the crowd.

Rowdy made it over to him, still rubbing his chest. "She might be small, but she packs a mighty wallop."

Leo laughed. "I've been on the other side of that fist a time or two."

The night sped by with good food and music and danc-ing. His attention was on Phoebe most of the time, and he could tell she wasn't happy. She could laugh and pretend all she wanted, but she couldn't hide the truth from him.

At nine he gave Stella a parting hug, said goodbye to Bev and Neil, and headed for the door. He'd booked a room in a Seattle hotel, so he could be at the airport by five for his seven o'clock flight.

The clear sky was full of stars glimmering and lighting up the night, highlighting the mountains in the background. His decision to take the San Francisco job had been impulsive. And stupid. He didn't want to leave Eden Falls. Especially with all the farm renovations coming up. He wanted to be here for every step. Otherwise, he'd feel like a frog in a slow boil.

Before he reached his car, he heard Phoebe call his name. He turned and watched Phoebe walk toward him, her arms wrapped around her middle.

"Are you going to leave without saying goodbye?"

"You seemed a little preoccupied."

She came toward him. "That's unfair."

Yes, it was. "Sorry." And here he was apologizing again.

"Are you okay?"

Leo rubbed that back of his neck. "Yeah."

"Are you sure?" She studied him for a moment. "You don't seem okay."

He looked away from her gaze. "How do I seem, Phoebs?"

"Not yourself. Are you mad at me?"

He was mad, but not at her. Just life. Everything seemed to be coming apart at the seams, but instead of leaving straight lines, the world was suddenly sharp with jagged edges. His new job, his parents leaving, Phoebe dating someone he didn't like while his feelings for her escalated to something he didn't know how to handle. He'd never tell Phoebe about those feelings while she was dating Keaton, even if she might be dating him for the wrong reason.

He glanced back at her. "I'm not mad at you."

"Is it the job? Your parents?"

He felt the all-too-familiar lump in his throat swelling. Things were changing, and he couldn't figure out how to change with them—wasn't sure he wanted to change.

He liked his life here in Eden Falls. Some people didn't

like small towns because they thought everyone paid way too much attention to your personal business, but it didn't bother him. He didn't have anything to hide. His parents used to embarrass him, but he'd gotten over that years ago.

He should be happy that Phoebe liked Keaton. He and Phoebe could forget all about the kiss they shared, and he could stop obsessing about it. They could just shift back to being forever friends.

Except for him, there wasn't any going back. He was intelligent enough to know what he felt wouldn't just go away. Like a disease, it filled him up, taking up too much space, stealing his sleep, and invading his waking hours.

Phoebe ruined everything in one impulsive moment. So he'd lied because suddenly he was extremely angry with her.

She walked even closer. Close enough that he could smell her perfume. "Talk to me, Leo."

He looked at her lips, remembering their blazing kiss, a moment he'd never forget. His gut reaction told him to reach for her and kiss her again. Instead, he opened his car door.

"I have to go." He slid behind the wheel and drove away, watching Phoebe recede in his rearview mirror.

CHAPTER 17

*P*hoebe stood in the parking lot for several minutes after Leo drove away, her emotions in turmoil. She was sad because of the awkwardness between them—and mad that she put it there.

Worst of all, she was in love with her best friend.

And not in a *best friend* kind of way.

He'd asked her to stay at his place to be with Willy tonight so he could drive the two and a half hours to Seattle to catch an early flight tomorrow.

She walked back inside and spotted Stella with girlfriends Misty, Alex, Carolyn, Jillian, and Jolie. Phoebe didn't have that girlfriend thing going for her. Her best friend had always been Leo. If she and Leo hung out with a group, it was with more guys. A stab of jealousy—a whole new experience for her—hit her right between the ribs. She wanted a girlfriend.

An arm wrapped around her neck. "I saw you go outside after Leo left."

Izzy might be her sister, but she still qualified as a girlfriend. "Yep. He's driving to Seattle because he has an early morning flight. We're staying at Leo's tonight."

"Okay, but that doesn't explain why you went out—"

"He's my best friend, Iz. I went out to tell him goodbye."

Her sister gave a knowing smile and led her to the buffet table. "I haven't had a chance to eat, and I'm so hungry."

Phoebe hadn't eaten much either. They both filled small plates with snacky foods.

"You okay?"

Dredging a chip through a mound of guacamole, Phoebe popped it in her mouth with a nod. The salty flavor of the chip settled pleasantly on her tongue, but with the first bite down, a little burst of spicy blended with the smooth of the avocado and the juice of a tomato perfectly. Rowdy made killer guac. "Sure. Wonderful. Fabulous. Never better," she mumbled around a mouthful.

"Yep. I believe you." Izzy looked around like she was searching for someone while crunching through a carrot stick. "How much longer are you going to try and force Keaton into your baby-daddy mold?"

Izzy's question hurt, but the truth usually did. "Why would you say that?"

"Because you don't seem like yourself when you're around him, which makes me think you don't really *like him* like him."

"You sound like you're in middle school." She nabbed one of Izzy's carrot sticks. "Can we talk about something else? Please?"

"Okay." Izzy led her to an empty table. "When I talked to Leo earlier, he seemed to be coping pretty well with his parents' relocation."

If anyone deserved a happy ending, Leo did. As if he didn't have enough to worry about, she'd filled his head with extra anxiety. "I don't think it's so much about them leaving as it is them leaving without saying goodbye."

"Leo deserves so much better," Izzy said, pulling out a chair.

"People say he should be used to his parents doing this kind of stuff, but who wouldn't hold out a little hope? They're his parents." Phoebe looked around for Keaton and finally spotted him at the dartboard with JT and Beam.

"He'll be better off with them in California," Izzy said.

Or not. "He'll probably worry about them more because he can't stop by to check on them."

Carolyn passed by their table with a wave.

"Hey, congratulations, Carolyn. Stella told me the good news," Izzy said.

"Thank you." Carolyn's cheeks bloomed a bright pink.

"What good news?" Phoebe asked.

"JT and Carolyn are expecting."

The ugly green monster raised its head and roared. Phoebe pushed her plate away and hoped her pasted-on smile conveyed a fragment of sincerity. "That's wonderful, Carolyn."

Carolyn's brows wrinkled. "I thought Leo would have told you."

"Leo knows?"

"He's the first person I told after JT and I found out. I just assumed he told you when he took donuts to the station last Monday."

Last Monday, the day she filled in on dispatch so Layne and Gianna could go for their ultrasound appointment. Leo knew and didn't tell her.

She snapped her fingers. "Oh, right. I was on the phone when he came in, so he just dropped off and ducked out. But that's fabulous news, Carolyn. Congratulations. And smack your husband for not telling me before tonight. He's had a whole week." she said in a teasing tone. *Leo had a whole week, too.*

"Thank you," Carolyn said, not committing to the smack. She was much too sweet a person.

"Don't read so much into Leo not telling you, Phoebs," Izzy said after Carolyn walked away. "The guy is freaking out so much he went to see Madam Venus."

That got Phoebe's full attention. "What? Why?"

Izzy frowned. "You know, he didn't really say. He asked if I knew that his mom went to see Vera, and I didn't. I told him Vera and I don't talk about her clients or my family."

Phoebe was bursting with questions that only Leo would be able to answer. Would he actually go to a psychic for a reading? "Did he say—"

Stella—the sister with impeccable timing—plopped into a chair next to Phoebe and stole a chip off her plate, scooping up the rest of the guacamole. "Why aren't you two dancing?"

Izzy scoffed. "Gunner hates to dance."

"Where's Keaton?" Stella asked, stealing another chip.

Phoebe pointed toward the dartboard.

"So, how are things going? Are you in love yet?" Stella asked, crossing her eyes.

Phoebe snorted. "If you keep doing that, your eyes are going to stay crossed forever," she said, mimicking their mom's voice.

"Phoebe doesn't date a man long enough to fall in love."

True, but Izzy's comment stung a little more than it should, and if she didn't shrug it off she'd be in tears again.

"Maybe this one is different, huh, sis?" Stella jumped up and slapped her palms against the table. "When did the Adams sisters ever need men to dance?"

"Never," Izzy said, leaping to her feet and holding out a hand for Phoebe.

Stella was right. The Adams sisters had been dancing

together since before Stella could walk. She, Georgie, and Izzy would wiggle to the music while she held Stella in her arms. Even after Oopsie was born they loved to dance every chance they got.

She let Izzy pull her to her feet and they hit the dance floor together and were soon joined by every female in the place. Phoebe let the music sweep her away for five minutes, only wishing Georgie and Adelaide were here with them.

And Leo. He'd be standing on the sidelines, watching some other woman and cheering. She wouldn't care, because at least he'd be near and smiling, which was exactly what he needed. A little carefree fun could go a long way toward healing hurts.

When the party broke up, Keaton walked Phoebe to her car. He leaned in and kissed her. And, again, she felt nothing.

"I'll call you tomorrow," he said.

She nodded, but when Keaton turned to leave, she stopped him with a hand on his arm. There was no need to prolong this. "Wait. I don't think this is working, Keaton."

He blew out a breath. Relieved? Disappointed?

Then he nodded. "I agree. I really like you, Phoebe, and I enjoy spending time with your family. I hoped tonight would—"

"I hoped the same thing. Things clicked so well the night we met. I couldn't believe how much we have in common. You were so easy to talk to that I just thought… Dating sucks, doesn't it?"

"I'm so tired of dating," he said at the same time.

They both laughed before he pulled her into a hug. "I hope you meet someone perfect for you, Phoebe."

"I wish the same thing for you." She released him. "Hey, maybe we'll run into each other sometime."

"I hope so." Keaton kissed her cheek and she stood near

her car watching until his taillights disappeared around the corner.

No need for Izzy to pose her hypothetical question to Madam Venus anymore. Keaton wasn't The One.

At Leo's, Willy greeted her at the door with his happy doggy wagging tail. She got down on the floor and let him try to climb into her lap. "You silly dog. Did your daddy stop to say goodbye to you?"

Willy yipped, which Phoebe took as a yes. She wished he was still here. Though she was a little upset that Leo didn't tell her Carolyn was pregnant, she understood. But she did have questions about him visiting Madam Venus.

With a final rub, she climbed to her feet and filled Willy's dish with food, which he started devouring before she got his water bowl filled.

"Izzy should be here any minute, Willy. I'm going to change, then I'll meet you in the family room for a good movie."

In the guest room she'd chosen, she changed into leggings, then snuck into Leo's closet and snagged a sweatshirt. Sitting on the edge of the bed, she breathed him in. If he was here, he'd think she'd lost her ever-lovin' mind.

Maybe she had.

Insanity caused by a medium.

~

*L*eo tried to settle into his new place, but everything seemed off-kilter. He woke up Wednesday morning stumbling toward the bathroom in the wrong direction. The furniture in the completely furnished condo was uncomfortable and colorless. The view, though beautiful on a clear day, wasn't Eden Falls in the distance with the surrounding mountains.

Generally, he didn't get attached to possessions, but today he wanted his cereal bowls, his spoons, and his coffee mug.

Yet this was his life now, the life he chose. Back in the city working for someone else.

It started to rain right after his plane landed yesterday and hadn't quit, so he drove his rental car to the office. Today was Greg's mandatory meeting, and Leo wanted to get in early to make some sense of his office.

He sat down with Casey yesterday and went over a few basics. All he really needed was someone to field his calls and take legible messages and notes during meetings.

When he got to his office, he turned the lights on against the gray day that sent him quickly sliding into a lousy mood. So he leaned back in his office chair and tried to understand why he felt the need to run from Phoebe. That question had plagued him since they said goodbye in Rowdy's parking lot two nights ago.

She was on duty last night and couldn't talk when he called. He tried again this morning before leaving his condo, but she didn't pick up. The thought of losing his best friend made him sick to his stomach. More than sick. The thought was unbearable, yet he seemed to be pushing her away as much as she seemed to be pushing him.

Had what Madam Venus said proved to be true? Was she still with Keaton, or did they break up the night of Stella's party like the psychic predicted? He felt bad that he couldn't be with her for their traditional pancakes if she and Keaton ended their relationship.

Leo had hoped to recapture their ease around each other this weekend on the boathouse, hoped to restore the friendship they enjoyed before their kiss, but he blew that too. With all the craziness going on in his life, he forgot to confirm his reservations. So no recapturing anything for them. He knew she'd be disappointed. Heck! He was disappointed. Too many things were going on, too many things bombarding him all at once—and most were his own doing.

After he got the email about the houseboat, he texted Phoebe to let her know and to apologize but she didn't text back.

His thoughts circled to the kiss they shared. He'd kissed a lot of women. Not one had ever been cemented into his brain like the kiss with Phoebe.

He turned his chair away from the windows to face his desk and the piles of files and messages stacked neatly on top, with the reminder of the all-hands meeting at ten o'clock on top of those.

The next message was a detailed description of a problem IT was having with a server. He took a swallow of coffee from his travel mug and got to work. The laptop was new, but ready for him as soon as he opened it.

"Good morning."

Leo glanced up. "Hi, Casey."

"Looks like you're already busy."

"Just getting started."

"Can I get you anything?"

"Actually, will you introduce me to Dex...?" He searched the papers in front of him for a last name.

"Harris?" she supplied. "Sure."

He grabbed the file he was working on and followed her down the hall and across the room full of cubicles to a corner where four desks were pushed together to make a big square. A woman and three men were all talking while they clicked away on their keyboards.

"Hey, Dex. This is Leo Sawyer."

A guy with long hair and a beard that was just as long jumped out of his chair. "Oh, hey, man. Glad to meet you."

Leo shook the hand Dex extended. "Same. Thanks, Casey."

After she walked away, he looked at the three other people that made up the group. "Are you all part of the IT team?"

"Yeah. Josh Johnson, Gillis O'Brian, and Thomas Frank," Dex said, pointing out each one as he introduced them.

"Nice to meet you," he said to the group. "I have your glitch figured out. Mind if I use your computer?"

Leo spent thirty minutes showing the team how to fix the first of many problems. Could this be done remotely? Yes. All he'd have to do is share his screen in a virtual meeting and walk the team through it. Easy.

By ten, they'd worked through two more problems, and Leo began to wonder where Greg found this team. These were time-consuming but easy fixes, and anyone with experience should have been able to figure out two of the three answers on their own.

Greg walked into the main room and whistled to get everyone's attention. He introduced the department leads, including Leo, then asked each to report. Leo had only agreed to be a consultant—not a lead. That reminder, along with discussing the IT team's inexperience, would be the first order of business once Greg finished his welcome presentation.

He and Casey walked back to his office together after the meeting. Her spiky hair wasn't standing up as much as the first day they met.

"Need anything?"

He handed her the notes he made while showing the IT guys how to work through the problems. "Can you type these up and send the file to my work email? Just do the best you can with my chicken-scratches. I'll make any corrections when you send me the file."

"Sure." She took the papers and settled at her desk. "When do you need these?"

He stopped in his office doorway. "By the end of the day is fine."

"Okay. Would you like to have lunch delivered?"

If he ate at his desk, he could get through a few more of the files. "That would be great. Any sub-sandwich places nearby?"

"A few. Do you have any preferences?"

"Turkey on white, lettuce, tomato, just a touch of mayo, and black olives if they have any. Thanks, Casey." He pulled out his wallet and handed her some bills. "Get something for yourself."

"Oh, you don't—"

"First full day treat for putting up with me."

She took the money from him. "Thank you."

"I'll take a bag of chips, too."

In his office, he shut the door, pulled out his cell phone, and scrolled to Phoebe's number. Her cell rang four times before he got a breathy, "Hello."

"You sound winded."

"No. Just aggravated with Rita. She keeps parking in the no-parking zone at the side of Noelle's Café. I'm done with writing tickets. Today I gave her a final warning and she flew off the handle. Next time I'll have her car towed."

Leo chuckled. "Sounds like nothing's changed in two days."

"Did you think it would?"

"No. Though I'm sorry about Rita, it's actually comforting to know things are the same." He sat in his desk chair and swiveled toward the windows. "I called to tell you I'm sorry I messed up with the houseboat. The management company rented it to someone else before I got back to them."

"Don't worry about it," she said. "I know you've got a lot going on right now."

He'd only been gone a couple of days and already couldn't

wait to get back to Eden Falls. He wished he'd been at Noelle's this morning. Rita and Phoebe probably put on quite a show. Rita was entertaining even when she wasn't in trouble.

"I better go. Another call is coming in."

"Okay," he said, though he wasn't ready to hang up. "I'll talk to you tonight?"

"No. I'm going out with Izzy and Stella. Sisters night."

"Have fun."

"Bye, Leo."

Phoebe hung up before he could say goodbye.

Leo stood and made his way to Greg's office. He was on the phone, but waved Leo in and gestured toward a chair in front of his desk. Leo spent the five-minute wait gazing out the window. The spires on the Golden Gate Bridge were shrouded in heavy clouds.

Leo wondered how his parents were doing and if they were glad about their decision to move. He shouldn't have been surprised or even hurt when they up and left without a goodbye. Rock and Sage would never change, and he needed to accept the way they'd been his whole life. As much as he hated to admit it, talking to Madam Venus eased his mind a little. It was hard to believe they had his best interests in mind when they decided to move, but he clung to the fragment she'd given him.

"How's the first day, Leo?"

He'd been so deep in thought he hadn't noticed when Greg ended the call. He crossed his ankle over the opposite knee. "Why have you got newbies running the IT department?"

"They aren't newbies."

"I showed them how to solve three problems this morning that would never have hit my desk if they had any experience."

"That's exactly what I hired you for."

"And that's the second issue. You hired me as a consultant, not a department lead."

"Like you said, you showed the team how to solve three problems in what? A couple of hours? Why be a consultant when you can be the head of IT?"

"I'm not interested."

"Come on, Leo. We're just starting out and the team could use your expertise."

"No. In fact, I was already planning to talk to you about working remotely. I have a big project coming up in Eden Falls and could do the consulting job from there."

"That won't work for me, because I need an IT lead."

This was just one of the reasons they severed their business association the first time. Greg was a manipulator who tried to win people over with his smooth talk and many promises while finagling another deal under the table. Leo dropped his foot to the floor and stood. "And being the IT lead won't work for me, so I guess we part ways before we get started."

Greg jumped up and held out a hand. "Wait, wait, wait. How about you head up the department until I can find someone else?"

Leo studied the man in front of him. "Thirty days, Greg. You have me over IT for thirty days, then I walk. I'll be happy to be a remote consultant, but nothing more."

"Why didn't you tell me about this big project when we talked in Eden Falls?"

"It was just an ember at the time." Leo rubbed the back of his neck. He knew deep down that San Francisco wasn't where he was happy, so why did he let his fears chase him away from home?

"Greg, the IT team can call me anytime with a problem. And I'll bill by the hour rather than take a salary, which will save you enough money to pay the IT team three times over. I can work the team through almost any problem in a virtual meeting. If I can't, I'll charge you an airline ticket—still much cheaper than the salary you'd be paying me. But I suggest you hire a team leader with more experience than what you have right now. If you do that, you won't need me at all."

"Thirty days, Leo."

Leo leaned forward and held out his hand. "Thirty days."

When Leo walked into his condo long after dark that night, he missed being greeted by Willy. That dog was such a part of him. He imagined Willy romping around the farm while the renovations were taking place. He had a big yard at home in Eden Falls, but nothing like the amount of land at his parents' place. Actually, soon to be his place.

Madam Venus said his parents knew he was buying the farm. He wondered how they found out, something he'd probably never know. More so, he marveled that his dad accepted the offer.

He went into the bedroom and kicked off his shoes before falling onto the bed. His eyes burned from staring at computers all day and spending the afternoon assigning the green IT team to different areas of the project, and then showing them how to fix the problems that cropped up.

He'd escaped home at eighteen, moving to San Francisco to find investors for his startup company. He missed Phoebe and his other friends, but he loved immersing himself in the busy, bustling life of the city. That love hadn't lasted long. Though he stayed for several years, he knew Eden Falls would always be home.

So why was he here?

This life isn't what he wanted. Especially when he already had a project he was anxious to start on. But first, he needed to close on the property, which would give Greg time to hire a department head and give Leo time to get the IT team up to speed.

~

*P*hoebe didn't have time to change out of her uniform before meeting her sisters at Rinaldo's Italian Restaurant. Stella and Izzy were already seated in a crescent booth.

"Hi, ladies."

Stella scooted to the middle, making room for her. "You're late."

"No, Layne was late, therefore making me late."

"I hear Gianna has horrible morning sickness," Izzy said.

"Except hers is stretching out to all-day sickness," Phoebe added. "Layne hates to leave her alone."

Stella held out a menu. "She and Misty are both struggling with their pregnancies."

"Are you guys ordering a pizza or pasta?" Phoebe asked.

"Salad for me," Stella said. As the curviest of the Adams' sisters, Stella always worried about what she ate.

Izzy set her menu aside. "I'm ordering a pizza. Gunner made me promise to bring leftovers home."

"How about I order a pizza and you can have a piece to go with your salad, Stella?"

Stella snorted. "Who's going to eat *your* leftovers? Leo's gone."

"I can eat a piece for lunch and a piece for dinner all week."

"Sold," Stella said.

After they ordered, they spent a few minutes catching up on each other's lives. Other than family dinners, they didn't get the chance to spend time together very often. Izzy's wedding, only four weeks away, took up a lot of their conversation. She ran several ideas past them. Most of the details were already nailed down, but she still worried about serving finger food rather than a sit-down dinner for the reception.

"There's going to be enough food for hungry people to get full. Quit worrying," Phoebe said.

"I agree. You've got a ton of choices, and I like the idea of carrying around a small plate of yummy tastes rather than sitting down for a full-blown dinner." Stella looked at Phoebe. "Is Leo going to come home for Izzy's wedding?"

"I can't imagine him missing it, but I have no idea."

"He'd better come or he'll be in big trouble with me and Mom. How's he doing with the new job?"

Phoebe shrugged. "Today's his first full day. He called, but I was at work and couldn't talk. I can ask him when we talk this weekend."

"I don't understand why you two don't just get married," Stella said with an eyeroll. "You talk every day, you finish each other's sentences, you spend the night at his house. You two know more about each other than—"

"I kissed Leo."

Stella's eyebrows almost hit her hairline, then a smile stretched across her face. "It's about time. You two should have a dozen babies by now."

Stella paused, looked between her and Izzy, then rolled her hand. "So, what happened?"

"Leo rejected me."

"That's not true," Izzy quickly interjected. "Leo has valid concerns. He's afraid to commit to a relationship because of his upbringing—which we all should understand since we grew up with him. We know how many times he's been disappointed by his parents."

"That's just dumb," Stella said. "Leo is nothing like Sage or Rock. Just tell him."

Phoebe wanted to laugh and cry at the same time. She'd been saying things along those lines since Leo was in elementary school. "Sometimes beliefs run too deep to change."

"Then I'll tell him."

"Sure, Stella. You can try."

"Leo is concerned that if things don't work out, the Adams family will reject him," Izzy said.

"That's just as dumb as him thinking he's anything like his parents. I'd pick Leo over Phoebe any day."

Phoebe blew a raspberry at her sister.

Stella wrapped an arm around Phoebe's neck. "You know I'm kidding because nothing would ever go wrong. I've always said you guys should be a couple. Sheesh, everyone in town already thinks you *are* a couple.

"Well, I'm not putting myself out there again. It was an incredibly embarrassing moment, and Leo has treated me differently ever since. Actually, not differently. Just…I'm not even sure how to describe the way he's acting. Our friendship seems on the verge of collapse because of that kiss, which makes me feel horrible. I don't want Leo to feel uncomfortable around me."

Phoebe leaned back while their dinners were set on the table, relieved that they'd all be too busy eating to continue the conversation.

CHAPTER 18

The rest of the week sped by for Leo. The IT team kept him busy with piles of questions and problems, so he finally had a desk moved out by them so he didn't have to keep walking down the hall. Thirty days wouldn't be enough time to teach the four team members all they needed to know before he left, so he hoped Greg let him be in on the hiring process for the man or woman who would take his spot.

His first weekend in the city started out lonely. He didn't have Willy or Phoebe or anyone he knew to hang out with. When Gabriel invited him to a family dinner, Leo jumped at the chance, but when he parked his rental across the street from a local gym and he saw people streaming inside, his enthusiasm waned. He thought it would just be Gabe, his wife, and kids. Obviously, his idea of family was very different from his friend's.

Inside, several different rooms were set up and both male and female basketball games were in full swing. In another room, two volleyball games were also going. A third room had a badminton net set up at one end and games for younger kids were assembled at the other.

Tables and chairs lined the middle of the fourth room. More tables overflowing with food were spaced out around the perimeter.

Family dinner to Gabriel looked more like a family reunion to Leo. He estimated about eighty people. And he felt out of place from the minute he walked in. His meager offering—a plate of brownies—wouldn't even feed the little kids in the group.

Gabriel's wife, Iolana, spotted him and waved. "Leo! So glad you could make it."

He hugged her. "I appreciate the invite."

"Gabe, Leo is here," she called.

"Leo!" Gabe came over and pumped his hand with the excitement of a linebacker who'd just won the Superbowl for his team.

"This is quite a family dinner." Leo looked around at all the happy faces. His first estimate of eighty people might be on the shy side.

"Oh, sorry, I should have warned you. Our family dinners have grown quite a bit since you were at the last one. In the summer, we meet at a park, but when it's cold or rainy we meet at my cousin's gym," he said, sweeping his arms out.

"Make yourself at home, Leo," Iolana said.

After Gabe introduced Leo around, all the games were put on hold and everyone gathered in a huddle so Gabriel's dad could deliver a prayer of thanksgiving for food and family. The group assembled in four lines, one on each side of the food tables, and filled plates. Leo attended many parties and barbecues, but he'd never seen such an array of choices. Everything looked so good, he followed suit and filled his plate to overflowing before finding a seat across the table from Gabe and his wife.

A gorgeous woman with a riot of long dark curls and huge brown eyes sat next to him.

"This is my cousin Penina, which means 'pearl' in the Samoan language," Gabe said.

"That's a beautiful name."

"Thank you," she said.

He spent most of lunch talking to her about interests and jobs. Normally, he would love the attention she showered on him, and he would have given right back, but all he could think about was Phoebe and how much he wanted to be sitting next to her in the Adams kitchen eating a meal prepared by Bev and the girls, shooting the breeze with Neil, Gunner, and Rowdy. He left Keaton out of his equation.

Was Keaton there? Or did Madam Venus call it right?

After dinner, the games picked up again before dessert. He played a round of volleyball. When he sat down to cool off, he paid attention to all the men who were carrying babies or watching toddlers so their wives could participate in some of the games.

Because his parents treated him like an inconvenience, he'd been of the same mindset about children, but no one here seemed to be missing out on the fun because they had a child or two.

Gabe sat beside him. "Crazy, huh?"

"Yes, but in a good way."

"You're welcome anytime. Feel free to bring Phoebe if she's visiting."

Phoebe. She'd love this and would fit right in with Gabe's huge, loving family. "I will if she *ever* visits."

Gabe tipped his head and studied Leo. "You guys have a falling-out?"

They seemed to have a falling out every time they talked lately. He was constantly apologizing for stepping over the line or coming on too strong or reading more into a situation than he should.

"Not a falling-out. We just seem to disagree about life a lot lately."

"Like an old married couple."

Something like that. "She has a crazy notion that we should—"

"It's about time," Gabe said with a laugh and a pat on the back. "You two have been dancing around each other for years."

"We've been best friends forever."

Gabe flipped his chair around and straddled the seat so he was facing Leo. "And you're afraid if things don't work out your friendship will be ruined."

"Wouldn't you be if you were in my shoes?"

Resting his folded arms on the back of the chair, Gabe ran his thumb along his chin. "Maybe. But if you don't take a leap of faith, you may be missing out on your life's greatest adventure. Iolana and I were friends for years before I asked her out. We went all through high school together. In fact, her brother is one of my best friends."

A lot like him and Phoebe.

"Iolana's my everything. I can't imagine my life without her and the kids."

Again, a lot like him and Phoebe.

Gabe stood up. "Enough seriousness. Let's get in on a basketball game. You can think about what I said later."

And Leo did. Despite what everyone else told him, Gabe's words stuck with him all through the next week. He and Phoebe talked every day. He paid attention to her voice, the cadence of her sentences, trying to read between the lines. She never mentioned Keaton, and he didn't want to ask. She also never mentioned the kiss.

They laughed at her crazy stories about Rita and Mr.

Polanski's Bigfoot chases. She told him about Willy and even put the phone to his dog's ear.

"Oh, you should see his tail. He misses you, Leo."

"I miss him." *And you.* "My condo is way too quiet."

When he hung up, he started a mental list of everything he loved about Phoebe. Not only was she his best friend, but he could count on her, no matter what. She made him laugh and was there when he cried. She went out of her way to help others, was kind and thoughtful, and had a huge heart. There wasn't anything about her he didn't enjoy—except when she called him out for being a dork, which she didn't hesitate to do when he needed to be set straight. He trusted her to tell him the truth and could always count on her to have his back.

She was sexy and sweet, all rolled up together. He loved the way her hair smelled and her smile and the way she wrinkled her nose like a bunny. Her laugh, her toes, and definitely the way she kissed....

Like a sledgehammer over the head, he realized he didn't just love these things about Phoebe. He *loved* Phoebe.

The thought flitted around his mind like a butterfly looking for a place to settle. He waited for the panic to hit. Instead, everything fell into place, because, deep down, he'd always known.

I love Phoebe.

~

*P*hoebe waved when Beck opened the door. "Hey, buddy."

"I knew it was going to be you."

"You did, huh?"

Mac opened the door wider. "How about we let her in the house, son?"

She stepped inside Mac's house, a place that had always been a comfortable guy's pad until he married Noelle. Since then, it evolved into a comfortable family home. The pang of jealousy she'd been anticipating all week hit, but it didn't hurt as much as she expected. Instead, a sweet happiness for her workmate and friend settled deep. Happiness because he'd found someone to share his forever with. Happiness for their sweet little family that would grow bigger as the years went by.

Noelle came into the room with a sigh. "I just got Lucas down. He's fed and burped and might sleep until we get home. If not, there's milk in the freez—" she scoffed. "Sorry. You already know where everything is. Thank you for watching my babies."

"I'm not a baby," Beck said.

Noelle tucked him under her arm. "You're my baby."

Phoebe's heart squeezed hard. She wanted this. All of it. From messy diapers to sloppy toddler kisses to angsty teenagers. If she needed to spend the money she'd been saving for a down payment on a house to adopt a child, she would.

"I'm glad you're letting me watch the kiddos again. I missed playing board games with Beck and having him beat the pants off me."

The tips of Beck's ears turned red just like his daddy's when Mac got embarrassed. "I didn't really beat the pants off her."

Mac laughed and wrapped his big hand around the back of his son's neck. "That's just a figure of speech. Phoebe likes to tease."

She'd never mention the red ears and embarrass him more. "Why don't you get one of those board games and let's see if I can win at least once?"

"Okay!"

"Hey," Mac said before Beck ran off. "Come say goodbye."

Beck wrapped his arms around his dad's waist, then he did the same with Noelle before running down the hall.

"Beck ate dinner," Noelle said. "And there's plenty of left-over lasagna in the fridge for you."

"Thanks. I just might have to try a piece."

Mac held out Noelle's coat. "We should be home by nine. Since it's a weekend, Beck can stay up until we get back. Call my cell if he gives you any problems."

Phoebe rolled her eyes. "I think I can handle him. Go have a nice time."

She and Beck stayed in the living room so she'd be closer to the baby's room while they played *Ticket to Ride*, a board game she'd never heard of. Beck won again.

"How do you do that?" she asked, ruffling his hair.

"I'm good at board games," he said with a shrug and a grin bright enough to light the town. "I'm going to get another game."

He jumped up just as someone knocked on the front door.

"I'll get it."

Phoebe put the top on *Ticket to Ride* and pulled herself up off the floor.

"Hey, Beck," said a low, very familiar voice.

"Hi, Leo. Did you come to help Phoebe?"

Leo chuckled as he stepped inside. "No, sir. Phoebe doesn't need any help. I'm here to help you keep winning board games."

Beck laughed and Leo's grin reached her over Beck's head, hitting her hard in the chest. Wow. She'd missed him way more than she realized.

"I don't need help either. Phoebe hasn't won one single game yet."

"Then I guess I'm here to watch."

"I'm getting another game," Beck said, heading down the hall again.

Leo shut the door and came toward her. "Surprise."

"It *is* a surprise. When did you get back?"

"I came straight here."

"Why? I mean, what are you doing in town?"

"I missed you," he said, stopping so close she had to look up.

Her pounding heart performed a breath-stealing somersault. Something in the air shifted. She'd never seen the expression on his face. Even his tone of voice sounded different.

"Are you hungry?" she said, grabbing the first subject that would get her out of the room.

He chuckled. "Starving."

She took a step back. "Noelle left some lasagna in the fridge."

"Sounds great."

"If you want to help Beck set up the next let's-humiliate-Phoebe game, I'll warm some up."

"You've got a deal."

She turned toward the kitchen, positive that if her heart beat any faster she'd need an ambulance. "Willy sure will be happy to see you."

"What about you?"

Beck came barreling into the living room. "I brought *Jaws*."

Leo laughed. "There's a game called *Jaws*?"

Phoebe took that moment to escape. She pulled the lasagna out of the fridge and cut two pieces. Even cold, the smell made her stomach growl. Sliding the pieces into the microwave, she leaned against the wall and listened to Beck and Leo laugh while her mind raced over Leo's question. Was his tone…suggestive?

She was being silly, reading too much into a simple question.

I missed you.

Willy will be happy to see you.

What about you? What about you? What about you? bounced around in her mind, looking for a place to take hold.

She took the lasagna out and set both pieces on the table along with forks, napkins, and glasses of water. "Beck, would you like a bowl of ice cream while Leo and I eat?"

"Yes, please."

Leo and Beck walked into the kitchen while she dished up the ice cream. "I could only find vanilla. If you want chocolate sauce, can you get it out of the fridge?"

She heard the fridge open and shut behind her.

Leo took a seat. She rounded the table and sat next to Beck, who was smothering his ice cream.

She took the bottle from him. "I think that's enough."

"I like a lot."

"It's a good thing," she said with a laugh. "You have more chocolate sauce than ice cream."

She looked up and caught Leo's intent blue gaze watching her. He smiled, but not his regular smile. Different from his I'm-enjoying-this-moment-so-much smile or his this-is-so-not-funny smile or even his I'm-glad-to-see-you smile. She didn't know how to read this unfamiliar expression.

"Noelle makes great lasagna," Leo said.

"Mmm-hmm," she agreed, taking a big bite to keep her mouth busy.

A little squawk came through the baby monitor, followed by a second one fifteen seconds later.

"Lucas is awake," Beck sing-songed from a chocolate-covered mouth.

Phoebe handed him a napkin. Then she turned on the water to let it warm while she pulled a plastic bag of mom's milk out of the freezer. Once the water was hot, she pushed the bag down to warm.

"I'll be back," she said, actually glad for another excuse to escape.

She walked into the baby's room and peeked over the edge of the crib. "Hi, Lucas." She lifted him into her arms. "Phew, you stink, little guy."

Lucas waved arms and kicked his little legs like he'd joined an aerobics class.

She carried a diaper and the package of wipes over to the little changing table on the low dresser. "Oh, baby, that is stinky," she said, smiling at the cute little face that seemed to be concentrating so hard.

After she cleaned the baby, she put on a fresh diaper and snapped up his cute little doggie pajamas. "There we go. You smell so much better."

In the kitchen, she put Lucas in his little bouncy seat so she could pour the warmed milk into a bottle. Tightening the top, she lifted him and touched the nipple to his lips. His head turned back and forth a few times before he latched on.

"We could hear you in the baby monitor," Beck said with a giggle.

"Lucas didn't smell very good when I went into his room."

"I told Leo you used about twenty-five wipes the last time you changed a poopy diaper."

"It wasn't quite that many." She met Leo's gaze, expecting him to be on his feet, ready to bolt or ready to accuse her of trying to trap him. Instead, he leaned back in his chair and stretched out his long legs, crossing one ankle over the other like he planned to stay all night.

The little swallowing sounds Lucas made sent a funny flood rushing from her chest to her lower belly. If asked to describe what she was feeling, she'd probably say her ovaries were rebelling because of neglect.

"You look good."

Leo wore that smile she couldn't decipher. "What do you mean?"

"Holding a baby. You're a natural."

How should she respond to that?

"Let me feed Lucas so you can finish dinner."

"Okay, who are you and what have you done with Leo. Aliens. That's the only answer. Aliens have landed and cloned you."

He held out his arms. "Nope, I'm still me."

She set the bottle on the table and turned Lucas to lay him in Leo's arms. Big Leo made Little Lucas look even smaller. Lucas started rooting around, so Phoebe handed her friend the bottle. Then she sat across the table and tried not to stare at Leo while he fed the baby, afraid to give him too much attention for fear he'd realize what he was doing and bolt.

"I'm done."

Phoebe rubbed a hand over Beck's back. "Put your bowl in the sink and the chocolate sauce in the fridge, please. Then wash your face and hands."

Beck went to the fridge before carrying his bowl to the sink. "Are we going to play the *Jaws* game?"

"After hands and face, set the game up. We'll play when Lucas has finished his evening snack."

Beck washed his hands, rubbed a wet paper towel across his face, and ran into the living room. "Hurry!"

Leo gazed down at Lucas with that smile again. Phoebe couldn't stand the suspense any longer. "Want to tell me what's up with you?"

"I figured if we're going to have twins I might as well learn how to do some of the stuff that goes along with kids."

She studied him for a long moment. "This isn't a good time to tease me." Except, he looked serious.

"I'm not teasing. Maybe Madam Venus is right."

Again, she didn't dare say respond for fear he'd run.

"I can see the million questions running through that pretty head of yours. Go ahead. Ask away."

"What changed your mind?"

"A friend gave me some things to think about."

Lucas sucked air, so Phoebe stood, took the baby from Leo, and put him over her shoulder. "Time for a burp, Lucas."

Leo pushed up from the table. "Babies need to burp?" he asked, rinsing their plates and Beck's bowl, then loading them in the dishwasher.

"Burping them gets rid of the air they swallow during feeding." *Pat, pat, pat.*

He came to stand right behind her and put a hand on her arm. She was glad her sweater would keep him from feeling the goosebumps that popped up all over her skin. *Pat, pat, pat.* His other hand went to the baby's head.

Lucas burped on cue and Leo chuckled. He was standing so close Phoebe felt the puff of air across her cheek.

"He's so small. And he smells good."

Phoebe put her nose against the baby's head, taking in his fresh lavender smell. Then she turned to put distance between her and Leo because he could so easily break her heart right now with a few simple words.

"His eyes are closed," Leo said.

Phoebe lowered Lucas to her arm. "Time for bed, little guy. Your big brother wants to play a game."

She walked down the hall pathetically grateful Leo didn't follow, because she definitely needed a minute to process what he just said. Since she was unsure what changed Leo's mind, she wondered if it might have been his visit to Madam Venus.

Just the fact that he'd come here and offered to hold Lucas was so out of character. And why didn't he tell her he was coming? He knew she'd be at Mac's babysitting because she reminded him during their call last night.

After tucking sweet Lucas in his crib, she went into the living room, where she found Leo sitting on the floor with Beck, looking like he was having the time of his life. The grin he flashed stole her breath and his gaze flipped her stomach upside down.

"Finally," Beck said, interrupting the moment between them.

CHAPTER 19

After goodbyes, Leo walked out of Mac's house with Phoebe. He opened her car door. "You up for a movie?"

Her eyes held questions with a huge dollop of doubt. "I'd rather talk about what's going on with you."

"Let's meet at the house, then."

He followed her through town, up the mountain road, and turned off at his house. All the while his heart was pounding in his throat. Why did it take him so long to realize he was in love with his best friend? After all, he put her through, how could he explain in a way that she would believe? How could he convince her he was all in? Marriage, kids, white picket fence, dog in the yard—all of it.

So many people had talked to him. So many friends tried to convince him he was nothing like his parents, but he was too stubborn to believe them. Why did it take Gabe, of all people, to convince him he was being an idiot? And why did Gabe's words resonate differently that what anyone else had told him?

He got out of his car and took a deep breath of fresh air.

He'd missed this place even more than he expected. Inside, Willy greeted him with yips of joy. He'd missed his dog as much as he missed home, and almost as much as he missed Phoebe. Dropping to the floor, he gave Willy a good rubdown while the dog tried to lick Leo to death.

He laughed. "Did you miss me, boy? Huh? I missed you too."

Phoebe hung up her coat and scooped dog food out of the bin he kept it in, pouring it into Willy's bowl, while Willy dashed into the kitchen, choosing food over his happy reunion with Leo.

"Ah, I see how it is. You missed me until food comes into play."

"You didn't tell me you were coming," Phoebe said, placing the scoop back into the dog food bin.

He pushed to his feet. "I decided at the last minute."

She trained her beautiful brown eyes on him. How could he have been so blind, so in denial for so long?

"You haven't really told me much about work. How are things going?" She leaned back against the kitchen counter, her hands behind her back.

"There isn't much to tell. I've been dealing with the green IT team Greg hired."

"Why did he hire a green team?"

"I'm not sure. He seems to think they know what they're doing, but I'm constantly showing them basics they should know."

"Can you teach them?"

He moved closer to her. "I can. I'm just not sure I want to."

"What do you mean?" she asked.

"I was hired as a consultant, not a teacher." He reached down and ran Willy's ears through his fingers when the dog nudged his hand. "I don't need to be in San Francisco to accomplish the job Greg hired me to do."

"Does that mean you're moving back?"

"I could. What do you think?"

"I think I'll be mad that it took three weeks for you to decide. I just gave away all my furniture, Leo."

"I won't kick you out of here if I come back."

She snorted. "We can't live in the same house. People will talk."

"Let them talk. When have you ever cared what people thought?"

"I care what my parents think," she said, crossing her arms over her chest. "And I know you do too."

She was right. Beverly and Neil wouldn't be happy if they lived in the same house. "I'll figure something out."

A worried expression crossed her face.

"You think I should stay in California?"

Pressing her lips together, she shook her head. "I think you should do what you want."

He moved even closer. "No, I'm asking for your opinion."

"That *is* my opinion. You should do what makes you happy."

"So you don't care one way or the other."

"Don't do that, Leo. You know I care." She looked down at the tile floor and toed a grout line.

"I have a confession."

She looked up at him with raised brows.

"Carolyn Garrett is pregnant. I found out three weeks ago and didn't tell you."

"Carolyn told me you knew."

"I'm sorry. I was trying to protect myself and didn't think of how it might hurt you when you found out." He crossed the kitchen, stopping two feet from her. "I also went to see Madam Venus."

"I heard about that, too." She tipped her head with narrowed eyes. "Why'd you go?"

"I wanted her to tell you she was wrong."

"What'd she say?"

He scoffed. "She didn't really answer me."

Phoebe became very interested in the floor again.

He stood close enough that he could see her making a meal out of her bottom lip. What was running through her mind right now? She'd always been so comfortable in her skin, so sure of herself. But it seemed her confidence had slipped a bit. Could it be his fault because he rejected her the night of Lara's party?

"Madam Venus told me you could possibly have twins with someone else."

She dropped her arms to her sides and headed for the fridge. "Great. You're off the hook."

He watched her pull out a soft drink from the bottom shelf and shut the door a little harder than necessary. His next admission tied his stomach in knots. "She also said you and Keaton would break up the night of Stella's party."

Phoebe turned to him in slow motion, her mouth open.

He crossed the space between them. "Are you still dating him?"

Willy's nails clicked along the tile floor, and he nudged his way under Leo's hand. He rubbed the dog's ears. "Phoebe?"

"No."

"Did you two break up the night of Stella's party?"

"Yes."

A shiver slithered up his spine. Madam Venus was right again. "Who did the breaking?" he asked, hoping she did.

"I was the first to say something, but he felt the same way."

He resisted the urge to tuck her golden strands behind an ear.

How easy it would have been to fall into a full life with Phoebe. How easy to imagine waking up next to her every morning. He could see her sleepy smile so clearly in his mind. He didn't need to fall in love. He was already there.

Becoming like his parents still worried him, but everyone was right. He *wasn't* like them. So many variables scared him, but like Gabe said, what if he threw away what could be his greatest adventure without ever trying?

He needed to go back to San Francisco because he owed Greg three more weeks, and he'd keep his promise, but it wouldn't be so bad if he knew he was coming home to Phoebe.

The image of Phoebe cuddling Lucas and hugging Beck settled in his mind. He'd never thought of her as a mother, but watching her tonight was eye-opening. She'd make a great mom.

He decided to follow through with his urge. He stepped close enough to tuck her hair behind her ear.

Her eyes opened wide

"What if we try this and it doesn't work?"

"Try…us?" Her question came out on a breath of air.

He nodded as his eyes roved over every detail of her face. The tiny white scar over her left brow from the time she fell out of a cherry tree. The pin-dot mole on the bridge of her nose—all as familiar as the shape of her eyes and the hollow at the base of her neck where her pulse jumped like a rabbit running for its life.

"What if we work better as friends?" he asked.

"We won't know if we don't try."

"You have to promise that if this doesn't work, we'll still be friends, Phoebs." He cupped her face. "I need you in my life. Always."

"I need you too, Leo. I've missed us since I ruined every-thing with that stupid kiss."

"You didn't ruin anything. You woke me up. You woke us both up."

She wrapped her fingers around his wrists. "I wish there were guarantees in life. I mean, we make sense, right? Together? I know everything about you, and you know everything about me. We're both miserable when we fight. We like the same things."

"I don't love all your girly movies and you don't love my shoot-'em-ups, but we're good at compromising. We know how to meet in the middle." He ran his fingers through her soft hair. "I love you, Phoebe. I've loved you since kindergarten. No. Actually, I was kind of scared of you in kindergarten, so maybe I fell in love in the first grade. Man, I was so jealous when Jason got to be your partner on that art project we did for Mrs. White."

She smiled and his world righted itself. His parents' abandonment drifted far away to a place he could live with. His job in San Francisco? Three more weeks and then ancient history.

"Why now, Leo? What friend changed your mind?"

He huffed out a breath. "Gabe. He told me the same things others have said, but for some reason, the way he said it make sense to me. I miss you when you're not around. I hate being away from you. I need to talk to you just so my day runs smoothly. You're my sunshine, Phoebe. My rock. My safe place."

She smiled for the first time since they got to his house. "I feel the same way."

"I watched you with Mac and Noelle's kids tonight and thought, *we can do this. Phoebe and I can do this.*"

"You looked pretty adorable holding Lucas."

"Yeah?" He looked at Phoebe's mouth, still stretched in a smile. Familiar and yet off-limits for so long. She wrapped her arms around his neck, her fingers playing with his hair, sending a cascade of goosebumps from his neck to his shoulders, arms, and back.

He pulled her against him, in awe of her intoxicating, comforting, so familiar, scent. He breathed her in and tucked her closer, all the crazy pieces of his life falling into perfect place.

He let her deepen the kiss, allowed her to decide just how much they should explore. Emotions he recognized from their last kiss washed over him. This was how you were supposed to feel when you kissed someone you loved. In all his thirty-four years no one had sparked the flood of passion Phoebe did with a simple kiss.

Her mouth was soft and warm and oh, so inviting.

She turned her head, deepening the kiss, and his heart shot off like a rocket. Unable to hold back, Leo cupped the back of her head and moved from her mouth to the tender skin under her earlobe. Her tiny moan heightened his awareness of her fingers in his hair, her nip on his neck.

"So, we're going to do this?" he asked, before moving back to her mouth.

"Yes," she mumbled against his lips.

~

*P*hoebe peeked an eye open. Willy had his chin on the bed, staring at her with his one soulful eye. He whined and his tail wagged—so, their usual every-morning routine. She reached out and scratched his head. "Good morning, Willy."

Woof.

Climbing out of bed, she walked through the house with Willy on her heels and opened the kitchen door so he could run outside. The sun was just peeking over the mountains with the promise of a glorious day.

Leo left for The Dew Drop at two this morning. Before all the kissing, she thought he was silly to stay at Eden Falls only hotel when he owned the house and had a perfectly good king-size mattress in the master bedroom. After the kissing, she knew he'd made a wise decision.

She got very little sleep after the kissing and Leo's change of heart, which happened so fast she was suffering whiplash and a boatload of doubt. She wondered what Gabe said. Wonderful Gabe and his cute family were so much fun to hang with when she visited Leo in San Francisco.

As much as she wanted to get her hopes up, she'd keep her feet on the ground. She loved Leo and wanted to be with him, babies or not, but before she truly committed, she needed to be sure he was really all in like he said.

Her phone pinged a message and she took it off the kitchen charger.

I have a free morning. Want to meet for breakfast?

Phoebe had made a decision while she tossed and turned and worried the rest of the night away. As much as she'd like to meet Iz and spill everything that happened last night, she needed to talk to someone else first.

Sorry. I can't.

Okay. See you tomorrow at church.

She wanted to talk to Izzy before dinner tomorrow, but it looked like that wouldn't happen. **I work in the morning, but I'll be at Mom and Dad's for dinner.**

See you then.

Phoebe set her phone on the cupboard before opening the door to let Willy in. He charged straight to his empty bowl, so she filled it up, refreshed his water, then went into her bathroom to shower while trying to brace for what was to come.

An hour later she got out of her car and stared at the

garish house. Maybe ghoulish would be a better word for the paint job Madam Venus inflicted on her place of business.

She'd never been here but remembered Leo telling her how to get here after he came with Izzy four or five months ago. The windows were blacked out, so she couldn't see if anyone was moving around inside. She looked up at the dead tree as she passed on the way to the front door, surprised it was still standing. A black cat sat on a branch staring down at her.

What was the old superstition—don't walk under a black cat—No, don't walk under a ladder. Bad luck followed a black cat crossing your path, which the cat did after jumping off the branch with a hiss, scaring her silly.

The whole place gave her the creeps.

As soon as she raised a hand to knock, the door swung open. "Hello, Phoebe."

Phoebe looked at the corner of the house for cameras—the only way this woman could have known she was on the porch.

"Please, come in. I was just making some tea. Would you like a cup?"

"No. Thank you," she added the "thank you" almost grudgingly, afraid the Goddess of Love would slip some hallucinogen in with the sugar. She didn't want anything from this woman but answers.

"Have a seat. I'll be right back."

Phoebe crossed the completely black room and sat in one of two chairs at a small, round table. The only light came from about twenty candles. *Fire hazard.*

With all the black fabric hanging from ceiling to floor all around the room, she understood why Izzy said there was no way Madam Venus could have known Leo was in the car with her that day. An exterior camera was the only answer.

A deck of cards sat in the middle of the table and Phoebe

picked up the top one. A knight riding a horse holding a sword aloft—she didn't even want to know what that might mean. Not that she believed.

The clinking of bracelets let her know Madam Venus was on her way back. The woman always dressed in flashy, bright colors. Today she wore a long black skirt and a flowy green blouse, which made her look almost normal.

She sat down opposite Phoebe and took a sip from a dainty teacup.

"I know it's early and I don't have an appointment—"

Madam Venus waved a hand. "I was expecting you. Are you sure you wouldn't like some tea? I have your favorite."

Phoebe refused to fall for any of this gibberish. She just wanted answers to a couple of questions. "You have turned my life upside down," Phoebe said pointing at the woman's nose.

"I'm sorry." Madam Venus set her cup on the table. "I didn't mean to hurt you in any way."

Phoebe leaned back into her chair and crossed her arms. "Well, you did. I kissed Leo earlier this month, and after that, he didn't want to have anything to do with me."

"He didn't kiss you back?"

"Yes, but then he pushed me away."

"Because he was scared? Because you were changing the rules on him?" The psychic lifted the top card. "Because you considered the possibilities before he dared to?"

"He had a rough childhood," Phoebe said.

Madam Venus nodded like she knew all about it. "Has he come around?"

"Last night."

She lifted her teacup, accompanied by more clinking of bracelets. "And you're worried about the quick about-face."

"If you're all-seeing and all-knowing, tell me why he changed his mind."

"Did you ask him?"

Phoebe ran an index finger along the edge of the table. "He told me a friend said something that changed his mind."

Madam Venus leaned forward, elbows on the table, teacup between her hands. "And you don't believe him?"

"It's not that I don't believe him. I'm just afraid to invest much if he's going to change his mind again."

"He won't." The psychic's smile lit the black room. She took a sip of tea and set the cup down. "He'll be your forever if you open your heart to the possibilities. Take a chance, Phoebe. You won't regret it."

"Did you do something to him when he visited?"

"Like cast a spell?" Madam Venus shook her head. "I don't do things like that. I'm not a witch. I can just see things. Leo came to the conclusion all on his own."

For some strange reason, Phoebe believed her. She thought this meeting would end with her putting the *fear of Phoebe* into this woman, but instead, she found herself leaving full of anticipation and optimism and a heart full of hope.

~

*L*eo woke with the sun in his eyes since he'd fallen asleep staring out at the stars. He wanted to spend every minute of the day with Phoebe. He wanted forever, and he wanted that forever to start right now.

He grabbed his phone, but his call to her went straight to voicemail. So he texted, **Where are you, Phoebs?"**

Hello? Are you at the house?

This isn't the time to play hard to get, P. Where are you?

Three texts in ten minutes and nothing. He jumped out of bed after deciding to go to the house. Maybe she'd gotten as little sleep as he did. Beautiful Phoebe…she haunted his dreams last night. He could still smell her perfume on his skin. Or maybe that was just part of the dream.

After a quick shower, he dressed in jeans and long-sleeved T-shirt, pulled on socks and boots, and headed for the door.

A knock sounded just as he flipped the lock. The joy at seeing Phoebe on the other side was indescribable. His heart stuttered when he realized that he'd measured every woman he dated against Phoebe.

He'd been scared for so long. But scared of what? Phoebe would never hurt him.

Being with her last night felt so right, kissing her felt right. The future seemed crystal clear. Them together in Eden Falls, her a police officer and him running the farm— exactly where they were supposed to be. They could stay in his house or build something closer to town. He was open to whatever Phoebe wanted.

"Good morning," he said, his husky voice sounding crazy to his ears.

She smiled and his heart stopped. "Good morning."

"I called and then texted."

"I know. I was driving."

"Where'd you go so early?" he asked, pulling her into his room, intoxicated by her floral scent mixed with clean, fresh air.

"I went to see Madam Venus. I know at one point you thought she filled my head with craziness, but she didn't, Leo. All she did was open my eyes to some things I never considered before. I want a husband and a family. Maybe I always did, but it took her comment to make me realize the truth."

Before last week, he wouldn't have believed a simple comment could make anyone turn such a sharp one-eighty, but Gabe made him see a truth in himself that no one else had been able to make clear.

"I love you, Leo." She quickly held up a hand. "I don't expect you to say it back. I just want to let you know. I truly love you. Maybe the reason I could never make any other relationship last, why I never wanted to move beyond a certain point, was because deep down I knew I belonged with you."

Leo took her hand. "I love that you know that. I hate that you discovered it before I did."

"Still competitive," she said with a teasing smile.

"My competitiveness is nothing compared to yours."

"True."

He pulled her down on the edge of the bed next to him. "For the record, you blew my socks off with that kiss at Lara's party."

"Really? You sure didn't show it."

"That's because you scared me to death at the same time."

She snorted. "I scared you so bad you ran off to flirt with a redhead."

"Not my finest moment. I'm sorry, Phoebs." He wrapped his arm around her shoulder, and she snuggled up against him. "I'm sorry about a lot of things."

"Me too."

Phoebe tipped her face up to his and he kissed the tip of her nose. That tiny gesture would have felt so wrong a week ago. Now, while still new, it felt like he'd been kissing her forever.

"Did you really mean it when you mentioned working remotely?"

"I gave Greg thirty days to find my replacement. I told him I'd work remotely or not at all."

"So, you're going to renovate the farm, and then what?"

"I guess we'll play it one day at a time. As long as I have you by my side, nothing else really matters."

"You really made me dizzy with your stunning about-face. What exactly did Gabe say to you?"

"Nothing that hasn't been said before. Maybe it was Gabe's family dinner I attended last weekend and when I say family dinner, there were probably eighty people." He thought about all the games and fun Gabe's family shared.

"Just watching the uncles and aunts and cousins all together with their kids…It had to start somewhere, right? A starting point. Two people fell in love and created this big, beautiful, loving family. Gabe said if I didn't take a chance, I might miss out on my greatest adventure."

He pulled Phoebe onto his lap and wrapped his arms around her. "All my greatest adventures have included you, Phoebs. You're my starting point. Let's find out where life takes us."

CHAPTER 20

*L*eo glanced in the dresser mirror and straightened his tie one last time, then slipped on his jacket. He couldn't remember ever being this nervous about meeting a woman. It felt like he hadn't seen Phoebe in months when it was only two weeks.

He pocketed his keys and turned to Willy. "What do you think, boy?"

Woof.

"Thanks for the vote of confidence," he said, rubbing Willy's ears.

He strode into the living room with Willie on his heels. Phoebe already left to get ready for the wedding with her sisters, so he was home alone for the first time in over a month. This house was as much Phoebe's as it was his now. She'd added little touches since moving in, little pieces of herself. He'd always liked this house, and knowing Phoebe was here eased his mind while he finished up in San Francisco.

He only had one more week in the city and then he'd be home for good.

And she'd move into Izzy's attic apartment.

Willy's whine got Leo's attention. "You can't come to the wedding, boy. Izzy loves you, but she doesn't love you that much."

He moved down the hall. "Come on, boy. Go outside for a quick run and then I have to leave. Phoebe won't be back until late."

Willy came back to the door about ten minutes later, and Leo gave him a good rubdown. "I'll see you tomorrow, boy. We'll head to the park before I have to go back to California."

Minutes later he drove into town. It was still too early for trees to be budding out, but daffodils and crocus were in bloom thanks to the warming weather. The river level was high with spring runoff.

Leo turned into the church parking lot. Izzy and Gunner planned for a very small wedding, but based on the number of cars, that plan must have changed. When he made his way inside, Beverly commandeered him immediately.

"Oh, Leo. You look so handsome," she fidgeted with his tie and brushed a dog hair off the shoulder of his black suit. "When are you coming home for good?"

He pulled the woman he loved so much in for a hug. "Next weekend."

She reached up and took his face in her hands. "No more leaving. Do you hear me?"

"Yes, Mom."

Her mouth fell open and tears misted her eyes. "You've never called me that before."

"Do you mind?"

"No," she said with choked voice.

"You've always been my mom, Bev." He'd never admitted it aloud before, and he wasn't sure why. Possibly because he always held out hope that his parents would change and maybe, just maybe, love him as much as Neil and Bev did.

"You're the best mom a boy could ask for. Thank you for all you've ever done to help me along the path of life. I love you."

"I love you too," came out on a sob.

"Whoa, whoa, whoa. Your daughters will have my head if they come out here and see I've made you cry."

"They're happy tears, Leo. Pure, joyful tears."

"Come on. Let's get us a good seat before this shindig starts."

~

*P*hoebe, Georgie, Stella, and Adelaide all crowded around Izzy while Phoebe fussed with her simple veil.

"You look so beautiful," Phoebe said.

Izzy ran a hand over her hip. "Do you think it's too much?"

"I think everything is perfect," Phoebe said of Izzy's dress with its bateau neckline and gorgeous lace appliques. Too frilly for Phoebe's taste, but the dress fit Izzy's personality perfectly.

Georgie straightened the slight train. "Gunner is going to have a hard time keeping his hands off you."

"He already has that problem," Phoebe teased, remembering the morning she caught them making out on the sofa in Izzy's office a few weeks ago.

So much had changed since that day. Leo was coming home. And they were dating!

"That's how a fiancé should act," little Oopsie added. "Or so I've heard."

They all laughed when she blushed. Madam Venus might be right about some things, but she was dead wrong about their big city Addie moving back to Eden Falls.

Just the thought conjured the woman to walk through the

door with her line of clinking bracelets and overly colorful outfit. She stopped in front of Phoebe. "I hear you and Leo are dating."

"Dating and having twins with a man are two very different things."

"You're having twins?" Addie asked with wide eyes.

Madam Venus shook her head. "Not yet, but she will."

Izzy stepped between Phoebe and the psychic. "Vera, I'm so glad you could come."

"You look stunning, Izzy." She took Izzy's hands and closed her eyes. "You and Gunner have many, many happy years ahead of you. Tell him to stay off the ladder on June twenty-eighth."

"What?"

"He'll be fine. Just keep his feet on the ground that day." She turned to Georgie and smiled. "Have you told them yet?"

The blood drained from Georgie's face.

"Told who what?" Stella asked.

The medium touched Georgie's arm. "He's very healthy. You have nothing to worry about."

"Who's healthy?" Stella moved closer to Georgie. "Who is *he*?"

"It's a he?" Georgie asked Madam Venus, touching her stomach.

"You're pregnant?" Addie asked, with raised brows.

"I was going to tell everyone after the wedding. I didn't want to horn in on your moment, Iz."

"Are you kidding? Let's announce it at the reception." Izzy took Georgie's hands and bounced up and down. "I'm going to be an auntie! I'm going to be an auntie!"

"Have you told Mom and Dad?" Addie asked

Phoebe glowered at the woman who'd kinda ruined Georgianna's big reveal. The woman had the civility to wince. And what if Georgie didn't want to know the sex yet? Her husband wasn't even in the room.

"Sorry," Madam Venus said. "She's been worried, and I wanted to ease her mind."

Phoebe ushered Vera out of the room. "You really need to work on your delivery. Some things are better left unsaid. Or maybe said in privacy. Aren't reveal parties the big thing these days? And you just took that away from Georgie."

"You're right." Madam Venus looked down at her skirt and Phoebe felt a twinge of guilt for being so harsh. Vera was actually a very pretty woman under all the mystic and fluff. Her tone and demeanor changed when she was just Vera.

"Just…be nice."

Vera nodded. "I will. I'm sorry. I felt the worry emanating off your sister the second I walked in and wanted to relieve her fear."

"Well, I don't want to know any more about twins or the sex of babies or anything to do with my life, so zip it."

"Can I just say—"

"No."

"—I'm happy for you and Leo?"

"You can go sit down and enjoy watching your friend get married. No scaring the guests, no readings at the reception, and you better stay out of Misty Garrett's sight. She may just stab you."

"Who's Misty Garrett?"

"Last October you congratulated her husband, telling him his night of lovemaking with his wife worked."

"Oh, the big guy. But why would his wife be mad at me?" she asked with wide eyes. "I didn't have anything to do with her conceiving a son."

"There you go again," Phoebe said waving an arm around. "Beam's mom is planning a big sex reveal party next month, so you need to put a lid on it so Misty and Beam can be surprised."

Addie stepped out of the bride's room. "Can I ask you something?"

The psychic persona swept over Vera instantly. "Of course, Adelaide. Your future husband will move to Eden Falls sometime in May or June."

Addie's mouth fell open and she shook her head. "I wanted to ask if you could be wrong about what you—" her glance bounced from Madam Venus to Phoebe and back "—told me?"

Madam Venus smiled. "Anything is possible."

Phoebe's face must have conveyed her urge to arrest the woman because Vera scurried away in a flash. She turned to her youngest sister. "Do not change who you are or what you want because of *Vera's* prediction," she said, emphasizing the woman's given name to humanize her.

"Her name is Vera?"

"Yes. Now, who are you dating? I hope he's tall and handsome and rich."

Addie wore a dejected look. "He is, but I'm thinking he's not the one. Tall, handsome, and rich is also very arrogant."

Phoebe threaded her arm through Addie's. "How so?"

"He, along with his parents, have been planning my life, from where we'd live, to how many kids I'd have, to being a stay-at-home wife rather than having a career."

"Wait. Did he propose?"

Sheepishly, Addie pulled a huge diamond ring out of the pocket of her dress.

"Ohmygosh! That rock must have cost a fortune. Why aren't you wearing it?"

"I haven't actually said yes."

"You got a rock that size for a maybe?"

Addie shrugged, then quickly shoved the rock back into her pocket when their mom approached.

"Come on, my sweet girls. It's time to find our seats. Gunner is getting anxious."

Phoebe gave Izzy one last hug and ushered her sisters into the chapel. Leo, looking so handsome in his suit, stood when she came down the aisle. His smile shot her heart rate up to overdrive while his devouring gaze made her knees weak enough to actually wobble. When she reached the seat he saved, he kissed her without a care in the world what anyone else thought.

He barely lifted his lips from hers. "I missed you."

"I can tell."

"Wrong response."

Her effort to behave more romantically around her best friend was a work in progress. Luckily, Leo was kinda going through the same thing. They both felt a little silly at times, but laughed their way through and moved on. "I missed you too."

"You can show me how much you missed me after the wedding."

"Deal."

He sat, pulling her down next to him. "Did you have fun with your sisters yesterday?"

She and the girls drove to Seattle for mani-pedis, some shopping, and then dinner. They'd spent a lot of time laughing and reminiscing. "We had a great time."

Preacher Brenner asked everyone to stand, and Mrs. Benson segued the organ music to Wagner's "Wedding March." Phoebe glanced toward the front and noticed Gunner running his finger around the inside of his collar. The poor guy lived in jeans and work shirts.

She turned just as Izzy stepped into the doorway.

"Wow," Leo said behind her.

"I know. She looks gorgeous, doesn't she?"

Leo rested his hands on Phoebe's hips. The weight and warmth felt good through her dress. So did the feeling of safety and consistency, two things Leo would always provide because of his inconsistent childhood. She leaned back against him.

Layne couldn't believe she named the cruiser Mr. Darcy, but she could be romantic. She laced her fingers through Leo's and pulled his arms around her despite the stares. Once Izzy started down the aisle on her dad's arm, all eyes turned to the bride rather than the couple townsfolk had always assumed were more than friends.

"You're playing with fire, gorgeous woman," Leo whispered, his minty breath gliding across her cheek.

Izzy passed them, her gaze on Gunner, her smile ethereal.

~

*L*eo finally had Phoebe in his arms, dancing to "Amazed" by Lonestar, one of the bride and groom's playlist picks. It was definitely not the first time he and Phoebe had danced together, but it was their first time as a couple, and he loved the feelings. He wanted to catalog each one to analyze later.

He wanted to remember the feelings because he'd never felt them to this degree before. He also wanted to hit himself over the head. Why hadn't he realized they were meant to be together years ago? They didn't need Madam Venus to tell them the obvious.

"What are you feeling right now?" he asked without pulling back an inch.

"A million good things."

They had their share of people staring during the ceremony. Even now he could feel the eyes and hear the murmurs. None of it bothered him, but he could tell Phoebe didn't love the attention.

At Sunday dinner, two days after they decided to give "them" a try, Neil said they had his blessing and Bev cried tons of happy tears—right after she made him promise he wouldn't drag Phoebe off to San Francisco. He'd assured her he had no intention of staying there himself. Other than an occasional visit to LA to check on his parents and some family vacations, he didn't plan to leave Eden Falls for any length of time ever again.

Well, except for the honeymoon—if Phoebe agreed to marry him. He decided to ask her today. She'd say yes because she loved him as enthusiastically as he loved her. And they were both anxious to get to the honeymooning part.

"Are you happy?" she asked against his neck.

"More than I've ever been in my whole life. I was just thinking we should have done this years ago."

She leaned back with a snort. "Right. Who knew?"

"Obviously Madam Venus," he said, glancing around for the crazy lady and spotted her on the sidelines of the dance floor talking to Preacher Brenner.

Phoebe turned to look. "Why on earth would Josh listen to anything a psychic has to say?"

"Maybe because he's polite and trained to listen to everyone, or maybe because she's not spouting mumbo jumbo after all."

"Nooo." Phoebe looked up at him so quickly she probably strained a neck muscle. "Don't tell me you believe her."

"I'm not saying I believe, but I've heard stories of people who have premonitions or get warnings before something happens."

"Or maybe she's just good at guessing."

He turned Phoebe so she couldn't see Madam Venus

without looking over her shoulder. "I don't want to talk about her anymore. I want to talk about us."

"What about us?"

The song changed and they simply upped their tempo. "We should discuss when we're going to get married. It's not like we need a lot of time to get to know each other or decide if we like each other enough to move on to the next step."

"But we do need to get to know each other as partners. I might not like all this kissing we've been doing."

Leo barked out a laugh. He knew better since she usually initiated their kissing at least half the time. She ducked her head, but he saw the smile twitching the corners of her mouth, tempting him to kiss it away. "Do you want a big wedding?"

Phoebe looked around the room. She'd never been a flowers and tiered cake and fancy dresses kind of woman, but she might want all those things for herself.

"No. I think I'd rather skip all this. How about you? Do you want a big wedding?"

"I don't need the hoopla."

She played with the hair at the back of his neck, creating millions of goosebumps. "When are you going to visit your parents in LA?"

Okay. She obviously didn't want to talk about weddings. "I thought I'd fly down after I wrap up in the office next week."

"Maybe I'll meet you there and we'll drive to Vegas for a quick, no-fuss wedding."

"Oh," he said, not able to hold back his smile, but wiped it away just as quickly as it showed up. "Your mom would kill us both."

"So, we invite Mom and Dad to join us," she said with a shrug.

The music stopped and the DJ took the mic. "Ladies, the

bride is getting ready to toss her bouquet. Then the groom will be giving a lucky gent the bride's garter."

"Isn't it tradition that whoever catches the bouquet is the next to marry?" Leo asked Phoebe.

Her pretty smile appeared. "I believe so."

"I've seen you play baseball and you're great at catching." He squeezed her bicep. "You might have to knock a few of the other ladies out of the way, but you can do it." He gave her a kiss for luck.

Gunner carried his bride to the middle of the dance floor and stood her on a chair, holding her steady with hands on her waist.

Squawk! "Out of my way, Phoebe. This one's mine," Rita Reynolds said, elbowing Phoebe aside.

The crowd laughed.

"Don't let Rita push you around, Phoebs," Leo called to her. "You've got this."

"One, two, three!" Izzy shouted and threw the bouquet in the wrong direction. The bouquet landed in Tatum Ellis's hands without her even reaching for it.

"Isadora, you throw like a girl!" Rita shook her bony fist in the air.

Gunner lifted Izzy off the chair, and she sat down. He put on quite a production of burrowing through the layers to get to the garter they picked up yesterday on their Seattle shopping spree. Gunner eased it slowly down her leg while Izzy feigned embarrassment. Once off, to the hoots and whistles of the men at the reception, Gunner stood and hooked it over the thumb of one hand while pulling it back with the index finger of his other. Then he shot it straight into the air. As bad a shot as Izzy, the garter sailed over Leo's head and hit Mike Stettler square in the chest.

After they waved the new husband and wife on their way,

Leo pulled Phoebe to him. He couldn't wait to get her alone, away from this crowd.

Her smile made it hard to breathe in a way that he wanted to last forever.

"Do we really need a garter and bouquet?"

"I don't need a bouquet, but that garter looked kind of fun," Leo teased.

She fake slugged him in the chest. "I'm going to like being married to you, Leo Sawyer."

"It will be an adventure, won't it?"

"Our whole life has been an adventure from the moment we met." Phoebe took his arm.

"Running barefoot around the farm to swimming at the pool to making snow angels, we've always found some kind of fun to fall into. Do you think marriage will change us?"

He stared into her beautiful brown-gorilla-eyes. "Yes, but in a good way. We'll find new places to visit, new restaurants to try. We've always talked about going to Hawaii and hiking to waterfalls. There's nothing holding us back, Phoebs. We'll do it all. As long as we're together, nothing else matters."

She pressed close to him. "I can't wait."

What better time to propose? He dropped to his knees and pulled the box he'd been carrying around for two weeks out of his pocket.

A gasp escaped her as well as others standing close.

"Phoebe, will you marry me, put up with me, and spend the rest of forever with me?"

"Yes!"

Phoebe whirled around. "Stella! He's not asking you."

"I know, but you're taking too long to answer," Stella said before Rowdy pulled her back against him and covered her mouth with his hand.

Phoebe glanced back at Leo, still on his knees. "What was the question?"

These Adams girls would be the death of every male in town. "Will. You. Marry. Me?"

"She will," Georgianna said at the same time Adelaide added another, "Yes."

They'd gathered quite a crowd and everyone, including Leo, was waiting for an answer. Phoebe couldn't get a word in edgewise with her sisters around, so Leo stood, took her hand, and pulled her into the bustling kitchen.

Phoebe looked around and smiled. "This isn't exactly a romantic spot."

"No, but your sisters are on the other side of that door. Besides, anywhere we're together can be romantic." He pulled her close.

"You laughed when I asked you if I was romantic," she said, faking a pout.

"And you've told me I'm a dork more times than I can count—so include that moment among them."

"I will, and yes is my answer."

He slid the modest emerald-cut diamond engagement ring onto her finger. As he did, the delicate vines, adorned with sparkling round and marquise diamond buds, surrounding the main diamond, glittered in the light. He could afford so much more but knew Phoebe wouldn't wear anything that attracted attention. So he'd spoil her in other ways.

She smiled up at him, her eyes shining with tears, and he gathered her close, pressing his lips to hers. This moment would never happen again, so he immersed himself in the feel of her against him, the taste of her mouth, lemon cake, and raspberry filling, with sweet cream cheese frosting. Breathing her in, her scent was as familiar as the feel of sunshine on his skin.

She leaned back a breath's distance. "I love you, Leo Sawyer. I always have."

"I love you right back, Phoebe Adams, and I always will."

If you enjoyed the Eden Falls Series, grab my *Second Chance Romance Collection* which includes *When You Love Someone, Endless Love* and *Rhythm of Love.*

To keep up to date on new releases join my newsletter at TinaNewcomb.com.

Following is an excerpt from *When You Love Someone.*

EXCERPT FROM: WHEN YOU LOVE SOMEONE

CHAPTER ONE

In the split second between hearing what his attorney said and the news actually sinking in, Jared McAlister took note of the photo of Connor's kids on his desk, how one slat on his window blinds hung crookedly, and the healthy plant on the file cabinet must be watered by an assistant. Connor would never take the time.

When the information finally registered, Jared laughed. "Are you still mad because I trounced you on the golf course last week?"

One side of Connor's mouth quirked down. That tiny motion effectively sucked all the air out of the room.

No. Jared inhaled, trying to expand his lungs. "There has to be a mistake."

"There's no mistake."

"Check again."

"I did. An assistant discovered the mistake, and I checked behind her. Twice. You are still legally wed to"—Connor glanced down at the papers on his desk—"Cecelia Chadwick." He looked up without moving his head. "I guess we need to add McAlister on the end."

Just the mention of her name set Jared's heart galloping. He pushed to his feet, strode to the window, and tried to straighten the crooked slat, which fell cockeyed as soon as he let go. Anything to buy a few moments as memories bombarded him. Connor watched him like a hawk at dinnertime. "This is the reason you insisted I come to this meeting alone."

Connor's crooked grin appeared. "Bad call?"

"No." Jared's fiancée wouldn't take this news well. They met with Stacy's attorney last week to discuss the fine points of their prenup. Her attorney and his assistants had obviously missed the "mistake" Connor's team caught.

Some telling expression must have crossed his face because Connor settled back in his chair and steepled his fingers under his chin. "Want to talk about it?"

Jared crossed to his chair and dropped into the soft leather, his mind racing to that sultry summer. "There isn't much to tell." Yet, given the chance, he could talk about those three months for hours. The long horseback rides, the lazy afternoons spent at the lake, the evening concerts, getting caught in a rainstorm, the way his pulse picked up every time Cecelia was near. "We were young and stupid and fell in love —or lust—too quickly."

Though at the time, it sure felt like love.

He left out the part that Cecelia wouldn't sleep with him until after they were married. If it had been anyone else, he would have suspected her of trying to trap him, but not Cecelia. She had specific moral beliefs on the subject of premarital sex and refused to bend. Though frustrated at the time, he'd admired her for her beliefs.

"We got married two days before I flew to California for my first year of law school, and a week before she left for her freshman year at Arizona State University. We were married for two months, exchanging emails, phone calls, and texts. I thought everything was fine. I sent her a plane ticket to visit for a long weekend and received divorce papers in reply. Uncontested, with no property or children, the divorce was finalized before Christmas."

"Is she going to hit you for back alimony when she discovers you're still married?"

"She didn't ask for alimony the first time, so no. That's not Cecelia's way."

"That *wasn't* Cecelia's way. Did she know your family's net worth?"

"Yes, she was well aware of the McAlister wealth. She didn't ask for anything in the divorce. Nothing."

"That was then, Jared." Connor shuffled through the papers in front of him. "It's been eleven years."

"She won't ask for back alimony."

"Tell me about her."

Jared jumped to his feet and retraced his steps to the window, shifting so Connor couldn't see his face, afraid of what his expressions might reveal. "Cecelia was—is younger than me by four years. Sweet, honest, book-smart, yet naïve of worldly ways.

"She never felt like she belonged in my world. Her family didn't have money. My family didn't help. Dad and Mom always looked down on her like an annoying puppy that had followed me home. Her mother hated me. She told Cecelia rich boys never married poor girls, and I was only after her for the sex."

"Were you?"

Jared twisted to face Connor. "*I* married her. *She* divorced me."

Connor nodded for him to continue.

"She raised her brother and sister because her mom and

dad weren't very good parents. And when I say raised, I mean she did everything from making their lunches and dinners to doing their laundry, setting curfews, and making sure they were home when they were supposed to be. Cecelia didn't need or want my money. With a full-ride scholarship to Arizona State, she had plans and hopes and dreams for the future and a better life."

"Do you have any idea where she is now?"

"None." Jared rubbed the base of his skull where a headache threatened.

"Any idea why she wanted the divorce?"

"No. When the divorce papers arrived by courier, I lived in shock for several days while I tried to contact her. My messages went unanswered, my emails undelivered. I flew to Arizona, but she'd left school, which didn't make sense. Her family didn't have money. That scholarship meant everything to her. From Arizona, I flew to Dallas, where I hit another dead end. Her parents wouldn't give me any information, wouldn't even answer the door or my phone calls. Her brother and sister swore they didn't know where she'd gone."

He'd even threatened Cecelia's attorney that he wouldn't sign the papers until he could talk to her. Still, no word. "Eventually, I signed on the dotted line and mailed the divorce documents back."

"You mentioned her family."

"They used to live in Mesquite. I'm not sure if they still do." He paced in front of Connor's desk before retaking his seat. "So, what now?"

A million emotions warred against each other, hitting Jared's mind, his stomach, and, unfortunately, his heart all at the same time. His fiancée's parents were planning an elaborate wedding ten months from now. Flowers, photographers, caterers. The venue had been reserved two days after Stacy had a ring on her finger. She, her mom, and his, along with a wedding planner, were chin-deep in plans and arrangements.

"Since nothing was ever filed, I guess we start over."

"How is it possible that someone overlooked something so life-changing?"

Connor stood the papers on end, tapped them until they were aligned, then slipped them into a file folder. "A paralegal forgot to file it with the court before he or she quit. A clerk neglected to record it in the court records. The document fell behind a file cabinet. Any number of things could have happened. Did you ever receive the final decree?"

If he did, he'd probably shredded it upon receipt, not wanting to be reminded. "I don't remember."

Jared read the astonished *how-could-you-not-remember?* look on Connor's face.

He'd been in a dark place at the time. Maybe the decree was in a box in his guest room closet, and all this panic about still being married would be for naught. "I'll look when I get home."

"Do you want me to use our in-house investigator to find *Mrs. McAlister?*" Connor asked, his lopsided grin in place.

"You're having way too much fun with this."

"Sorry." He pressed his lips together. "I'm astonished, is all."

Me too.

"Do you want us to find her, or do you want to take care of it?" Conner asked again.

If Jared hired an investigator, his dad would somehow find out, and chaos would ensue. If he used the investigator at the law firm where he worked, again, somehow, his dad— with his far-reaching connections—would find out. "You find her. I'll tell Stacy you had to cancel our appointment tomorrow because—"

"A case came up, and I have to be in court," Connor

inserted. "Want me to draw up new divorce documents and have them sent to your office to look over? Things should be pretty cut-and-dried. Like you said earlier, no property, no children."

"Draw them up, but I'll come here to get them." Though he received documents by courier all the time, he didn't want them to fall into the wrong hands accidentally.

Jared stood to leave. "Let me know when you find Cecelia."

"You don't want my investigator to serve her?"

"Not yet."

Connor quirked a brow. "Letting someone else take care of this for you would simplify your life."

Jared paused at the door and glanced back at Connor. "I've never done things the easy way. Just ask my dad."

ACKNOWLEDGMENTS

Thank you to my editor Faith Freewoman at Demon for Details.

Thank you to Sara Olds for proofreading.

Thank you to Dar Albert of Wicked Smart Designs for my cover.

Thank you Jeanine Hopping, Holly Hertzke, Marnie Giggey, and Chris Almodovar for always being my first readers.

Thank you to Rick for all you do.

Thank you to my family for your encouragement.

And last but not least, thank you readers for sticking with me and loving my books.

I couldn't do this without all of you.

xox

Tina

ALSO BY TINA NEWCOMB

The Eden Falls Series

Finding Eden

Beyond Eden

A Taste of Eden

The Angel of Eden Falls

Touches of Eden

Stars Over Eden Falls

Fortunes for Eden

Snow and Mistletoe in Eden Falls

Rumors in Eden Falls

Second Chance Romance Collection

When You Love Someone

Endless Love

Rhythm of Love

Second Chance Romance Collection

ABOUT THE AUTHOR

Tina Newcomb writes clean, contemporary romance. Her heartwarming stories take place in quaint small towns, with quirky townsfolk, and friendships that last a lifetime.

She acquired her love of reading from her librarian mother, who always had a stack of books close at hand, and her father who visited a local bookstore every weekend.

Tina Newcomb lives in colorful Colorado. When not lost in her writing, she can be found in the garden, traveling with her (amateur) chef husband, or spending time with family and friends.

Follow Tina on:

facebook.com/TinaNewcombAuthor

instagram.com/tinanewcombauthor

bookbub.com/authors/tina-newcomb

goodreads.com/tinanewcomb

pinterest.com/tinanewcomb

www.ingramcontent.com/pod-product-compliance
Lightning Source LLC
Chambersburg PA
CBHW030401200726
48286CB00015B/1904